KING OF TEDS

INCEPTION

by

Dave Bartram

with Dean Rinaldi

Published by Blue Mendos Publications
In association with Amazon KDP

Published in paperback 2022
Category: Fiction
Copyright Dave Bartram © 2022
Copyright Dean Rinaldi © 2022
ISBN : 9798353615613

Cover design by Jill Rinaldi © 2022

Dedication

To the thousands of Showaddywaddy fans who have remained loyal and supportive since the band's inception in 1973. For the Teddy Boys & Girls, Edwardians, Rockabillys, Rockers and the generation who kept the love and spirit of Rock 'n' Roll alive

Acknowledgements

Jill Rinaldi for designing all the King of the Teds book covers and my friend and ghostwriter, Dean Rinaldi.

Chapter 1

London 1974

"See you in the morning and don't be late," Gary, works foreman at Harrington's Garage said.

"Since when have I ever been late," Ricky Turrell, the apprentice motor mechanic answered with a chuckle, slipping his blue works overalls off and hanging them up.

"I know what you youngsters are like. You'll be down the boozer tonight getting off your head and then when the alarm goes off in the morning, you'll be no good to man or beast," Gary said as he pulled on his donkey jacket.

"I'll be in, Gary, and I'll do that Saturday morning no one wants for you too," Ricky said as he opened the door out onto the main road. "You've gotta love a bit of double time."

He looked up when he heard a car hooter. He had to take a second look at the Olympic Blue RS 3100 Ford Capri parked with two wheels on the pavement.

"Is that Neil?" Ricky wondered.

The driver of the Capri leant across and swung the passenger's side door open. Ricky, still not sure if it was Neil, his friend since junior school, walked warily towards the car. He stopped and bent down. It was Neil.

"Hello mate, I thought I'd drop by and give you a lift home," Neil said, beckoning him in.

Ricky shook his head and smiled as he climbed into the car.

"So, what's with the Capri, Neil?" Ricky said as he pulled the seat belt across and closed the door.

"Well, let's just say I've borrowed it," Neil said with a broad, mischievous grin.

"You, Neil, are a bloody thief," Ricky said bluntly.

"Yes mate, I am. I'm the best car thief in the whole of London. There isn't a car anywhere that I can't get into," Neil boasted.

Ricky and Neil had been friends since they were eight years old. Ricky and his parents had moved to the Milton Road Estate as part of a council home exchange scheme. Neil was one of the first lads at his new school to befriend him shortly after Ricky had a run in with Karl Thomas, the class bully. At eight years old, Karl already looked much older than his age. He was well built and stood head and shoulders above most kids of ten and eleven years of age. Karl enjoyed bullying and intimidating the other kids in the class. The first time that Karl purposely knocked his shoulder as he walked down the school corridor, Ricky let it go. As much as he wanted to stand up for himself, he found Karl's size and persona intimidating. Even the kids in the higher years were scared of Karl. For days afterwards Ricky found it difficult to look at himself in the mirror as he washed and dressed before school. Allowing Karl to get away with the psychological attack was eating away at him. Even at eight years old, Ricky knew that once you show fear to a bully, they just keep coming at you, only harder. It was a Monday morning at break time when Karl and several lads approached him as he talked to Jackie, one of the girls in his class.

"Who said you could talk to Jackie, new kid?" Karl said, with his hands on his hips.

"I don't know what you mean mate," Ricky said, innocently shrugging his shoulders.

"Mate? Mate? I ain't your mate and I don't take too kindly to people trying it on with my girlfriend," Karl said, clenching and unclenching his fists.

"I'm not your girlfriend, Karl Thomas. I wouldn't go out with you if you were the last boy alive on the planet. You're nasty, mean and a bully!" Jackie said sharply.

Some of the kids behind Karl began to laugh.

"Shut it!" Karl bellowed. "You're in for it now, new kid!"

Karl stepped forward and threw a punch. He missed. Ricky fired a right hook and then a left jab. Both connected and Karl looked startled. He yelled out and ran forward, trying to make a grab for Ricky. The attempt was clumsy, and Ricky managed to sidestep him. He grabbed Karl around the neck and pulled him down onto the ground. The two boys grappled and wrestled while a growing numbers of school kids cheered and clapped as the two lads fought. Ricky managed to turn Karl over and clambered on top of him. With his knees now pinning Karl's shoulders down, Ricky fired punch after punch at Karl's face, much to the delight of the cheering crowd around them. The next thing Ricky knew he had been grabbed by the scruff of the neck and flung across the playground. He looked up with gritted teeth and clenched fists only to see it was the head teacher.

The two lads were frog marched into the school and given a dressing down by the headmaster. Both boys were given three whacks each with the cane and told to shake hands. As the two lads left the headmaster's office, Ricky spotted Neil waving him over. From that day the two boys had remained friends. And then, once

Neil discovered how easily he could break into cars, joyriding had become an almost daily ritual. He had often boasted how he would take and joy ride as many as three cars during an evening.

***

Neil turned the ignition key and the throaty V6 engine roared into life. He thrust the gear shifter into first gear and then adjusted his rear-view mirror.

"Let's see what we have on here," Neil said, pushing the cassette tape into the Sharp cassette player.

As the beginning of *'Teenage Rampage'* by Sweet played, the two lads smiled and nodded their heads. Neil looked in the rear-view mirror and gave the engine several revs before dropping the clutch. The Capri's tyres screeched as the car began to slide across the road with burning tyre smoke belching out of the rear wheel arches. The Capri weaved from left to right as Neil fought to straighten the car. He slammed the gear shifter into second gear. There was a short screech before the tyres gripped and propelled the car hurtling down the road. It was a 30mph limit and Neil had just reached 50mph as he slid the shifter into third gear. Ricky pushed himself back into the seat as Sweet yelled out *'Teenage Rampage'*.

The traffic lights ahead were changing to red. Ricky gripped the seat belt as Neil hit the brakes and short shifted back down into second gear. He came to a complete stop at the traffic lights.

"It goes well, doesn't it?" Neil gloated. "This is a works special you know. It's not like your normal three litre Capris. I mean they're fast enough straight out the showroom, but this is something else. I'd like to keep this."

10

"You keep driving like that and the only thing you'll have is a picture of it on your cell wall," Ricky warned.

"Nah, not me Ricky. I'm too fast, too good and I only nick fast motors," Neil said as he reached over to turn the music down before looking in his rear-view mirror.

Behind him was a bright red Ford Zodiac MK1 with black tinted windows. Both Ricky and Neil turned towards the back window when they heard the roar of the highly tuned American V8. The front of the Zodiac rocked from side to side.

"That's Jeff Harris," Neil said.

"Who?" said Ricky.

"You must have heard of the Harris's?" Neil said, feigning a shocked expression.

Ricky shrugged his shoulders and shook his head.

"Where have you been Ricky? The Harris family, that's Jeff, Andy and their dad Ron, build really fast street legal Zephyrs and Zodiacs with monster V8s."

The Zodiac pulled out from behind the RS Capri and lined up alongside it at the traffic lights. The front of the Zodiac rocked from side to side as the throaty V8 revved.

"Come on the, let's have it," Neil muttered before sliding the shifter into first gear and looking up at the traffic lights. The red changed to amber and then green. Neil dropped the clutch and floored the throttle pedal. The sound of the Capri's RS engine was dwarfed by the Harris Zodiac. The rear wheel spun as Neil fought with the steering wheel to keep the car straight, but the Zodiac had launched with the front wheels lifting a few inches from the ground while thick tyre smoke belched out of both wheel arches. The Zodiac was ahead with the rear end of the car sliding back and forth leaving thick black tyre marks on the road. Neil slammed the gear shifter into second gear and the Capri pulled violently to the left. He fought with the steering wheel as the Capri swerved, veered sideways and out of shape. Pedestrians on both sides of the road stopped and looked at the two cars. The Harris Zodiac straightened with the rear sitting down and gripping the tarmac. Sounding like something monstrous from the Jurassic period, the Harris Zodiac raced ahead, leaving Neil and the RS Capri behind. Neil knew he was beaten, took his foot off the throttle pedal and gently slipped the gear shifter into third.

"Hey, if you're going to get your doors blown off then I suppose it's okay if it's a Harris motor. Did you see that thing go?" Neil said excitedly.

"That was something else. I've never seen anything like that," Ricky agreed.

The traffic lights ahead were red, and the Harris Zodiac sat motionless as pedestrians crossed the road. Neil pulled up behind. As the last person crossed over, the traffic lights changed. The Zodiac let out a loud, ferocious roar. It sat still with both the rear wheels spinning frantically, trying desperately to grip the tarmac. The burning tyre smoke got thicker and thicker, covering the Capri and the roadway. Both Ricky and Neil watched as the Harris Zodiac slid away sideways, leaving two thick, snaking, tyre streaks behind.

"I want one of those," Ricky announced.

"You ain't the only one mate," Neil said as he pulled away slowly from the traffic lights. "Here, check under the seats?"

Ricky reached down and pulled out a magazine.

"What's that?" Neil said as he glanced over.

"A girlie magazine," Ricky said, looking at the cover.

"Yea, what one?" Neil said.

Ricky looked down at the magazine. There was an image of an attractive brunette dressed in white stockings and suspenders. She sat suggestively by the text 'The erotic thoughts of AMY'. In the left-hand corner it read, 'The sex shots of our readers' and 'TESSA and her sexy secrets'.

"Climax," Ricky said.

"Oh, nice one. I'm having that," Neil said with a broad grin.

"Really?" Ricky said, putting the magazine on the floor mat.

"Bloody right I am," Neil chuckled.

Neil indicated and turned left. They were only a mile or so away from the Milton Road Estate where they both lived.

The Milton Road Estate was constructed in 1962. The estate had over one thousand high rise, pre-cast concrete flats and maisonettes that were heated by a central communal boiler house. The eighteen hundred homes were filled with residents from all over London. The area gained a reputation for being rough and dangerous to outsiders. The local newspaper often referred to it as a 'no go' zone.

Neil looked in his rear-view mirror as he edged the car forward to turn left.

"Shit, it's the old bill!" Neil hissed.

Behind them was a white Ford Escort MK1 police car with a red stripe running down its side and a POLICE sign and blue light on the roof.

"We don't need this, Neil," Ricky said as he glanced over his shoulder.

"Don't worry mate. It's all in hand," Neil said as he took a firm grip on the steering wheel.

The police car siren came on.

"Hold tight," Neil said as he indicated to pull over by the side of the road.

Neil brought the Capri to a halt and sat calmly with the engine still running and his hands firmly on the steering wheel. Ricky and Neil sat in silence for several seconds before the police officer opened his door and stepped out.

Neil turned to Ricky and began to grin.

"You'll like this," Neil said with a wink.

Neil looked into his side view mirrors and just as the police officer got to the rear wheels he slowly edged forward.

"Stop!" shouted the officer as he trotted after the car.

Neil stopped just ahead of him. There was now a good thirty feet between the Capri and the Police car. Again, just as the officer got closer to the car, Neil drove slowly away, again taunting the officer.

"Stop in the name of the law!" the officer shouted, waving his arms in the air.

"Bollocks!" Neil shouted back as he revved the engine, dropped the clutch, and sped away. He began to laugh almost uncontrollably as he watched the police officer scamper back to his car in his rear-view mirror.

"He ain't got a chance in hell of catching this," Neil said with a manic grin. "It'll pass just about everything except a petrol station."

Neil sped along the main road and then slung the Capri sideways into the opening of Milton Road Estate. Under the sign somebody had painted graffiti. It read: 'Turn Back or Die'. Neil took a quick left and then a right while still checking his rear-view mirrors and keeping tyre squeal to a minimum.

"Lost him," Neil said with a triumphant grin.

"Yeah, cheers for that," Ricky said with an exaggerated sigh. "The last thing we need right now is a tug by the old bill."

Neil pulled the car up outside a set of garages. Ricky got out and produced a set of keys from his pocket. He leant down and undid a padlock and then opened the steel door.

"You'd better stick it here and dump it later," Ricky said as he stepped back to reveal an empty garage.

"I dunno," Neil said as he admired the Capri. "I might keep this one."

"Yeah, right. You say that every time I see you in a nicked motor," Ricky said as he held up the keys.

Neil drove the car into the garage and Ricky closed the door and locked the padlock. He twisted the key from his ring and handed it to Neil.

"Let me have it back later when you're done," Ricky said.

"Sure, no problem. When you gonna get your motor sorted then?" Neil asked.

Ricky had bought a Rover P5B from a face on the estate. The car's interior had been savaged by the owner's Doberman Pinscher and he'd run the engine low on oil causing it to seize. Other than that, the car was immaculate, and Ricky considered it a steal at one hundred and fifty pounds. The owner would have had the repairs carried out, but he was due in court on a robbery charge and didn't think he'd be back for a while. He needed the cash for his wife and kids.

"I've been doing the rounds looking for an interior and a replacement engine but there's been nothing at the right price yet," Ricky said as he slid his right hand into his pocket.

"It's a bloody nice motor," Neil said.

"Yeah, it will be when she's all sorted."

"Here, are you going down the Arms tonight?" Neil said as he placed the Climax magazine inside his jacket and zipped it up.

The Milton Arms was the local pub on the estate and known as 'The Arms' by its customers.

"Yeah, course, its Thursday night," Ricky said.

"Great, see you there, mate. I'm gagging for a pint and whatever else is on offer" Neil said as he turned, waved and strode off.

***

"Nice driving mister," a young kid riding past on his orange chopper bike shouted.

"If the old bill say anything, you didn't see anything, alright?" Ricky said with a wink.

"Course," the kid said with a cheeky grin, "I ain't no grass!"

Ricky walked past the garages, through the alleyways and then across the main road. One of the new, red, square shaped buses with automatic doors came to a halt by the bus stop. He carried on past the newsagents and noticed that it had just been refurbished with a Players No6 Cigarettes logo placed along the top of the window. Just below it was a board with handwritten adverts of unwanted goods for sale on the estate. Ricky browsed over them for a few seconds. Outside, by the entrance door, was a new Walls Ice Cream sign. Out of the corner of his eye, he spotted Deano the Dog and two of his lads.

Deano was a Teddy Boy. The Teds originated in the 1950s and wore flamboyant drape suits, ruffled collar shirts with bootlace ties and crepe soled brothel creeper shoes. They were hard, working-class men, smartly turned out and not afraid of confrontation. The Teds were back in full force and Deano the Dog was the number one, not just on the estate, but right across London. With his brown, greased back hair and sideburns, he had gained a reputation for fighting and beating many of the area's tough guys. It was rumoured that he joined a boxing gym and the trainer, aware of his growing reputation, put Deano, on his first night, in the ring with an ABA (Amateur Boxing Association) champion fighter. When the bell rang, Deano steamed straight in to his opponent firing punch after punch until the champion boxer was forced back against the ropes and slowly backed into the corner post. Deano was relentless with precision and hard, bone breaking, punches. Finally, without landing a single punch, the champion boxer collapsed into a heap on the mat. Deano pulled off his gloves and threw them down at his opponent before climbing out of the ring. The trainer had called him an animal and Deano stopped at the door, looked back at the stunned onlookers and said, 'that's right, Deano the Dog.' From that day the name stuck. Deano and his gang were known as the Milton Road Teds or MRT's. On the estate he was legendary. His gang would engage in vicious, violent brawls with gangs from other estates. He was fearless, unbeaten and his very presence commanded respect. Ricky was in awe of Deano and his gang. He had often daydreamed about becoming part of the gang, to hang out and wear a smart drape suit. To be more than an average working Joe, getting married, having kids and paying bills for the rest of his life. Ricky looked on the Milton Road Teds as a group with purpose and meaning. They were carving out their own place in the world, living an active front line life and not being merely spectators.

Ricky looked on as Deano and two of his lads disappeared into the bookies by the community centre. He passed by Doreen and two of her girls by the wall. The wall was where Doreen, the matriarch, and her shoplifting crew would meet customers and sell their daily takings.

Doreen was a platinum blonde with hair that toppled over her shoulders. She had alluring, galaxy blue eyes and a supple, curvaceous figure. On the Milton Road Estate Doreen was the number one supplier of cut-price stolen goods. She had a team of four girls, all professional shoplifters. They would drive to different parts of London and move from shop to shop stealing easy to sell goods like school uniforms, baby's formula milk, make-up, perfume and electronic goods. Doreen would also take forward orders for clothing, shoes and handbags for presents. On Saturdays, Doreen and her crew would visit large supermarkets and load their shopping trollies to the brim with pork chops, bacon, chickens, branded sausages and other foodstuffs then push it out of the doors and return to the wall outside the community centre where it was all sold off at discount prices in minutes.

"Alright Doreen," Ricky said with a brief wave of his hand.

"Hello, Ricky, isn't it?" Doreen said with a warm smile.

"Yeah, you know me and my mum," Ricky said.

"Course I do," Doreen chortled. "Here, I've got something for you."

"What's that?" Ricky said.

Doreen reached into a large black sports bag and produced a new, boxed, lava lamp.

"Your mum will love this. They're all the craze now, you know. I can't get enough of them," Doreen said as she handed Ricky the box.

"What do want for it?" Ricky said, trying to hand the box back.

"Because it's a present for your Mum, it's yours for three quid," Doreen said, rubbing her hands together.

"Three quid!" Ricky said.

"Alright two quid for you but you don't go telling anyone, alright?" Doreen said with a smile that showed off her dazzling angel-white teeth.

"Yeah, alright," Ricky said, reaching into his pocket and handing over two pounds.

Doreen snatched it out of his hand.

"Thank you darling. Now you say hello to your mum from me, alright?" Doreen said as she looked over Ricky's shoulder as another potential customer approached.

"Sure, catch you later," Ricky said.

The estate's parade of shops consisted of the newsagents who also sold foodstuffs, mostly supplied by Doreen, the Community Centre, the Bookies, a Fish & Chip Shop, the Chinese Take Away and the Milton Arms pub.

Ricky entered the fish & chip shop.

"Hello Tony," Ricky said.

"Hello Ricky," Tony the Greek, the owner of the fish and chip shop replied.

Tony always wore a white lab style coat, and his wife wore a green one. Everyone on the estate liked Tony. He would always give his customers an overly generous portion of chips. Outside the chip shop he was known by the locals as Tony the Bubble because bubble and squeak was rhyming slang for Greek.

"Is it the usual?" Tony asked with a smile.

"Yes, please Tony. Three medium size cod and chips with lashings of salt and vinegar," Ricky said before turning to look at the Corona shelf by the side of the chip fryer.

There was a line of bottles that included Lemonade, Cherryade, Orangeade and his mum's favourite, Cream Soda.

"Do you want a Cream Soda?" Tony asked as he placed a large cod on the greaseproof paper and covered it with chips.

"Yeah, go on then," Ricky said. "It's for my mum and she loves the stuff."

Chapter 2

"Hello Mum, Dad," Ricky called out as he entered his parents' two-bedroom flat.

"Is that you Ricky?" his mum called back.

"I hope so," Ricky chuckled, "or you're being robbed."

"Don't even joke about stuff like that on this estate," his dad said in a grumpy tone.

"Alright Dad. I picked up the fish and chips," Ricky said as he held up the brown paper bag.

"What do want, a medal or something?" Ricky's dad said as he stomped off into the kitchen.

"What's up with him?" Ricky said as he placed the bag of fish and chips on the kitchen table and handed his mum the bottle of Cream Soda.

"Take no notice of him, the miserable git. Oh, Cream Soda! My favourite, thank you," Ricky's mum said as she pecked him on the cheek.

"Here, I got you this," Ricky said as he handed his mum the boxed Lava Lamp.

"What a little darling you are," Ricky's mum said with a sigh, "Thank you."

"Here, less of the little," Ricky retorted with a cheeky grin.

"You'll always be my little boy," his mum said.

The fish and chips were put on plates and taken through to the front room. Ricky's dad was slouched back in his favourite chair with the plate on his lap. His mum took a sip from her glass of Cream Soda just as Top of the Pops started. Ricky watched as the intro music played and the countdown of numbers flashed across the TV screen. Finally it stopped at number one and the Top of the Pops appeared as the intro music came to its conclusion. The camera zoomed in through the studio crowd to Tony Blackburn as he jumped up and down in his roll neck jumper and gold chains, welcoming everyone to Top of the Pops. The top thirty artists were shown with the camera flashing back to a bunch of pretty girls dancing at number twenty. Ricky could see a rare smile on his dad's face. It seemed that the only time he smiled was when Top of the Pops was on, and especially when Pan's People danced.

"Did you see that?" his dad asked.

"See what, Arthur?" Mum said.

"Bill Haley and The Comets at number nineteen in the charts. Is this generation so hard up for good music that they have to wheel in a balding old timer from the 1950s?" Arthur said as he scowled at the television set.

"I don't know Arthur, but it strikes me that if people didn't like the song, it wouldn't be at number nineteen," Mum said.

"Don't be a smart arse, Caroline. It doesn't suit you," Arthur said sharply.

"Oh, look Dad," Ricky said, "Its little Jimmy Osmond. You like him, don't you?"

"Don't you start!" Arthur said with a growl.

"I could have sworn I saw you jigging about in the kitchen to Jimmy Osmond last Sunday," Ricky said as he shot a wink to Caroline.

"No, no, no! I wasn't doing anything of the sort. I was just exercising," Arthur said a little sharper than intended, before looking back at the television.

Ricky looked over at his mum, smiled, and winked again.

"I told you 'Waterloo' by Abba would be number one," Caroline said triumphantly.

"Yeah, alright I'll give you that," Arthur said with a heavy sigh. "I suppose it beats them bloody Wombles from Wimbledon Common. I mean, who in their right mind goes into a record shop and hands over good money for that load of drivel?"

Top of the Pops presenter Tony Blackburn tried and failed to get a young blonde girl in a white dress to sing before introducing 'Shang-a-Lang' by the Bay City Rollers.

Ricky ate the last of the chips and rose from his chair.

"Where are you off to then?" Arthur said abruptly.

"I'm meeting Neil for a pint in the Arms," Ricky said.

"The Arms! That place needs to be pulled to the ground brick by brick and replaced with a police station. The place is full of old lags, crooks and brasses," Arthur said as he shovelled a large piece of battered cod into his mouth.

Ricky glanced down at his watch.

"I've got to get ready, or I'll be late," Ricky said as he closed the living room door behind him.

Ricky shut his bedroom door firmly. The lock mechanism had been faulty for as long as he could remember. On the walls he had a movie poster of 'Enter the Dragon' starring Bruce Lee, and above his bed was a framed Ziggy Stardust and the Spiders from Mars by David Bowie album cover. Ricky turned on his blue Bush Record Player. He'd bought it for just three pounds after seeing it for sale on a handwritten card in the newsagent's window. He opened the lid and put *'Sugar Baby Love'* by the Rubettes on the turntable. He watched the arm automatically move across and land on the vinyl before opening his wardrobe to choose what he would be wearing. Ricky settled on a pair of Oxford Bags trousers with the three-button waistband, a white Ben Sherman shirt and his highly polished, ten-hole, Ox-Blood Doctor Marten Boots with the yellow stitching and air wear labels. Ricky had bought the boots from Doreen a few months back for just five pounds.

Ricky put his unopened wage packet in his bedside cabinet and took out the bundle of notes from his work trousers. He checked himself in the mirror and combed his hair into a middle parting. He smiled before opening his shirt and spraying on a healthy dose of Brut Deodorant. As he tried do the buttons back up, a button popped off.

"Shit!" Ricky thought as the button landed on the carpet.

"Mum, I've got a problem!"

"What's up sweetheart?"

Ricky walked back into the living room and handed her the button.

"That's not a problem. Go and get my button box from the sideboard," Caroline said as she pointed to the teak sideboard.

Within minutes Caroline had the button sewn back on.

"Right, I'm off, I'll see you later," Ricky called as he opened the front door.

"Make sure you have your front door key with you, or you'll be locked out," Arthur shouted after him. "Did you hear me?"

"Yes, Dad and if you shout just a little louder so will all the neighbours," Ricky called back as he closed the front door.

"He can get right on my wick sometimes," Ricky thought as he walked across the estate to the Milton Arms. *"He wants to get up off his backside and do something with his life instead of just whinging and moaning about all and sundry while watching the bloody television."*

Chapter 3

To the casual onlooker, The Milton Arms pub didn't appear to be any different from pubs all over the manor. Its dark red brick and four pane windows made it stand out from the community centre. A sign had been placed above the entrance doors. It read Truman // The Milton Arms. There was nothing to suggest that it had a long history of violence, slashings and even a murder. Ricky had witnessed outsiders enter the pub and the atmosphere radically change in an instant. As they ordered a beer, all eyes would turn to the outsiders and follow them back to their seats. Those that had chosen to stand at the bar would find two muscle-bound, intimidating, characters from the estate stand either side of them. All strangers were made to feel thoroughly unwelcome. Very few stayed to finish their beer. For many, the Milton Arms was a place of business. Criminals would be talking shop, brasses plying their trade and moody gear being openly traded. It's a place where severe, bloody, violence could erupt in an instant without a single customer witnessing a thing and a place where the police were unable to carry out any undercover surveillance safely.

Ricky opened the pub doors and peered in. As usual it was packed just as it was every Thursday night. He caught Neil's eye and made a drinking gesture. Neil nodded and ordered an extra pint of Watney's Bitter and a bottle of light ale. Ricky spotted John sitting on the salmon pink upholstered chairs.

"Alright mate?" Ricky said as he sat down.

"Alright Ricky," John said before taking a large gulp from his pint. "I'm on a right roll tonight. This is the third pint and I'm going to break my personal record."

"Your record John?" Ricky said, sounding surprised.

"Yes mate. Last Saturday I managed to put away seven pints and tonight I'm going for eight."

"Eight pints! John, mate, you've only got eight pints of blood in your body," Ricky said, shaking his head in disbelief.

"Yeah, but some things have just got to be done," John said as he took a Rothmans cigarette from its packet.

He offered the packet to Ricky.

"No, mate. I don't smoke," Ricky said, shaking his head.

"There you go lads," Neil said as he approached the table with beer spilling over the glasses' rims.

Ricky looked up and saw Jackie, his friend since junior school. She smiled and waved from behind the bar.

"Get that down your Gregory," Neil said as he handed Ricky the pint of bitter and a bottle of light ale.

Ricky understood Gregory Peck to be rhyming slang for neck. On the estate rhyming slang was commonplace.

"Cheers mate," Ricky said as he took his first sip.

"So, it looks like you're on the firm tonight," Neil said as he raised and lowered his eyebrows several times and nodded back towards Jackie at the bar.

"What?"

"With Jackie. I've seen the way she looks at you. I'm telling you mate, half a shandy and you'd be right in there," Neil said with a raucous laugh.

"Give it a rest," Ricky said as he put his pint on the table. "You know as well as me that it ain't like that between us. She's just a friend. A good friend, granted, but that's it. We don't have any hold over each other."

"I'd be in there like a rat up a drainpipe," John slurred as he finished his fourth pint.

"Well, you would be," Ricky said.

"What do you mean by that?" John said.

"You're all talk and," Ricky paused for a second, "and you're a virgin."

"Bollocks am I," John retorted.

"Only if self-abuse counts," Neil said as he winked at Ricky.

"I got off with that bird, what's her name, Shirley. That's it, Shirley, at Steve Ward's party," John said as he slammed his empty glass down on the table.

"John that was four years ago and no you didn't have sex with Shirley. I know Shirley and she told me that all you did was try and kiss her, but she wasn't having none of it," Ricky said.

"Yeah, and she told me you kept on telling her that you loved her and wouldn't stop begging her for sex," Neil said. "Mate, that is embarrassing."

"Bollocks to the pair of yer! You both know that ain't true," John said adamantly.

"I don't know so much," Ricky said in a jovial tone, "I've been half expecting you to kind of come out the closet for some time."

"It's funny that, Ricky. I had my suspicions for some time that John was a bit that way inclined," Neil said as he pushed his upper body tight against the back of the chair.

"What, a back door merchant?" Ricky said, bending his hand and hunching his shoulders.

"You two are well out of order now, so you need to shut the hell up before this gets personal," John said with a scowl.

"Oh, shut up you tart," Ricky said with a short laugh. "You couldn't punch your way out of a paper bag. We're just having a laugh, winding you up and John, mate, you bite every time."

"Yeah, well, I'm just saying," John said.

"Here," Ricky said, handing John a couple of notes. "Go and get another round in."

John took the cash and traipsed over to the bar.

"Here Ricky, have you seen Doreen over there?"

"Yes mate," Ricky said as looked over Neil's shoulder.

Doreen stood at the far end of the bar surrounded by her shoplifting crew. She wore a knee length black leather skirt and a tight, rose red, designer blouse that accentuated her pert, rounded, breasts.

"Tell you what, I don't half fancy her," Neil said, before knocking back the last of his pint.

"Fancy Doreen? Are you having a laugh? She's old enough to be your mum."

"Take a good look at her Ricky. That woman is a living, breathing, encyclopaedia of experience. Imagine what she could teach a guy in the bedroom," Neil said, leering in Doreen's direction.

"But she's old, Neil, and to her you'd just be the boy that's been babysitting for her kids for the last three years while she was out on the prowl" Ricky said.

"Nah, there's something there. I can feel it," Neil said.

"What you feel is the same thing all blokes feel when the wind changes direction mate," Ricky said.

"I'm telling you now Ricky. I would drink Doreen's bath water with a straw and do it twice on a Sunday."

"You're a sick man Neil. You need help," Ricky said with a laugh.

Just then, in front of their table, Double Bubble, the estate's hard man money lender, bumped into a group of guys. Ricky could see that the man was ready to give the person a mouthful for spilling his beer but when he saw it was Double Bubble, he bit his lip and remained silent.

Double Bubble earned his name as a money lender because anyone who borrowed five pounds on a Friday had to repay ten pounds the following week and if you couldn't pay then it was doubled up again. He stood at just over six foot tall and had a chest size of fifty-four inches. At an early age he had been convicted for shop breaking, larceny and had been in and out of youth centres. He eventually wound up in Borstal. Once inside the prison system he was violent towards the screws and built a reputation amongst the other inmates. He was extremely strong and powerful. Double Bubble was always working out in the gym doing endless press ups and lifting prisoners or officers with one hand. During one altercation he bear hugged a prisoner until he collapsed. The violent outbursts secured him a place at Broadmoor where he honed his money lending skills. It was rumoured that he took an axe to a prisoner over three pounds. On the Milton Road Estate Double Bubble preyed on the weak and vulnerable. He ruled with fear and was, quietly considered by most, a loathsome thug, a nasty piece of work but an essential economic ingredient for those living on government handouts and to the scores of petty thieves.

"I hate him," Neil said in a whisper.

"I heard that he waited outside one bloke's place of work and just took his unopened wage packet straight from him. The bloke was apparently in tears, begging to let him keep some of the money to feed his family but Double Bubble was having none of it," Ricky said softly.

"Yeah, I heard that. The bloke is a right liberty taker. One of these days he'll have what's coming to him," Neil said.

"Maybe, but I wouldn't hold your breath," Ricky said.

"I'm surprised that Ronnie, the landlord, hasn't shown him the door," Neil said.

Ronnie, the landlord, was a well-known London face from the early 1960s. He had worked with Bruce Reynolds, the mastermind behind the Great Train Robbery after they met while he was serving time in Wormwood Scrubs for petty crimes. He was brought in to turn over a security van carrying wages in North London, but the team had been grassed. The Cozzers were ready for them and swooped in, tooled up, and nicked them all. Ronnie said nothing throughout the trial at the Old Bailey and was weighed off for ten years. He did his time, came out and went straight, despite several offers of work, and ended up running pubs. And because he was known and respected, the brewery placed him in their most difficult pubs. Ronnie ran a straight establishment. No regular punter would take out and out liberties. There were unwritten rules on estates like Milton Road and Ronnie knew just how to work it.

"Here Neil, John's only trying to give it the big one with Trudy over there," Ricky said.

"Doesn't he know that she's a brass?" Neil said.

"There's nothing wrong with a brass mate. Everyone has to get by in any way they can. Trudy is a single parent with two kids from two fathers and neither are coughing up child support. She doesn't have a lot of choices and if turning tricks is putting food on the table then good for her," Ricky said.

"I didn't mean anything by it," Neil said.

"Good, she's alright is Trudy," Ricky said.

"Maybe John wants to lose his virginity," Neil said with a snigger.

"I guess he'd have to get in line right behind you then," Ricky said with a smirk.

"Yeah, right, as if," Neil said.

John returned to the table with a tray of drinks.

"I think someone's been having a right good chin wag about me. My left ear is hotter than Sally James stark bollock naked!" John said.

The lads all laughed.

Ricky looked down the bar to the far tables where he knew that Deano and the Milton Road Teds were sitting. Deano was surrounded by his top Teds. Micky Deacon was his number two and best known for his temper and short fuse. Specs had been named that because he wore black framed national health glasses. He was married with a little boy and was well liked by everyone on the estate. Kenny, with his big blue eyes, fluorescent porcelain white teeth and boyish good looks, was the womaniser. If it wasn't for the Teddy Boy drape suit and Blue Suede shoes, he could have passed for a Donny Osmond lookalike. Kenny could sweet talk a nun out of her habit and took great pride in his appearance. Girls of all ages, social backgrounds and sizes were drawn to him like a moth to a flame. Lee was… Lee. He talked a great talk about past conflicts and conquests, but no one was ever there to substantiate his claims. After a few beers Deano would invite Lee to stand and give a speech. The whole group would join in chanting 'speech, speech, speech'. Lee would stand and then ramble on about how proud and honoured he was to be part of the Milton Road Teds, much to the amusement of the other lads.

To Deano's right were three very attractive girls. Melanie was Deano's ex-girlfriend. Their on/off relationship was complex, passionate and emotionally intense. Her magma-red hair spiralled down over her shoulders and rested on her white and red tartan polo shirt. She had an hour-glass figure and wore a white pleated short skirt, stylish white leather knee length boots with a sassy platform heel. Her friends Donna and Kaz were twins, and both

34

wore short red pleated skirts with Bay City Roller T-Shirts and red patent leather high heel shoes. The three girls were inseparable and turned heads wherever they went.

Ricky's attention was drawn towards a group of four workmen standing at the far end of the bar.

"Do you know who that noisy lot are?" Ricky said as he nodded towards the group.

"Yeah, I've seen them in here a couple of times. They're a scaffolding team working on the estate. Normally they pop in for a pint after finishing up and bugger off, so no one has really paid them much attention," Neil said as he handed Ricky a pint from the tray.

Ricky looked back at the group. One of them was a similar size to Double Bubble. He stood in the middle waving his pint jug around, spilling beer onto the carpet as he spoke.

"Right lads, my shout," Ricky said. "What you having?"

"Give it a rest," John said. "It's my turn to get them in."

"No, mate I insist. I've had a good week and I'm feeling flush," Ricky said as he patted his side pocket.

"Well in that case I'll have a Southern Comfort and lemonade," Neil said.

"I'll have another pint," John slurred, slouching back in the chair, opening his mouth wide and letting out a long, loud, beery burp.

"John, that was disgusting," Ricky said, fanning the smell of beery breath away from his face.

Neil, having finished his third pint, was in fits of laughter.

"Ricky I couldn't help it mate. I could feel it building up in my throat and I tried, trust me I really tried to swallow it back down, but it just wouldn't have it. I gotta say though I'm feeling much better for it now," John said as held out both his arms and then put them on his stomach.

"It's no wonder you don't get any birds," Ricky thought.

Ricky crossed the pub and stood at the bar. Jackie was serving Doreen but looked over and nodded.

"How are you, Ricky?" Jackie said as she started to pour the drinks

"Yeah, I'm good, thanks. How are you?"

"I'm okay. Working here keeps me busy most nights. I do miss standing on the other side of the bar sometimes and of course our chats. When I think back, we must have talked about everything at some point over the years. I miss that, don't you?"

"We've been good friends for a long time Jackie," Ricky said as he handed her a five-pound note.

Jackie opened the till and then returned, putting four one-pound notes and a pound in change into his hand. Ricky quickly put it into his pocket.

"I should be finished up here just after midnight. Do you fancy coming back to my place for a coffee?" Jackie said with a slight flutter of her eyelids.

"I can't tonight, Jackie. I've got to be up early for work. Maybe another time," Ricky said as he picked up the tray of drinks.

"Are you sure?" Jackie said, puckering her lips to feign disappointment.

"Sorry, I can't tonight," Ricky said.

"Maybe another time then?" Jackie said before turning away to serve another customer.

"Yeah, sure," Ricky said.

Ricky and Jackie had been good friends since junior school. At the age of thirteen Ricky began to look at Jackie in a whole new light. He no longer saw her as the little tom boy that would run wild through the swing park or the girl he would talk to for hours upon hours about music, pop groups and people on the estate. Jackie began to develop breasts and curves. Ricky found himself thinking about her constantly, but felt awkward and difficult about sharing his feelings. He wanted to hold her hand, take her into his arms and kiss her sweet lips. On one occasion, after what he felt was a series of mixed signals, he built up the courage to open up a little, but Jackie promptly changed the subject. Jackie was attracting significant attention from lads at school and around the estate. Whilst walking back home one night he turned the corner by the garages and saw Jackie kissing an older lad passionately against the wall. Everything changed that day. Ricky felt betrayed and let down. He found it difficult to process how his long-term friend, that he had developed strong feelings for, could still look upon him as just a friend and then openly flirt with other boys around him.

At home Ricky began to argue and become hostile towards his parents. Increasingly he had become uncooperative and antagonistic and would often just retreat to his bedroom. His mother, Caroline, understood that Ricky's behaviour was just puberty, but his father, Arthur, had no patience for anyone at the best of times. As time moved on Ricky remained friends with Jackie but he conditioned himself to look upon her and their relationship as just good friends, almost sisterly. When Ricky began to get attention from other pretty girls around the area, he found it became easier to hide his vulnerability, the pain of rejection, and shelve his inner turmoil, emotional confusion and true feelings for Jackie.

"You're mad you are," John said shaking his head slowly

Ricky handed them their drinks.

"There's a right cracking looking bird over there who clearly fancies the pants off you and you do nothing. If I was you, I'd be all over it like a rash," John said.

"Jackie and I are friends, nothing more, and you would be over anything that was drunk enough to let you," Ricky said abruptly. "Now give it a rest."

Melanie, Donna and Kaz strutted over to the Jukebox. The coin dropped in and they made their selection. The three girls turned around and stood in a line.

"Do You Wanna Touch" by Gary Glitter blasted out of the speakers.

The girls swayed their hips back and forth while running their tongues over their succulent, sultry, and velvety soft red lips. All eyes were on the girls as their short skirts lifted and dropped to the rhythm of the song. They slowly swirled their hips around and then thrust them forward in perfect harmony.

The builders had put their drinks on the bar and stared as the girls turned around slowly, with each girl placing their hand on the other's rear and patting it suggestively in time to the music. The larger of the builders made a playful grab for Melanie, but she swept his hand away and continued with their routine. The builders began to cheer and egg him on with one of the men patting him on the shoulder and encouraging him to try again. The builder stepped forward with his legs apart and began to emulate the girls dancing by swivelling his hips back and forth. His friends were in hysterics and urging him to do more. Melanie and the girls continued to dance, ignoring the builder's drunken antics. He made another intoxicated attempt to grab Melanie, but again she pushed his hand away. The builders were laughing and cajoling him to try yet again. He did, only this time Melanie pushed him away with both hands

"Get your filthy hands off me!" Melanie yelled.

The record came to a stop and both Donna and Kaz stood either side of Melanie.

"Crawl back into your corner," Donna said firmly.

The builders were still laughing. The expression on the larger of the builder's face changed. He lunged forward and grabbed Melanie and pulled her in tight to his body and placed a hand on her backside.

"Get off me!" Melanie screamed as she wriggled and tried desperately to pull away.

"Take your hands off her!" Deano warned.

He stood just inches away in his immaculate red drape jacket, white shirt with a bootlace tie made up of two crossing silver colt 45 guns and matching red drainpipe trousers. On his feet he wore white brothel creepers with red stitching.

The builder let go of Melanie and faced Deano. He looked him up and down slowly.

"Well I never, the circus is in town," the builder said with a sarcastic laugh.

Before the last word left his lips Deano lunged forward and head butted the builder 'SMACK' on the nose. There was a loud, sickening, crack, and blood shot out onto the bar stool. The builder's knees buckled as he grabbed his face with both hands and slid down the side of the bar. One of his friends moved forward. Deano launched a punch and struck him hard in the stomach. Just as he tumbled forward Deano sent a second upper cut with such ferocity that the builder's head jerked so far back, he lost his balance and collapsed onto the floor.

Deano shook his fingers on both hands as he looked down on both the floored victims.

"You two fancy your chances?" Deano said calmly as he clenched both fists and stared menacingly at the remaining builders.

Neither one of them moved. They were like animals caught in the headlights of a car. Finally, one of them spoke.

"Look mate, we're sorry alright? It's been a misunderstanding."

"Alright I think we've had enough for tonight," Ronnie the landlord said. "Get your pals off the floor and out of my pub."

"Yeah, no problem, mate. We don't want any trouble," the builder said as he leant down to help his mate up.

"You're not welcome here, alright?" Ronnie said firmly.

"Sure, whatever you say," replied the builder as they helped their injured friends towards the door.

"Go on, sod off and don't come back!" Melanie screamed as she stood with both hands firmly on her hips.

"You're all barred" Ronnie called as they opened the door.

Chapter 4

"Ricky your breakfast is on the table."

"Thanks Mum, I'll be out in a minute," Ricky said.

Ricky had been awake for hours thinking about how Deano the Dog had handled the builders the night before at The Arms.

"What a legend," Ricky thought. *"He smashed the pair of them builders up then offered the other two out and looked so damn cool while he did it. I wanna be a Ted and I want the clobber and the respect that goes with it."*

Ricky pulled on his work jeans and steel toe capped boots, checked his reflection in the mirror and then joined his parents in the kitchen.

"I did you cornflakes, is that alright?" Caroline said as she put the breakfast bowl on the table.

"Yeah, cheers Mum," Ricky said, picking up his spoon.

"He'll be grateful for whatever you make him," Arthur said gruffly.

"Good to see you got out the bed on the right side this morning, Dad," Ricky said sarcastically.

"I don't want any of your cheek either," Arthur said stabbing his finger at Ricky.

"Did you have a nice time last night?" Caroline said, patting his head affectionately.

"Yeah, it was alright Mum, just a few beers and a laugh with the boys."

"That Neil is a bad influence. You do know that, don't you? I've been saying that for years. He steals cars you know, and joyrides them about at night. Everyone knows it and mark my words he'll land you in trouble, and when that happens, I'll just tell you how I told you so," Arthur said reaching for his tea.

"Neil is my mate, and you don't want to believe everything you hear," Ricky said firmly.

"Well, I'm telling you this, my boy, if the old bill come knocking on my door you're out of here. Do you understand?"

"Arthur, why do you always have to start?" Caroline said as she put a mug of tea on the table.

"You watch your mouth and stop sticking up for him," Arthur said in a soft, slightly menacing, tone.

"I don't need anyone to stick up for me," Ricky said.

"Really!" Arthur said, slamming his spoon down on the kitchen table.

"You don't scare me Dad," Ricky said as he calmly put his spoon on the table.

"Please, please stop this, for heaven's sake," Caroline pleaded.

"Sorry Mum," Ricky said as he stood up. "I better get going. Do you need me to bring anything in for you later?"

"No thank you darling. I'm going to the Fine Fare Supermarket later so I can get my Green Shield Stamps. I've got four books now, only a couple more and I'll be able to get that glass fish ornament I like for the coffee table or a set of six of those crystal cut Ravenhead glasses. I've not made up my mind yet," Caroline said with a broad smile.

"I'm sure the stupid glass fish will go great with that picture of the Spanish Flamenco dancer on the bloody wall!" Arthur said.

"I like that picture, Arthur. Maybe one day. You know, when we win the pools, we'll go to Spain and then I'll see them dance in real life," Caroline said as she rubbed her hands together. "Oh, and I am watching the Dick Emery show tonight. You promised Arthur."

"Got to go, see you later," Ricky called as he opened the front door.

"I've got to think about the future. I can't be putting up with that miserable, cantankerous old duffer for much longer. I need change and only I can make that happen," Ricky thought as he crossed the kids' play park and walked out onto the main road.

He spotted the milkman, dressed in his white jacket and black trousers tucked into his wellington boots, in his open back float. Ricky gave him a wave. He had planned to take the bus in to work but Neil was there in the RS Capri.

"You have to got to be off your head still smoking about in this," Ricky said.

"Yeah, and good morning to you too. This is going to be a tough one to walk away from," Neil said as he patted the roof. "So, do you want a lift into work or what?"

Ricky hesitated for a moment and then got into the car.

"Yeah, go on then, but none of the racing about stuff alright?"

Neil shrugged his shoulders and said "Alright."

As they drove out of the estate, Ricky took a deep breath.

"Do you ever want to just change stuff Neil?"

"Yeah, of course. Everyone wants that, don't they?" Neil said, changing gears as the traffic lights turned red.

"Everyone might say they want it, but very few actually make a real change, do they? I mean just take a look around the estate. I could give you countless examples of people doing the same stuff today that they were doing last year and the year before and most probably the year before that," Ricky said.

"What's your point?" Neil asked.

"My point is that change is something we have to do ourselves. We have to create and forge our own future. I've got some ideas that could make a big difference if you're interested," Ricky said enthusiastically.

"I'm in," Neil said.

"Neil, mate, you don't even know what they are yet," Ricky said with a chuckle.

"Yeah, but knowing you they'll be well thought out, so, mate, I'm in, especially if it'll take me closer to getting laid by the delightful Doreen," Neil said as he puckered his lips.

"I can't promise you that," Ricky said.

"Well, I'm babysitting for her again on Saturday night as she's going to the Cadillac Club. She asked me last night after Deano the Dog bashed seven sorts of shit out of those loudmouth builders."

"And you just said yes, bolloxing up a Saturday night?"

"What can I say, mate? I just can't get her out of my head. You've got to admit she doesn't look her age, does she?"

"No, I'll give you that. She does look good for her age," Ricky said.

"I just love the way she struts about in her heels and is so full of self-confidence. There's nothing needy, clingy or desperate with a woman like that. She makes all her own money and doesn't rely on any man for anything. That, my old son, I find incredibly sexy."

"Fair play Neil, I ain't judging. None of us can help who we're attracted to," Ricky said.

"I'm getting a stiffy just talking about her," Neil said, laughing out loud.

"Mate, I don't want to know!"

Just a few hundred yards before Harrington Garage, Ricky spotted a grey coloured PA Cresta parked on the side of the road with the bonnet up. It was Deano.

"Neil, mate, can you drop me here?" Ricky said, undoing his seat belt.

"Yeah course," Neil said as he checked his rear-view mirror, indicated and brought the car to a halt.

"Listen, right. Do not dump the Capri. Take it back to the garage and lock it away. I'll meet you there tonight at 7.00pm," Ricky said.

"Alright Ricky, see you later. You be lucky mate," Neil said as he drove away.

Ricky walked slowly towards the parked the PA Cresta.

"Everything alright Deano?" Ricky said.

Deano glanced up and looked Ricky up and down.

"No, the bloody thing has broken down," Deano said.

"I'm a mechanic, well, an apprentice. Do you want me to take a look?"

Deano stepped back from under the bonnet.

"Be my guest. I can't tell one end of a motor from the other," Deano said as he rubbed his hands down his trousers.

Ricky rolled up his sleeves and took a look. He had learnt very early on that providing a car has a spark, fuel and air then an engine will run. It wasn't rocket science. Ricky checked that the spark plugs lead was on tight and then noticed that the coil lead to the distributor wasn't attached.

"There's your problem," Ricky said, reaching in and reattaching the lead. "Can you turn the ignition key for me?"

Deano climbed into the passenger's side door and slid across the bench seat until he sat in front of the steering wheel. He reached down and turned the key. Instantly the car leapt into life. Ricky pulled the carburettor cable several times so the engine revved.

"It's only a quick fix but it'll get you out of trouble," Ricky said.

"Cheers mate. I know you, don't I?" Deano said with a quizzical smile.

"We both live on Milton Road Estate and drink at the Arms," Ricky said.

"Were you there last night?" Deano asked.

"Yes, I watched you iron out a pair of those builders, nice one!" Ricky said.

"Oh, that was nothing. They just overstepped the mark and got a slap for being out of order."

Deano looked down at his watch and shook his head.

"I can't hang around here all day talking bollocks or I'll be late for work," Deano said.

"Yeah, right no problem," Ricky said as he rolled his sleeves back down.

"I appreciate what you did here. So, the next time you're in the Arms I'll get you a pint, alright?" Deano said as he clambered into his car.

"Yeah, great. Cheers mate," Ricky said.

"What's your name?" Deano said abruptly as he put the column change gear shifter into gear with a loud clunk.

"Ricky, Ricky Turrell."

"Cheers Ricky. I'll catch you later," Deano said as he pulled out onto the main road and drove away.

"How bloody cool was that?" Ricky thought. *"I'm right in there now. Deano the Dog knows who the hell I am and he's going to buy me a pint at the Arms."*

***

Ricky had been treated to a Vesta Beef Risotto by his mum for dinner. They were on special offer at the local Fine Fare supermarket. His dad was plotted up in front of the television drooling over Barbara Windsor.

"I'm going to be late Mum, so don't wait up alright?" Ricky said as he opened the front door.

He waited for a sarcastic or confrontational comment from his dad, but it didn't come.

"Alright darling," Caroline said as she carried a pot of tea and two cups on a tray into the living room.

Ricky was still dressed in his work clothes and was surprised that neither his mum or dad had questioned him or passed comment.

Over at the garages, Neil was standing by the garage with the up and over door open.

"Well I put the Capri back as you said. Now what's the plan?" Neil asked.

"You and I are going into the car spares business, Neil," Ricky announced with a grin.

"I've never lifted a spanner in my life," Neil chuckled.

"You don't have to. I think we could both do with a few extra quid, and it strikes me that we have that right in front of us," Ricky said, pointing to the RS Capri, "A highly desirable car with parts that are in demand. What I want for us to do is strip this motor right down to its chassis and then I'll sell all the parts on."

"Do you have someone in mind?" Neil said.

"I'll take care of the sales," Ricky said confidently.

"What about the chassis?" Neil said.

"No problem. I'll remove the chassis plate and the scrap man will hoist it away without any questions. Neil, it'll be crushed within hours with no come backs," Ricky said.

"Bloody hell, you've thought this through," Neil said.

Chapter 5

"Mick, I wouldn't do her with yours. She's got a face like a blind cobbler's thumb," Kenny said as he scrunched up his face.

"Yeah right. You, Kenny, are a two-bob slag. If it has a pulse, you'd be all over it. Now tell me I'm wrong and remember, before you open that big gob of yours, that we've all known you since school," Mick said.

"I'm hurt that you think of me like that Mick," Kenny said, letting out a long raucous laugh while holding both hands on his chest.

"I'd give it a go," Lee said.

"Lee, you'd shag a corpse if it was still warm," Deano said.

"Err, no I wouldn't Deano," Lee said.

"I've still got the hump with you," Deano said softly.

"What for?" Lee asked, shrugging his shoulders innocently.

"You bloody well know why Lee. When we had it with those lads on the Kings Road, you bottled it," Mick said.

"Nah, I didn't," Lee whimpered as he shook his head.

"Yes, you bloody did!" Deano said with a menacing glare. "The minute it kicked off you had it on your toes. By rights I ought to give you a slap, right here, right now!"

"Nah, nah, Deano, I explained it to everyone. I had to be home and didn't want to miss the train," Lee pleaded.

"Really?" Mick said. "Is that why you were legging it down the middle of the main road with your arms waving about like you were trying to flag down a taxi?"

Deano, his number two, Micky Deacon, Kenny, Specs and Lee were in the Wimpy Bar, a fast-food restaurant on the High Street. The waitress brought them over their order of cheeseburgers, a Wimpy Special Grill for Kenny, french fries and a Knickerbocker Glory for Lee.

"There you go Kenny," Specs said, nodding towards the waitress after she left the table.

"Not a chance," Kenny said. "She's got a face like a grieving cod."

"I bet she bangs like a bog door in a gale," Mick said as he took a huge bite out of his cheeseburger.

"Yeah, my money says she could suck a golf ball through a straw," Specs said as he pushed a handful of french fries into his mouth.

Kenny looked up to take a second look at the waitress.

"Maybe, but she would have to ask nicely," Kenny said as he shovelled a mix of fried egg and chips into his mouth.

"Told you lads, he's nothing but a two-bob slag that would shag anything with a pulse," Mick said.

"Right, have you lot finished?" Deano said as he placed his knife and fork on the dinner plate.

Kenny and Mick nodded.

51

"Okay, what's going on around the manor? Who has been having it with who?"

"Well," Mick said, "I heard that the Cambridge Flats lot had a run in with that mob from over Streatham way. From what I've heard they did them up like kippers and it was all over some bird."

"That doesn't surprise me," Kenny said.

"What doesn't surprise you?" Deano asked sternly.

"That the Cambridge Flats lot came out on top. They're a bunch of pretty game lads. I mean they don't run off at the first sign of trouble like Lee here," Kenny said.

"Leave it out Kenny," Lee said.

"I heard there was a run in on Chelsea Bridge between two biker gangs," Specs said.

Deano shrugged his shoulders and dismissed it as not being of interest.

"What about the Bedford Boot Boys?" Deano asked.

There was silence around the table.

"I've not heard anything," Mick said finally.

"Me either," Kenny said.

"What, nothing at all?" Deano said, as he slowly shook his head.

"Nah, nothing," Specs said.

"Well that tells me that either our information ain't as good as it should be, or Clifford Tate and his gang of twenty odd skinheads

52

have given up having rows and have taken up carrying old ladies' shopping home or something," Deano said.

"Maybe we'll find out a bit more when we get down the Cadillac Club on Saturday night," Mick said.

"Yeah, maybe," Deano said.

Deano got everyone to pay for what they ordered and sent Lee up to pay the bill.

"I might pop into the bookies," Deano said.

"Have you had a tip or something?" Lee asked.

"Yeah, a little bird told me that were a bottle job Lee," Deano said.

The lads all laughed.

Outside on the high street, Kenny spotted three Skinheads walking towards them. They wore skin-tight blue Levi jeans, with ox-blood high leg Doctor Marten boots, short sleeved shirts and braces.

"Well fuck my old boots," Deano said sarcastically. "Look what we have here."

Instinctively the Milton Road Teds spread across the pavement to prevent them passing.

Deano took a cigarette from its packet and lit it. He inhaled deeply and blew the smoke skywards.

"You look like Bedford Road Boot Boys to me," Deano said. "Is that right then?"

The three Skinheads stopped just a few feet away from the Teds.

"We ain't looking for any trouble," one of the Skins said.

"You speak for yourself," the biggest of the lads said.

Deano looked down at the Skin's right arm. He had a tattoo of a large blade, swallows and 'Saturday Night's Alright for Fighting' written in a scroll with two dice underneath. Deano knew that it was the image featured on the inside cover of the 'Goodbye Yellow Brick Road' album by Elton John.

Deano smiled and raised his eyebrows in mock surprise.

"So, you're the big bollock then," Deano said.

"I'm Eddy, Eddy Boyce, and you Milton Road Teds don't frighten me one bit," Eddy said as he puffed out his chest and squared up to Deano.

"That's good to know," Deano said as a manic smile spread across his face.

Deano's right arm shot out like a loaded mortar rocket. His clenched fist smashed into the Skinhead's chin. Deano sent a second and then a third punch, each strike faster and harder than the last. Eddy's knees sagged. Deano kneed him straight in the face. Eddy keeled over and fell into a heap on the ground.

The other Skinheads didn't move. One held his hand up, clearly indicating that he didn't want any trouble.

"Eddy Boyce. Yes, I'll remember that name. You might want to do your homework before opening your big mouth next time. You tell that jug-eared bellend Clifford Tate that you had a run in with Deano the Dog and the Milton Road Teds and he might want to keep his mongrel puppies on a lead if he doesn't want to see them bashed up," Deano said.

Eddy didn't respond.

Deano buried his blue suede brothel creeper deep into his stomach. Eddy winced with the pain.

"Did you hear me?" Deano said menacingly.

"Yeah," muttered Eddy.

"Good. The next time you see a Drape suit you might want to cross the road."

Deano turned away slowly and led the Milton Road Teds towards his parked PA Cresta.

Chapter 6

Ricky stripped the Ford RS3100 Capri of everything saleable. The V6 Essex engine, gearbox, axle, suspension, body panels and all its interior. Only the bare shell was left. Ricky removed the chassis number plate and called the scrap man to cart it away to be sold off for the price of its weight in metal. With all the parts now ready for sale, Ricky bought a pack of clear postcards and hand wrote 'Breaking RS Capri' and his parent's telephone number. A card was placed in the windows of newsagents and convenience stores within a five-mile radius. By the time he returned home the phone had already started ringing. Within just 24 hours Ricky had sold everything. To avoid being left with anything he discounted some of the parts to motor traders and back street garages. Ricky had made just over £400 in cash. It was the equivalent of four month's wages, before stoppages, as an apprentice motor mechanic at Harrington's Garage.

Ricky put Neil's share of the money in his black and gold money box by the side of his bed. With a pocket full of cash, he took a walk to the train station. As he passed by the community centre, he spotted Double Bubble by the wall. There was an orderly line of hard-up couples and single mothers waiting to either repay their loan or to borrow money. Ricky bought a ticket and travelled through London on the underground and got off at Sloane Square. He walked around the corner on to the Kings Road, Chelsea. Ricky passed the Antiquarius Antiques market but stopped outside Acme Attractions. They were pumping out Reggae tunes and had a rail of electric blue zoot suits and juke boxes for sale. Ricky was looking for Malcolm McClaren and Vivienne Westwood's shop 'Let It Rock' on 430 Kings Road, Chelsea. The Kings Road was infamous for large gatherings of Teddy Boys and 'Let It Rock' was the go-to place for the very best in Teddy Boy gear.

Ricky had concluded that if he was going to become a Ted then he wanted the best clobber available and with a pocket full of cash it was now more than a dream. He walked up and down the Kings Road but failed to find the shop. He walked back again slowly rechecking the door and shop numbers. Ricky stopped outside a shop with the giant four-foot shocking pink lettering spelling the word 'SEX' above the door. Ricky took a long look to his left and then his right. Taking a deep breath, he entered the shop. Inside there were various ensembles of rubber and leather fetish goods. He was approached by a shop assistant with long bleached blonde hair and thick black eye make–up. She wore a short black leather skirt and matching blazer.

"Excuse me, but can you tell me where I'll find 'Let It Rock'?" Ricky asked.

The assistant looked Ricky up and down and smiled.

"You're standing in it, or should I say you're standing where it once was," the assistant said.

"Damn," Ricky muttered.

"What was it you were looking for?" the assistant asked.

"Teddy Boy gear," Ricky said.

"Well, you might be in luck. We still have drapes, shirts and stuff out the back. Do you want to take a look?"

Ricky beamed and followed the assistant through a door to the back of the shop where he was met with several rails of drape suits, shirts, socks and boxes of Brothel Creeper shoes.

Ricky began to browse enthusiastically through their stock. The assistant looked him up and down and began to take out suits that looked to be his size.

"Everything here has to go so we can probably work out some special prices if that helps," the assistant smiled.

Ricky bought three drape suits, four white silk shirts, socks, a handful of bootlace ties and a black leather belt with a silver tiger's head buckle the size of his fist. There were four different pairs of brothel creeper shoes in his size. Ricky bought them all. The assistant threw in two additional black silk shirts and showed him a heavy, biker style, black leather jacket with silver studs which he declined. When Ricky asked if she could recommend a good hairdresser, she made a phone call to Ricci Burns Hairdressers on the Kings Road. Her friend said that he had a cancelled appointment and would see Ricky. The assistant agreed to let Ricky leave his new wardrobe at the shop and strolled down to Ricci Burns. The shop was surprisingly empty with just two clients. Ricky had hair his cut and styled with a middle parting that, with a little Brylcreem, stayed in place. The Canadian woman to his left had her dishwater blonde hair bleached and then coloured with a bright, vibrant, blue, and styled into a David Bowie–esque Diamond Dogs-like hairdo. Ricky was thrilled with his new look and left before the Canadian woman's hair was finished. As he walked back towards SEX, he caught a glimpse of several Teddy Boys crossing the road. He couldn't be sure, but he thought he recognised Deano. Thinking that they may be going into SEX he quickly dived into the red telephone box next door to the shop. He picked up the receiver and turned his back to the pavement. Ricky could hear the group talking and laughing as they passed by. Ricky was almost certain it was Deano and a couple of the Milton Road Teds.

Ricky collected several bags from SEX and flagged down a London Taxi. It was too much for him to carry home on the Tube. He managed to strike a deal with the cabby and was taken all the way back to Milton Road Estate off the meter.

Chapter 7

"What the hell are you wearing?" Arthur said as he rose abruptly from his armchair.

Ricky stood in his parent's front room wearing a Royal Blue drape jacket with powder blue velvet cuffs, collars and side pockets. His matching Royal Blue trousers fell a little short of his blue suede, crepe soled, brothel creeper shoes showing off his luminous green socks. Ricky opened his jacket to show off his white silk shirt and bootlace tie. Taking a comb from his inside jacket pocket he peered briefly into the gold framed mirror on the wall and combed his hair back.

"Caroline, have you seen this?" Arthur shouted.

"Seen what?" Caroline said as she entered the room.

Ricky stood upright and put his hands in the trouser pockets.

"Oh, my, now that is a smart suit," Caroline said as she looked him up and down.

"Cheers mum," Ricky said.

"You what? Have you both gone off your rockers?" Arthur said as he threw his newspaper to the floor. "You look like a Teddy Boy thug! What's next? Flick knives and a bicycle chain?"

"Well I do look like a Teddy Boy, Dad because that's what I am now," Ricky said calmly.

"Ricky couldn't be a thug, Arthur. He's just wearing a nice suit," Caroline said as she continued to admire his new clothes.

"Teddy Boys are known for fighting on the street and running around causing trouble," Arthur said.

"So the newspapers say," Ricky said.

"That's right, they do, and I've read about it!" Arthur said.

"Have you ever thought that what they write may not be completely true and what they really want is to sell newspapers, so they exaggerate or even make things up?"

"Newspapers would never do that," Arthur barked out defiantly.

"Really and I suppose police officers don't lie either," Ricky said.

Arthur was silent.

"That's right, we all remember Santa from around the estate. He was a lovely old fella. Always had time for us kids and never said boo to a goose, but the gavvers swooped around to his home, smashed in the front door and carted him off to the Old Bill station where he was charged with the murder of his best mate. No one expected it to stick as there was evidence that he couldn't have been there at the time of the murder, but the newspapers were full of stories that anyone who didn't actually know Santa, would think he was some kind of a monster. Then, when it finally got to court, the evidence that clearly showed he couldn't have committed the crime was not allowed. I mean what is that all about? Santa was dished out a twenty-five-year prison sentence. He ain't ever coming home so, no, dad, you cannot believe everything you see on the news, read in the newspapers or hear from the lips of every police officer. I've become a Ted because I like the music and the clobber looks bloody smart and right now, dressed in all this," Ricky said, slowly turning a full three hundred and sixty degrees, "I feel like a million dollars."

"I'm not happy about this Caroline. You need to talk to your son!" Arthur said firmly.

Ricky leant forward, kissed his mum on the cheek and winked.

Arthur looked on and was becoming increasingly agitated.

"It'll be your fault when all this goes wrong, and I'll be right here to remind you Caroline. You're too weak with the boy and look where it has led. We have a bloody Teddy Boy living in the house now!"

"I don't have to explain or justify my choices, Dad. This is my life to live, not yours," Ricky said.

"You mark my words young man. The day you bring the police to my door you'll be booted out on your ear!"

"See you later Mum," Ricky said.

Ricky swaggered across the estate. He was tingling with excitement from head to toe. He had an overwhelming need to belong and be part of something, and just watching Deano the Dog and the Milton Road Teds had convinced him, beyond any doubt, that becoming one of them would satisfy his innermost secret hopes, dreams and desires.

Ricky stopped outside the Milton Arms pub and looked briefly at the red and white sign on the wall. It was an outline of a man running with 'Suspicious? Call the Police' in the red section and 'Watch out! There's a thief about' written into the white section.

"This is the Milton Road Estate so the chances of somebody actually grassing up anyone to the gavvers is zero!" Ricky thought.

Ricky took a deep breath, wriggled the fingers on both hands and then opened the pub's old wooden door. He looked around at the ornamental mirrors, the cast iron bars over the stained-glass windows and the yellow stained ceiling from clouds of cigarette smoke that seemed to float permanently just above the bar.

Ricky was met with a broad smile from Jackie, his friend and barmaid.

"Ricky, Ricky, Ricky, you look... Wow!" Jackie purred as she poured his pint.

"Thanks Jackie. You don't look too bad yourself," Ricky said.

"You know I've often wondered what you'd look like in a drape suit," Jackie said, "and out of it."

"You are bloody bad," Ricky said as he handed her a pound note.

"And you, Ricky Turrell, are a tease," Jackie said with a grin before handing him back his change. "Is Neil not with you tonight?"

"Nah, he's babysitting for Doreen."

"What and given up a night out on the lash?" Jackie said as she poured drinks for the two guys standing by him.

"He promised to help out and you know Neil, he's a man of his word," Ricky said.

"Not like everyone I know," Jackie said with a discreet grin.

Ronnie the landlord beckoned Jackie over to the far end of the bar where Deano and the Milton Road Teds were standing.

Ricky took a look around the pub. In his new drape suit he felt as though he stood out as being different from the other lads on the estate. He felt proud and had an almost imposing effect on others around him, which changed their demeanour. There were plenty of people he could have sat with, but he knew what he had to do. He picked up his pint and walked slowly down the bar. *'Devil Gate Drive'* by Suzi Quatro was blaring out of the juke box.

"Smart, very smart," Melanie said as he passed by.

"Hmm, delicious," Kaz said as she licked her lips while looking him up and down.

Ricky smiled awkwardly. He could feel himself blushing.

Ricky approached the five Teds.

"Alright Deano," Ricky said.

Deano put his pint on the counter.

"Yeah, hello mate," Deano said.

"It's Ricky, Ricky Turrell. I helped you with your motor and you said you'd get me a pint."

Deano ran his eyes back and forth.

"Sorry mate, I didn't recognise you. What you having?"

"Light and bitter, cheers," Ricky said.

"Well, what's all this then?" Mick said.

"Hello mate," Ricky said.

"What time are you due back in the window?" Mick announced as he looked to the lads for a response.

The Teds all laughed.

"Probably about the same time as you're due back on the Dad's Army set in that get up," Ricky retorted.

The Teds continued to laugh.

"He got you there," Kenny said. "That whole look you've got going on is a bit suspect."

"Well maybe I should take the pair of you outside and teach you both some manners," Mick said.

"Always with the threats of violence," Specs said.

"And you can watch your mouth too," Mick said.

"At this rate we'll all be outside, and Deano will have to drink alone," Ricky said with a chuckle.

"Leave it out Mick. I asked Ricky to have a drink with us, alright? He's a good bloke and he helped me out the other day," Deano said as he handed Ricky his drink.

"Since when did you become a Ted?" whispered Deano.

"I bought all the clobber today but in my heart I've been a Ted forever," Ricky whispered back.

"Good answer. I wouldn't say too much about it to these guys though," Deano said.

"Ricky, this is Mick, he's my second in command," Deano said.

Ricky held out his hand, but Mick didn't take it which caused a burst of laughter from the Teds.

"He's a sad, tragic case but we love him, don't we?" Deano said. "This is Kenny, Specs and Lee. These boys are my inner circle."

Ricky shook hands with them all.

The lads drank their drinks, laughed and bantered about.

Ricky watched as Deano interacted with his gang, the girls and the people in the pub. He oozed charm and charisma and had an unmistakable air of authority about him. He was confident, powerful and self-aware. Deano the Dog was the real deal and Ricky was in awe of being in the presence of the King of the Teds.

"I think Deano must have taken a shine to you," Kenny said. "He doesn't usually invite outsiders, and by that I mean non-Teds, to drink with us."

Ricky nodded.

"I suppose he'll be organising your initiation then," Kenny said.

"Initiation?" Ricky asked.

"Yeah, you didn't think you just get to become a Milton Road Ted simply by invitation, did you?"

"I never gave it any thought," Ricky said.

Kenny shook his head.

"Mate, you are going to do some serious shit to get in with us. I mean Deano might just go and point out the biggest bloke you've ever seen, and I mean even bigger than that arsehole Double Bubble and tell you to go and smack him one just to prove yourself and your loyalty to us. Ricky, I've seen Deano pick out two, three and four guys and have first time Teds march over and start a fight. It was never pretty. We actually lost one poor sod," Kenny said.

"Lost?" Ricky asked with a quizzical expression.

"Yeah, they kicked seven sorts of shit out of the poor bugger and then stomped on his head. By the time the ambulance arrived it was too late; he was brown bread."

Ricky took a sip of his drink.

"Ain't that right Deano?"

"What?" Deano said.

"I was just telling Ricky about the initiation and how we lost someone," Kenny said with a wink.

"Don't you be taking any notice of him," Deano said with a chuckle. "He's a wind up merchant and bloody good at it too. You seem like an alright bloke, so if you want to hang around with us you can. There is no initiation, just my say so. I will tell you this though. There will be times when it can get a bit rough going and we will expect you to stand by us no matter how outnumbered we may be. The Milton Road Teds have a formidable reputation, and I will not allow that ever to be tainted by bottle jobs."

Ricky called Ronnie over and bought all the Milton Road Teds a drink.

"All joking aside, Ricky, you do know that by wearing that drape suit you're flaunting your affiliation with us. It's a bit like painting a target on your back because, believe me, we do have enemies," Kenny warned.

"Anyone in particular?" Ricky asked.

"Like my todger, mate, the list is long," Kenny said. "Rockers, Greasers and biker gangs have a natural affiliation with Teds. That's probably because of our mutual love for Rock 'n' Roll music. We don't have a lot of time for Skinheads and have an on-going feud with the Bedford Boot Boys. Funnily enough Deano gave one of their lads a slap the other day. That will lead to retaliation just as night follows day. Clifford Tate and Deano hate each other."

"Who is Clifford Tate?" Ricky said.

"Well, if Deano the Dog is King of the Teds, then that would make Clifford Tate the Prince of the Skinheads. Then there's just Milton Road Estate business and as you probably know there's an on-going rivalry between us and the Cambridge Flats Lot, the Chandler Road Boys and the Temple Drive Mob. You know what it's like, school against school, council estate against council estate and just young working-class men all mobbed up and wanting to have a row but it looks like you're with us now, so you've come in with the number one. We're not the biggest, but we are the baddest and most vicious, blood thirsty lot when it kicks off. Now if that little lot hasn't frightened you off, then welcome to the Milton Road Teds," Kenny said.

Chapter 8

Ricky and Neil, both carrying Party Seven tins of Watneys Bitter, climbed the concrete stairway to the flats on the third floor. Neil had been invited to a party on the other side of town and extended the invitation to his mate. Ricky, with his new Teddy Boy wardrobe, wore a pair of black drainpipes, luminous green socks and black brothel creepers with a tiger's head silver buckle. He wore a black satin shirt with the top button done up and a bootlace tie with two crossed over colt 45 guns finished in silver, and a black leather bomber jacket.

"It's going to take some getting used to seeing in you in all this get up," Neil said.

"It's like I've said before. I've always loved the gear and have wanted to be with the Milton Road Teds since, well, for ages. It doesn't affect our friendship mate," Ricky said.

"No, I know that. We're like brothers and have history," Neil said.

"Too right," Ricky said. "We're going to the Cadillac Club tomorrow night, you coming?"

"What with Deano and that lot?"

"Yeah, it should be a crack. I've never been so I'm right up for it," Ricky said.

"Nah, I said I'd baby sit for Doreen. She asked me a few days ago and I just said yes, so I can't let her down now, can I?"

"I suppose not. Do you really think you'll crack it with Doreen?"

"Maybe, who knows? But to me she's way more appealing than some silly tart who's trying to look big in front of her mates," Neil said.

As they reached the right floor, they heard the sounds of *'Hang On In There Baby'* by Johnny Bristol. The front door was open, so they went in and walked straight through to the crowded kitchen.

"Ricky, hello mate," Kenny said.

"Alright Kenny, what you doing here?" Ricky said.

"Ricky, I'm just going to check out who's here. I'll catch you in a while," Neil said.

"Yeah, catch you in a bit," Ricky said.

"What can I say? The choice was venture up into London to listen to Crazy Cavan and the Rhythm Rockers with Deano, the lads and another hundred or so Teddy Boys giving it the big one or chance my arm at a local party packed to the rafters with available muff. No contest," Kenny said, roaring with laughter.

"Alright, Ricky," Melanie said as she passed by to grab a drink from the kitchen worktop.

Melanie was wearing a pair of white 'Roller Coaster' trousers that stopped a couple of inches above her ankle with a red tartan turn up. Her red tartan short sleeved top had a three inch white stripe over her left breast.

"Yeah, good, you?"

"Always," Melanie purred.

"Hey, you gotta be careful with that one," Kenny said. "She can get a bit, well you know, flirty when she's had a drink or two."

"I know that she's Deano's bird and I wouldn't be stupid enough to put myself in it, no matter how tempting," Ricky said.

"Well, technically she's not with Deano, but that said it wouldn't be a wise move for anyone to be seen to try it on. You saw what happened to those builders the other night and believe me, mate, having known Deano for as long as I have, that was nothing," Kenny said before taking a large gulp from his glass of bitter.

"I thought they were an item, you know. I just thought that everyone automatically thinks of Melanie as Deano's bird," Ricky said.

"Nah, it's not as easy as that," Kenny said as he handed Ricky a glass of Watneys Bitter. "Those two have a long, complex, history. Look if I tell you, you have to keep it to yourself, alright?"

"Yeah, course. I know the rules," Ricky said.

Kenny lowered his voice.

"Deano and Melanie were kind of boyfriend, girlfriend back in school. They were inseparable, always together. That's every break-time, lunchbreak and even after school when they should have been doing homework. Then, once they left school and Deano spent more and more time with us lot, you know The Milton Road Teds, and travelling to see Rock 'n' Roll bands play and visiting other Teddy Boy gangs from all around the manor, I think she just got a bit pissed off with it and so, and this is just my theory, because she was bored and impatient with their relationship, she got off with someone at a party to get his attention back. Well, it did alright, and they've kind of been on and off ever since. When they're on, it's full on and unbelievably intense. They can appear to be emotionally and physically passionate with each other. Melanie would throw the term 'soulmate' around and how they were destined to be together, and you can almost see Deano becoming overwhelmed by her enthusiasm and it's when he doesn't respond as she wants, the sarcasm and back handed criticism starts and that's when me and the lads, without ever actually saying it, back off and keep things to a nod or shake of the head. We have all seen Deano go and trust me; you do not want to be on the end of that. It's like a cycle because Deano will just fuck her off, but she doesn't go. She stays around and begins the full-on flirting. That thing the other night with the builders, trust me, she knew what she was doing, we all did and knew it could only end one way. That night they left together and now she's back in with Deano, but it will all happen again," Kenny said.

"I appreciate the heads-up Kenny," Ricky said.

"He likes you," Kenny said.

"Sorry?" Ricky said with a quizzical expression.

"Deano. He likes you. I think he was impressed that you bowled up in the Arms with your new drape suit and when Mick started giving it his usual bollocks you just shut him down with a few sarcastic remarks. It was impressive. Getting in with us is one thing but if you want to really impress Deano and the others, make sure you're there to be counted on if and when it kicks off," Kenny said.

"I won't run," Ricky said firmly.

"Yeah, I gathered that. I can remember back to when Deano and I were supposed to meet up with a few Teds at this pub. Now this particular pub can get a bit lairy, so much so that the landlord stuck two bouncers on the door. Well, they decided that they were not going to let Deano in. One of them said something like 'no dogs allowed'. I was quite prepared to walk away and have a drink somewhere else, but Deano was having none of it. He knew that the pair of them were just trying to mug him off and make him look bad. I didn't even see the first punch go as this six-foot monster has flown back with an almighty thud and slid down the door with claret spurting out all over the place. The other bouncer has lunged forward, and Deano just piled in punch after punch until this geezer is on his knees and gasping desperately for breath. I watched as Deano took a step back and just looked down on this penguin suited twat, then he casually brought out a bunch of coins from his pocket, placed them between his fingers and wrapped a handkerchief around his fist. It was the first time I'd seen a homemade knuckle duster. There was a bit of a crowd forming and Deano just let this geezer have it, and I mean the crunch from this fella's jawbone was sickening. He was out. I mean spark out and all done. Deano then calmly unwrapped the handkerchief, put the coins back into his pocket and went inside the pub, bold as you like, and ordered a round of drinks. The landlord came over and handed him back the money for the drinks. He apologised for the behaviour of his bouncers and said that the night's drinks were all on him. Deano the Dog is a bloody legend and is known by Teds, Greasers and Rockers from all over London. That's Bromley to Wembley and Islington to Croydon and to most of them he's just known as the 'King of the Teds'."

"King of the Ted's. That's some reputation," Ricky said.

"It was hard earned with fists, blood and broken bones. A more loyal friend would be hard to find. I love the man like my brother, as we all do, because there isn't anything he wouldn't do for each and every one of us, even Lee," Kenny said with a chuckle.

Ricky looked over Kenny's shoulder and could see Neil laughing and dancing with a bunch of girls to *'Rock the Boat'* by The Hues Corporation.

73

"Have you seen anything here you fancy then?" Ricky asked.

"I'll have a couple more drinks and then take a proper look around. The bird whose place this is had a party here a few months back. It got a bit embarrassing. Mate, I'd gone all day without eating and then chowed down on this really hot Chilli Con Carne at the Café. It was bloody tasty, but my guts were having none of it and started playing up almost immediately. I could feel myself get a bit hot under the collar, but I wasn't about to miss out on a party, especially one filled with crumpet. So I've turned up, cool as you like, and sunk down a couple of drinks but my guts are not giving up. It was like a spin dryer on the wonk in there. A bit of self-control and this cracking little blonde sort has really started throwing herself at me. She wanted some and truth be told, if it hadn't had been me it would have been someone else, so come 11.00pm we're having this slow dance and I've just placed my hand on her ass and she's pulled herself right in tight. So, now I know I'm on and her panties are coming off. So, when the record finished, we kissed and I led her through to the bedroom. I didn't turn the light on as there were two other couples at it. We managed to squeeze by them and get to the bed. We began kissing frantically and she was moaning and groaning and I'm proper excited. Then I could feel something brewing in my stomach and now I'm worried, proper panic stricken because this wasn't going to be good. I knew a fart was coming and I clenched my ass as hard as I could. I somehow managed to let it seep out quietly, but it went on and on and fucking on. It was relentless and kept on coming. Then, the horrendous, evil, smell of steaming hot shit was upon us. I tried to ignore it and carried on undressing this bird and then she's yelled out 'What the fuck is that' and started gagging, and I mean being properly reaching like she was going to throw up. I had to think quickly so I got off the bed. This was when other voices in the room started saying 'What the hell is that horrible smell' and 'What dirty bastard has dropped one?' I've marched over to the light switch and turned it on. They were all in various states of undress and squinting because of the bright light. So, while I'm doing my trousers up, I've just said 'Whoever did that should be bloody ashamed of themselves because that was well and truly out of order!' This red-faced lad has gone 'It wasn't me' and so I just stared him down and shook my head in disapproval. You should have seen this bloke's bird. She was livid and pushed him off and started calling him a dirty rotten pig and then this other bird has thrown a pillow at him. Ricky, I just slipped out of there lively and plotted back up back in the kitchen. I didn't see the blonde again that night, but who knows, maybe she's here tonight and game for another round, only this time there's no chilli to spoil things."

Ricky was laughing, he was bent down and laughing almost uncontrollably as Kenny told his story.

"You are bloody funny," Ricky said as he wiped tears of laughter from his eyes. "I'm just going to check out Neil, alright? I'll catch you later."

Kenny winked and refilled his glass.

Ricky stood by the doorway and looked into the living room. The suite had been moved back against the walls so there was room for people to dance. A young girl sat rifling through a box of records and then enthusiastically placed 'Me and Baby Brother' by War on the turntable. Instantly some of the girls, including Melanie and the Twins, formed four lines and moved their arms and shoulders from left to right and then on every fourth beat they jumped to their left together. Neil joined them which raised several smiles, so Ricky, encouraged by Melanie and the Twins, joined in too. When the record finished, the girl playing DJ slipped on 'Gee Baby' by Peter Shelley. The lads from the kitchen swooped in and began slow dancing. From the corner of his eye, he spotted a beautiful girl with locks of sable-black hair that that surged over her shoulders and veiled her heart shaped face. She was pulling her arm away from a guy who was trying to make her dance with him. Ricky watched as the intensity of the guy's grabbing intensified.

"Excuse me, but is he bothering you?" Ricky asked.

"Yes, he won't leave me alone," the girl said.

"That's not true Michelle. I just wanted a dance, that's all," the guy replied.

He was tall, slim and had a military style haircut. He wore smartly pressed Farah trousers with shiny black shoes and a white open neck shirt.

"I told you a hundred times to just leave me alone, Kevin," Michelle said.

"Oi, Kevin, you heard her. Now leave her alone," Ricky said.

"What's it got to do with you?" Kevin said loudly.

Ricky stared back at him and clenched his fists.

"I won't ask you again!" Ricky said sharply.

"Or what? What will you do?" Kevin said so loudly so he could be heard by all around the room.

The record came to an end and there was silence as the party goers looked on.

"I'm very happy to take this outside, if you're game enough," Ricky said.

"Really, and do what? I'm a police officer. That's right, I'm an officer of the law!"

"I couldn't care if you were Bruce Lee, the King of Kung Fu. Your badge and the uniform mean nothing to me. Neither will help you here! Now you need to respect Michelle's wishes and leave her alone and walk away."

There was a moment's silence as the two young men stared each other out.

"This has just got very silly," Kevin said, "I'll call you in the week Michelle."

Ricky stood firm as Kevin passed him by. From the corner of his eye, he saw Kenny by the doorway. He was nodding his head slowly, winked with a smile, and returned to the kitchen.

"Are you okay, Michelle?" Ricky said.

"Yes, thank you. You're like my knight in shining armour. Sorry, I'm so rude. What is your name?" Michelle said.

"Ricky, Ricky Turrell."

"It's nice to meet you, Ricky.

Ricky couldn't help but look into Michelle's lambent jade green eyes and then down at her pert nose and blossom-pink lips. He felt the aroma of her pungent Cristalle Chanel perfume envelope his entire body. Ricky had never found himself so completely captivated by a girl before.

There was a loud crackle through the speakers and then *'Sad Sweet Dreamer'* by Sweet Sensation played.

"Would you like to dance?" Ricky asked.

Michelle stepped back and looked him up and down.

"I'd like that, but are you sure, being a Teddy Boy, you can be seen slow dancing to a song like this?"

"Being a Ted means that I don't care what anyone thinks," Ricky said, reaching out and placing his hands on the small of her back.

The record played and Ricky and Michelle swayed back and forth. He was lost in her arms and hoped that the song would never finish.

"Thank you, Michelle," Ricky said as he stepped back. "Do you fancy a drink?"

Michelle revealed her bewitching bleach-white teeth and cherubic smile.

"Okay."

Ricky took her by the hand and led her through the living room, down the hallway, past the queue outside the toilet and stopped by the kitchen door. Somebody had dropped and then opened a tin of Watneys Party Seven and the beer had soaked the floor. Ricky watched as one guy slipped, recovered, and then slipped again but just managed to stop himself from going over. In the living room *'Kung Fu Fighting'* by Carl Douglas was playing. In the corner he saw his friend Neil sitting on a chair holding a bowl of crisps. He pushed handful after handful in his mouth and chomped down on them without even looking up. Ricky had seen this before several times. Whenever Neil had too much to drink, he would eat whatever he could to try and soak up the alcohol. Kaz, one of the twins, edged past Ricky and Michelle carrying an empty plastic cup. As soon as she stepped onto the beer-soaked floor she began to slip. She let out a yell but managed to straighten herself up only to slip again.

This time she tried to reach for the safety of the kitchen worktop, but her legs slipped from under her, and she fell backwards onto Neil's lap. There was a loud cracking noise and all four of the chair's wooden legs snapped and shot off in different directions. Ricky and Michelle burst out laughing as they looked down at Neil with his head still in the bowl of crisps and Kaz sitting on his lap, just inches off the kitchen floor.

"That's my mate Neil," Ricky said.

"I think he's had too much to drink," Michelle said.

"Yep, he's off his head and well out of it," chuckled Ricky. "You alright down there, mate?"

Neil looked up and slurred, "Yeah, sweet, mate."

In the living room the record had been changed to *'Juke Box Jive'* by The Rubettes and people were clapping. Deciding that it wasn't safe yet to venture across the kitchen floor for a drink, Ricky and Michelle went back to the living room where both guys and girls had formed a circle around Kenny as he danced.

Kenny bent his knee and kicked his left foot out, pulled it back, then did the same with his right foot, in perfect time to the music. Then he dropped down onto one knee, jumped up and dropped down backwards with his knees bent and his palms spread either side. He sprang back up onto his feet and continued to dance. Ricky was in awe of Kenny's dancing skills. All around them people clapped and swayed from left to right as Kenny danced. As the record came to an end the girl, who was the acting DJ, slipped on *'Tiger Feet'* by Mud.

"Come on Ricky," Kenny called, "Let's show them how it's done.

"Nah, I'm alright," Ricky said.

"Go on," Michelle said, egging him on.

Ricky beamed and stood alongside Kenny. Together they took a step forward, then a step to the right before taking a step backwards, then left and doing the whole move again. Together they squared off the dance area and just as the song began to chant the chorus, they turned and faced each other, placed their thumbs either side of their large chrome belt buckles and rocked their shoulders and bodies back and forth. Other lads in the room began to do the same. Ricky could see Michelle smiling.

"Nice one Ricky, now you see that proper little sort in the corner with the yellow hot pants?" Kenny asked.

"Yeah," Ricky said, looking over at three girls smoking and chatting by the open window.

"Well, my son, I'm going to be all over that like a tramp with a free bag of chips," Kenny said before playfully punching Ricky on the arm.

"Get in there, mate," Ricky said with a wink.

Ricky and Michelle eventually managed to get a drink in the kitchen without falling over, and Neil had sobered up a little. It was just after 12.30am when everyone at the party sang along, at the top of their voices, to *'Gonna Make You a Star'* by David Essex. Ricky was merry and feeling incredibly comfortable with Michelle.

"I've had a really good time tonight. What about you?"

Ricky touched her lightly on the hand.

"I've had a lot of fun," Michelle said as she gazed into Ricky's eyes, "and thank you again for chasing off that idiot earlier. You turned what was beginning to look like a mistake by coming here, into a great night."

Ricky held her gaze, squeezed her hand gently and then leaned in slowly. Michelle tilted her head to the right and closed her eyes as their lips met. After just a few seconds Ricky pulled gently away, looked deep into her eyes and smiled. Michelle returned his smile and leant in for a second kiss. After the kiss Ricky pulled her gently towards him and wrapped his arms around her back. His eyes were closed as they cuddled. When he opened them, he saw Jackie standing by the doorway with her arms tightly clenched across her body. She had a face like thunder. She turned away abruptly and stormed off towards the kitchen.

"Hey, Ricky," Michelle said, looking down at her watch, "My dad will be waiting downstairs to pick me up."

"Okay, I'll walk you down," Ricky said.

"My dad can be funny about me and boys. Maybe just to the bottom of the stairs?" Michelle said.

"Of course, no problem," Ricky said. "Have you got a coat?"

"Yes, it's in the bedroom. You can't miss it. It's a red one with gold buttons."

"No problem, I'll get it," Ricky said as he turned to leave the room.

Ricky opened the bedroom door and was met by a series of loud moans and groans. It was dark and the light from the hallway wasn't enough for him to make out a red coat, so he found the light switch and turned it on.

"What the hell!" Kenny yelled out.

He was on the bed with his trousers around his ankles and lying on top of the girl with the yellow hot pants.

"Sorry mate, I've just got to get a coat," Ricky said, trying hard to look away.

"Oh, it's you Ricky. Do me a favour mate? Turn the light off and close the door on your way out."

"Will do, see you later," Ricky said as he placed Michelle's coat over his arm.

"Were they... you know?" Michelle asked.

Ricky nodded and grinned.

"Well I never," Michelle said and she pulled her coat on.

Ricky opened the front door and walked Michelle down to the bottom of the stairs and just out of view of the car parking spaces outside.

"Can I see you again?" Ricky whispered.

"That would nice. I'm meeting some friends at The Cadillac Club tomorrow night," Michelle said.

"Brilliant!" Ricky said with a broad smile. "I'm going there myself with a bunch of mates so with any luck I'll see you there."

Michelle leant forward and kissed him gently on the lips.

"Hopefully I'll see you tomorrow, Ricky," Michelle said as she pulled away and walked towards a sable brown Jaguar XJ6 with white wall tyres. Ricky watched, discreetly, as she opened the car door, kissed her dad on the cheek and then drove away.

"Ricky, Ricky, Ricky my old son you have well and truly hit the jackpot. She is absolutely stunning! What a girl!" Ricky thought.

Ricky looked up the concrete stairway and remembered the look on Jackie's face when he held Michelle in his arms.

"I've had a bloody good night and I'm in no mood for petty drama. It's not like we're going out together. Jackie and I are just good friends and that's all we've ever been. I can't be doing with any old bollocks right now." Ricky thought as he turned back and began to walk up the road towards the taxi rank in the High Street.

Chapter 9

Neil arrived at Doreen's flat just before 7.00pm.

"Come in Neil. Listen, I really appreciate you doing this for me again," Doreen said before placing a delicate kiss on his cheek.

Neil inhaled the heavy scent of her 'Charlie' perfume by Revlon and slowly closed his eyes.

"I've left a couple of beers in the fridge if you fancy them and there's ham, cheese and porkpies if you're hungry. Are you on your own tonight then?" Doreen said as she pulled her coat on.

"Yes, well, I might have a friend pop round later. I'm not sure," Neil said.

"Well try not to make too much noise as the kids are both asleep and if it's a girl then you make sure you're wearing something. You don't want to become a daddy at your age," Doreen said with a cheeky grin, pushing him playfully on the shoulder.

Neil went bright red with embarrassment.

"No, no, nothing like that," Neil stuttered.

"I'm going to the Cadillac Club and should be home just after 2.00am. Is that alright for you?"

"Yes, of course Doreen. I'll watch a bit of television and then maybe listen to one of your albums if that's okay," Neil said as he glanced over at her record collection.

"Of course you can sweetheart, just be careful with the needle. Some of those vinyls can scratch so easily. You'll find a bit of Slade, Diana Ross and Alvin Stardust. Oh, and there's Band on the Run and Goodbye Yellow Brick Road. Just put them back in their sleeves for me when you've finished, alright?"

Neil nodded.

"Right, now, how do I look?" Doreen said, doing a little twirl by the front door.

"Stunning, absolutely drop dead gorgeous!" Neil said as he cast his eyes slowly over her body.

Doreen turned slowly, tilted her head to one side and smiled coyly when she caught Neil still running his eyes over her curves.

"See you later," she said as she closed the door behind her.

The inside of Doreen's flat looked like it belonged in a suburb of Chelsea. Every stick of furniture, ornament and piece of cutlery had been hoisted from the top shops around London and the home counties. Her wardrobe was packed with top quality clothing, shoes, boots and handbags from the best designer shops. Doreen had started shoplifting when she was fourteen and found it to be the fastest and quickest way to make money. Whatever she stole was sold at half the retail price. By the time she was fifteen years of age Doreen was making more money in a month than most working men would earn in a year. She was fearless, hard, and driven to make money and secure her financial independence. At eighteen she introduced two of her friends to the art of shoplifting. By this time Doreen had honed her skills. She insisted they wore their best clothes because they had to look like they belonged in the upmarket, expensive shops and boutiques they preyed on. She taught the new girls how to remove tags and avoid detection, but made it very clear that if it looks like it's coming on top, you run like mad because you're on your own. If you're caught you say nothing. Grass and you get cut. The worst that can happen is first time, with no previous, a warning and a slap on the wrist. Anything after that is a fine or two months inside Her Majesty's, of which you'll only serve a month anyway. Then, when you come out, it's straight back to work. The gavvers have nothing to threaten you with. There is no real deterrent compared with a minimum of five hundred quid a week and well over a grand come Christmas. Doreen would sell the goods at half price and the profit was shared equally between Doreen and the shoplifter. It was an arrangement that worked well with each of the girls very quickly becoming cash rich. Men were disposable playthings for Doreen. Many had tried to win her over, even when she fell pregnant with the twins, but she took only what she wanted from them. Doreen would groom younger girls with a hunger for easy money that she felt could be trained and trusted in the art of professional shoplifting. With a team of seven girls, Doreen was self-reliant, resilient and powerful.

The evening passed quickly with Neil drinking a can of Lowenbrau, a West German beer that had been branded as the world's most exclusive and expensive beer, and a small pork pie. He had watched and laughed at the antics of Benny Hill. He had invited Debbie, a girl from the other side of the estate, to join him, but she hadn't turned up. At 11.30pm he put the *'Band on the Run'* by Wings album on at low volume. He sat back in the chair and opened a second can of Lowenbrau. Suddenly he heard a key in the front door and the door open. Neil sat upright and put the can on the coffee table. The living room door swung open and there stood Doreen.

"You're back early," Neil said as Doreen entered the room.

"Yeah, I just wasn't into it tonight," Doreen said, removing her coat and putting it over the back of the chair.

"I know what you mean," Neil said as he reached for the can of Lowenbrau. "I could have gone along with my mate, Ricky, and the Milton Road Teds but I just didn't fancy it either."

"I have had this guy chasing after me for a while and I wasn't really that interested," Doreen said, as she poured herself a large gin and tonic from the drinks cupboard. "Well, he must have caught me on an off day, and I thought why not? So I agreed to meet him at the Cadillac Club. A few of my girls were there but I like to keep business away from my personal life. Anyway, I walked into the VIP lounge, and he was sitting at the bar surrounded by a bunch of plastic gangsters. You know the sort, all talk, and nothing to back it up. I've seen them in there before. If they were players, they'd be around or associated to Frank Allen."

"You know Frank Allen?" Neil said as he leant forward.

"Yes, I know Frank. He's the real deal and a proper gentleman. Frank has tentacles the length and breadth of the country. He knows everyone who is anyone and believe me, if you are someone then you know him. Anyway, I smile and walk up to this guy, and he's just given it 'Is that a ladder in your stockings... or a stairway to heaven?' and I knew there and then it was a mistake meeting him. His mates thought it was hysterical and I'm already looking for the door. I had one drink with him then went over and chatted with Frank and some serious people for a while before quietly slipping away."

"I'm sorry the soppy sod went and messed up your night out," Neil said.

"How have the kids been?" Doreen said as she slumped down onto the sofa.

Neil could smell the sweet, intoxicating, scent of her perfume.

"I checked in on them a couple of hours ago and they were spark out."

Doreen knocked her drink back in one and then stood up and walked back over to the drinks cabinet. Neil couldn't take his eyes off her. He traced her body with his eyes and savoured her every move.

"Would you like one of these?" Doreen asked, holding up her freshly filled tumbler.

"Err, no thanks. I'm okay with this."

"Do you mind if I change the record?" Doreen said as she lifted the needle from the vinyl.

"No, of course not. Hey, it's your house, right?" Neil said.

Doreen smiled and put 'Simon & Garfunkel's Greatest Hits' album on the turn table. The first song to play was 'Mrs Robinson'. As the song started, Doreen looked over at Neil and held his gaze for several seconds.

"Have you seen the movie, you know, 'The Graduate' with Dustin Hoffman?" Doreen said as she sat back down on the sofa, allowing her skirt to ride up as she parted her legs slightly.

Neil's heart began to race when he thought he caught a glimpse of flesh at the top of her stockings.

"Yes, I have. It's a great movie," Neil said after clearing his dry throat with a feigned cough.

"Was it the storyline or the music you enjoyed?" Doreen asked before taking a small sip from her drink.

"The music was good, not the kind of thing I would normally have listened to, but the storyline was unlike anything I'd seen before."

"What, do you mean about an older, sophisticated woman, being attracted to the younger man?" Doreen said with a suggestive grin.

"Yes, I suppose so," Neil said.

"So, would you be attracted to an older woman, Neil?"

"Yes, I could see how he would be attracted to Mrs Robinson. I mean he could learn so much having an adventure with a woman in her prime. I would imagine that women like Mrs Robinson, are more grounded and realistic about life and would see something in a younger man that maybe he doesn't see in himself. Perhaps even showing him the kind of man he could aspire to be. I would imagine that a woman like Mrs Robinson could motivate a guy to achieve much greater things with his life."

Doreen held his gaze for a few seconds and said, "Anything else?"

"Yeah, young girls like to play head games, you know, try and make you jealous with drama and stuff while an older woman would have matured beyond all that. They know who they are and have nothing to prove. I suppose they've got life all figured out. They know exactly what they want and wouldn't waste their precious time with silly girl's games."

"I think you're right," Doreen said in a soft, evocative, tone. "What about me, Neil? Do you find me attractive?"

Neil felt his heart thumping against his chest and his mouth go dry.

"Doreen, if I'm being honest here, I find you fascinating, enchanting, and dare I say captivating, and I don't mean just your sultry curves and drop-dead gorgeous body. You just have this way of drawing a person in without any effort. There's something very special about you that totally captures my imagination. I suppose what I'm saying, Doreen, is that I find you irresistible and absolutely ravishing."

Doreen stood up with her eyes fixed on Neil's. She slowly undid the buttons on her blouse revealing a black lace bra that held her pert and perfectly rounded breasts. She tossed her long, platinum blonde hair back and slowly removed her blouse, her galaxy blue eyes still firmly fixed on Neil. She reached around and undid the clip and zip at the back of her knee length skirt. She turned slightly to her side and then rolled the skirt down over her black stockings and then her brazen, breath taking, curvaceous ass.

Neil could feel a rush of intense excitement with his highly excited, aroused, manhood tightly bound by his trousers.

Doreen allowed her skirt to drop to the floor. She stepped out of it with her blue eyes burning deeper into Neil's. She stood upright in her matching black lace bra, black stockings, suspenders and satin red panties. She turned and faced Neil before reaching for the tops of her silky panties with both hands. She leant forward slightly and slowly edged them down over her stocking tops, knees and ankles. Doreen stood upright. Neil's eyes were fixed on her trimmed pubic triangle as she sat back in the chair and then slowly lifted her left stocking clad leg, so it rested on the chair's arm. She placed her right index finger into her mouth and ran her tongue around the tip before beckoning Neil over to her.

Neil stood up and gingerly walked towards Doreen. She gestured for him to drop to his knees in front of the chair. He gazed upon her perfectly trimmed lady garden. Doreen reached forward and brushed his hair back from his face. The electricity of her touch raced through his body. She extended her hand a little further and rested it on the side of his head. She took a handful of his hair and let out the most glorious, raw, intense, high pitched moan of pleasure as she slowly but firmly yanked his head down between her legs. Neil could feel her body shudder and her legs quake. He looked up to see Doreen's face glowing with passion. Her eyes were alive, wild and wanting. Neil opened his mouth and allowed his tongue to slowly leave its resting place. Doreen let out a moan and pulled him in closer.

***

Neil left Doreen's home just after 7.00am and went on the prowl. He stole a Ford Cortina MK 2 from just outside the Estate to take him out of the area where he found an almost new RS2000 Ford Escort in Sebring red with an orange stripe. Neil parked up the Cortina and within a few seconds the Escort's door was open, and Neil was driving away. By 8.00am the Escort was parked inside one of Ricky's three garages. He then walked out of the estate again and found an Austin mini which he stole to take him back closer into London where he stole a Cortina MK3. Neil spotted a Rover P5B Coupe on the opposite side of the road. After taking the Cortina to Ricky's garage he returned and took the Rover. By 10.30 Neil had stolen three motor vehicles.

Neil looked up as Ricky walked towards the garages.

"Hello mate," Ricky said.

"I've got a surprise for you," grinned Neil.

"Go on," Ricky said, beaming.

"Well, I've got some good news and some great news," Neil said.

"In that case I'll have the good news first," Neil said.

"Well, I was up and out early this morning, so in the garages you'll find an RS2000 and an MK3 Cortina. Plus, down the end in that empty garage I've got you a mint Rover P5B Coupe so you've no excuses for not finishing your motor. Believe me, it drives a treat. I've never driven a Roller, but it can't be much better mate. Both the engine and gearbox are sweet, and the interior is like new. So, my old mate, you're well and truly sorted.

"Neil, you are a bloody good mate!" Ricky said, shaking him firmly by the hand.

"We are going to make some serious money with these cars, and I've got a couple of back street garages that have already said that providing the price is right they'll have everything we get. You're probably looking at the best part of eight hundred quid here if not more," Ricky said.

"Nice one," Neil said. "So, do you want to hear my great news?"

"Bloody right I do," Ricky said.

"Well, you know I was babysitting for Doreen last night?"

"Yeah," Ricky said, leaning in.

"Well, I did the business, mate. I mean I got well and truly stuck in there balls deep. It was incredible mate, she just kept going and going. I was drained, nothing left but a smile."

"No way," Ricky said.

"Oh, yes, mate, and I mean everything. Whatever you've read in the dirty books... I did," Neil said, thrusting his hips and making a playful grab at his crotch.

"Well good for you, Neil. If it makes you happy then I'm happy for you too," Ricky said.

"Yeah, but don't go saying anything alright. She made me promise when we were all done and dusted. Trust me mate I don't want to bollox this up. Doreen is something else."

"You know me, mum's the word. I ain't saying nothing to no one," Ricky said.

"Yeah, I know you won't, but I just had to tell someone, you know. Anyway, what about you? How did it go at The Cadillac Club last night?" Neil asked.

"You know that good looking bird, Michelle, from the party the other night?"

"Yeah, I remember. She was the pick of the litter for sure," Neil said, raising his eyebrows.

"Well, she was there so we kind of hooked up. It's funny because some things are just supposed to happen, you know?" Ricky said.

"What, you mean like me and Doreen?" Neil said.

"Sort of. I mean who would think that you would meet someone at a party that you're kind of attracted to, and then a few days later there she is in a club with hundreds of people but you find each other. We chatted for ages and even went to the burger stall round by the Ponds after and were still chatting."

"So, are you like on the firm now or what?"

"We'll definitely be seeing each other again and I did kiss her goodnight. I really like her Neil. She's different, not like the girls around here, there are no obvious hard or rough edges. Michelle is, just, well, you know what I mean. She told me about some bloke that has been pestering her," Ricky said.

"What like an old boyfriend or something?"

"Yeah, she chucked him, but he just wasn't taking no for an answer. He is supposed to be old bill. You'd think someone in a uniform would know better," Ricky said.

"We all know what the old bill can be like. They make the bleedin' rules up as they go along. One for us and one for them. We all know they're bent as nine bob notes. How many people on the estate do we know that have been fitted up by the old bill at one time or another. That's not to say that they weren't at it, but they got fitted up for something they didn't do. You know Alan Clarkson?"

"Yeah, I know Alan."

"Well, his old man was nicked and imprisoned for a murder he didn't do. The bloke was having a drink with a mate when it happened, but the gavvers held back evidence that proved he couldn't be there. That poor fucker is doing a twelve stretch. Can you imagine being banged up for something you ain't done?"

"Yeah, well, I will sort it one way or another if he doesn't back off and leave her alone," Ricky said.

"If you need me, I'm there, you know that," Neil said.

Ricky nodded.

"Other than that, it looks like we're both sorted on the bird front," Neil said. "So, why don't we make a start at getting these motors broken up and turned into cash."

"I've got a mate from work called Monkey," Ricky said.

"Monkey?" Neil said.

"Yeah, his name is Dave Wrench and because wrench, monkey wrench and being that he's a mechanic, everyone calls him Monkey. Anyway, he said he'd pop around later to help me pull the V8 motor out of my Rover. He's a good guy, staunch, and I trust him, so I might bung him a few quid to help us break these motors down into parts, no questions asked. Knowing Monkey, he'll be right up for earning a few bob," Ricky said.

"If it's alright by you then it's fine with me, mate. As soon as you're ready, Ricky, I'll sort out another couple of motors."

"Have you ever been to an auction? You know, a car auction?" Ricky asked

"Nah?" Neil said, shaking his head.

"I did a few years back. You can see how motor traders pick up bargains, do a few repairs or add value with special wheels and upgrades before selling them on. So, I've been thinking that in addition to breaking motors up for spares, we could use some of the parts on cheap motors bought from the auction and then knock them out for retail money."

"Sounds like a plan," Neil said, rubbing his hands together.

"Here, tell you what. If we bought a few motors and then you nicked identical cars but in tip top nick and we just changed the chassis and number plates and put them back through the auction

95

we'd make a bloody fortune. We'd make a few quid from the parts and then a quick trade sale with the ringer."

"Ringer, what's that?" Neil said.

"A ringer is when you steal a car and change the chassis and number plates with either one from an accident, an MOT failure or has been written off by an insurance company."

"Bloody hell Ricky, that's a licence to print money. Why don't we just bypass buying from an auction and just buy accident damaged cars that have been written off and just ring them and then stick them through an auction?"

"Now, that I like. We could buy a written off motor for say a hundred or two hundred quid and then ring it and bang it out at auction for five, six or seven hundred quid. Once a motor trader gets his hands on it it'll be passed onto retail and then on again, so there'll never be any come back. I don't know why I never thought about this before," Ricky said.

"I think we could be talking proper money here," Neil said.

"Yeah, so we have to keep it quiet and not a word to anyone. This is our bit of business. Loose lips and all that."

"Agreed," Neil said, shaking Ricky's hand.

Chapter 10

Ricky had stood checking himself out in front of his bedroom mirror for almost twenty minutes. He wore his powder blue Drape suit with the royal blue velvet cuffs, collar and pocket trimmings. The white silk shirt was buttoned up with a silver skull and cross bones bootlace tie. He checked out the luminous green socks against his blue suede crepe soled brothel creeper shoes. Ricky picked up his comb again, dipped the end into his tub of Brylcreem, ran it through his side parting and neatly down into the traditional Teds D.A (duck's arse).

Ricky heard the front doorbell.

"Ricky, it's one of your friends. What is your name, darling?"

"Kenny, Mrs Turrell."

"Call me Caroline."

"It's Kenny," Ricky's mum called out.

Ricky strutted down the hallway and into the kitchen where Kenny, dressed in a black pin stripe Drape jacket, black trousers, white socks and black suede brothel creepers was chatting to his mum. Kenny turned to face him.

"Looking good Ricky," Kenny said with a smile.

"You too, mate," said Ricky.

"Isn't Neil going with you Ricky?" Caroline said.

"No, not tonight. He's got something on," Ricky said.

"So, where are you boys off to tonight?" Caroline asked, putting the kettle on the stove.

"We're going to the Cadillac Club, Mrs Turrell. Sorry, I mean Caroline," Kenny said.

"That sounds nice," Caroline said.

"We're going to see a brilliant new Rock 'n' Roll band called Showaddywaddy," Kenny said. "They've been playing all over the Midlands, and this was a last-minute booking."

Ricky looked at his watch and shot Kenny a look.

"Oh, I've seen them on the television. That's right, it was on New Faces with that nice Derek Hobson. Oh, I do love that song 'You're a star, super star'. Those Showaddywaddy boys sure looked like they were having fun," Caroline said.

"Mum, we've got to go. There should be a taxi waiting to pick us all up from the Arms," Ricky said.

"It was nice meeting you," Kenny said, shaking Caroline's hand.

"Have a lovely time, you boys."

"See you later Dad," Ricky called out as he opened the front door.

There was no reply.

Ricky and Kenny walked across the estate to the Arms where they saw Mick, Specs, Lee, Melanie, the twins and several Teds from around the estate surrounding Deano.

Deano was dressed in a smart black drape suit with red velvet cuffs, collar and pocket trimmings.

"Loving the suit Deano, very sharp," Ricky said.

"Seductive, I'd say," giggled Melanie.

"Yeah, I picked it up this morning. Check this out," Deano said, leaning forward.

On the red velvet left breast pocket trim was 'Deano the Dog' embroidered in thick gold stitching.

"That is the nuts," Ricky said.

"Very cool," Kenny said.

"You should get one done," Mick said to Ricky. "Yeah, it could read 'Rick the Prick'."

"What's your problem?" Ricky said.

"You, you're my problem. We don't like strangers!" Mick said, shaking his head.

"Strangers? Are you having a laugh? I've lived on this estate most of my bleeding life!"

Mick clenched his fists and took a short step forward.

"Make your move," Ricky said, his eyes firmly fixed on Mick.

"Leave it out Mick," Deano said. "He's with us, and if it's good enough for me then it's good enough for you, alright?"

"The taxis are here," Kenny said.

Ronnie, the landlord, had arranged for five private mini cabs to take them to the Cadillac Club.

"We'll finish this another time," Mick said.

"Don't take too much notice of Mick," Deano said. "He can be a bit of a twat sometimes, but you'd definitely want him in your corner when it kicks off."

"I thought we are all Teds together, you know, one force. But Mick always seems like he's itching for a ruck with anyone," Ricky said as he climbed into the mini cab.

"We are one force but he's just letting you know the pecking order. Mick's my number two. I reckon he's just letting you know, that's all," Deano said.

"I ain't trying to upset the apple cart," Ricky said.

"Of course you're not," Deano chuckled. "By the way, nice drape, mate."

The mini cabs drove in convoy across South London to the Cadillac Club.

Ricky clambered out of the cab and brushed himself down. He looked up at the large bright neon lights spelling out 'Cadillac Club' spread across the front of the club's entrance. Beneath it stood three, well built, professional bouncers wearing smart tuxedo suits and Dicky Bow ties. On the left of the club was a large sign spelling out: 'Showaddywaddy: One Night Only!'

The Cadillac Club was the 'go to' club in London with a rich, notorious, history. It had hosted many of the biggest musical artists and was a regular haunt of many of London's criminal underworld including the Kray firm, Charlie and Eddie Richardson, Frankie Fraser and George Cornell.

Ricky had put Mick to the back of his mind and allowed the evening's excitement to flow through his veins. He was a Ted, with

Deano the Dog and the Milton Road Teds on a night to see Britain's newest and biggest Rock 'n' Roll band.

One by one they paid their entrance fees. Inside the foyer there were several tables covered with Showaddywaddy merchandise. Melanie and the twins joined several girls picking through the pens, scarves, mugs, badges and posters. One of the team encouraged the girls to join the official Showaddywaddy Fan Club with the offer of a lifetime membership. All three girls completed the forms. Melanie bought a bootlace tie in the shape of a club from a deck of cards with Rock and Roll written either side.

Once everyone was inside the foyer together, they strode towards the double doors and into the club. As they entered the dimly lit club, the sounds of *'Hey Rock 'n Roll'* was being performed live on stage by Showaddywaddy. The dance hall was ram packed with Teds, Rockers and Greasers bopping around to the rock 'n roll beat. Deano was the first to start bopping about, quickly followed by the others. Ricky had been practising at home and could hold his own. He allowed the music to flow through him as he dropped down to his knees and then flipped backwards onto his hands, as he had seen Kenny do at the party where he met Michelle. Mick was furiously bopping, spinning around and dropping down to his knees. Ricky thought how, with gritted teeth, Mick looked so angry while everyone else in the club was happy smiling, dancing and singing along.

The Milton Road Teds continued to dance while Melanie and the girls bought drinks and secured several seats by the bar. The eight lads on the revolving stage performed a mix of covers including *'Johnny Remember Me'* and *'Bony Moronie'*. At the close of the session everyone around the dance hall stood and applauded their brilliant performance. Dave Bartram, the band's lead singer, remained on stage briefly and thanked everyone for coming to support them.

The Cadillac Club's resident DJ opened with *'Miss Hit and Run'* by Barry Blue with girls from all over flocking to the dance floor.

"They're all here tonight," Mick said.

"I've seen the Wandsworth Teds, Clapham Junction, Putney and Croydon," Kenny said, looking around him.

"Who's going to be banker?" Lee said.

"You are," Deano said.

"Why did I know that was coming," Lee hissed.

"Banker, what's all that?" Ricky asked.

"We always do this when we come here. We all toss up a couple of quid and hand it to the nominated banker. Which, as Lee has made abundantly clear, is almost always him. The banker's job is to go the bar and order for everyone, but with a difference," Kenny said.

"What's that?" Ricky said.

"We get double or triple rounds in. So, if there's, say, ten of us then Lee will get maybe twenty or thirty pints in to avoid queuing up again. We had a right laugh here on Spec's stag night. There must have been about fifty of us from all around the estate and we had Lee order triple rounds for everyone. Mate, I'm not kidding when I say we were all sinking them as quickly as they were being poured. Can you imagine some poor tart behind the bar pouring one hundred and fifty pints and then when she thinks it's all done and dusted Lee has ordered the same again? We were cracking up," Kenny said.

"Love it," Ricky said, handing Lee two pounds.

"Cheers Lee," Ricky said.

"You should be doing this by rights," Lee said. "Being the new bloke."

"Yeah, but what are you gonna do," Kenny said, shrugging his shoulders and smiling.

"This ain't fair, you know," Lee grumbled.

Melanie returned to the table briefly, handed Deano the bootlace tie she had bought him earlier and placed a kiss on his cheek.

Ricky watched as almost every Ted in the place passed by and acknowledged Deano. Finally, a group of seven Teds in full drape suits approached their table.

"Budge over," Mick said to Ricky.

Ricky looked at Lee's empty chair. Deano nodded and motioned Ricky to move so that Mick was alongside Deano, Kenny and Specs.

"Hello Deano, how's it going my old mate?" the largest of the Teds said. He wore a white drape suit with red tartan cuffs, collar and side pockets.

"Jock. How are you son?" Deano asked.

"That's Jock Addie, the leader of the Croydon Teds," Kenny whispered to Ricky. "Him and Deano are old mates. He must have a good forty if not fifty hard-core Teds about him. They're game fuckers as well, and all ready for a tear up at a moment's notice. Month in and month out you hear stories of how they took on so and so."

"Yeah, all is good Deano. I heard all is not so good for you though, mate," Jock said.

"You must know something I don't then," Deano replied.

"What, you mean you've heard nothing through the grapevine?" Jock mocked.

"Get to the point!" Mick said.

Jock chuckled. "You always act like you have so much to prove Mick. I'm here to pay respect to the King of the Teds, not one of his obsequious minions."

"What did you say?" Mick said, smashing his fists onto the table.

"Mick," Deano said calmly, "Allow our friend to continue."

"Deano, I've been hearing all kinds of stuff," Jock said.

"Like what?"

"Well, it looks like after your little dust up outside the Wimpy Bar, that nutty skinhead, Clifford Tate, and his Bedford Boot Boys are trying to build some kind of super gang. They've been talking with the Cambridge Flats Lot and plenty of others from all around the manor," Jock said.

"And you know this how?" Deano said, before calmly taking a sip from his pint.

"My little sister has been seeing some guy from the Cambridge Flats and he's been spouting on to her about how they are going turn you lot over," Jock said.

"Really?" Deano said, before revealing a manic smile.

"Yeah, but there's more," Jock said.

"You're really milking this, ain't you?" Mick said.

"What else do you know?" Deano asked.

"Clifford Tate is building a super mob to come down and take you all on. They're planning to hit the Milton Arms mate. They want to hurt all you lot where you live and breathe," Jock said.

"They must be off their heads if they think they can take on the estate," Deano said.

"I'm just telling you, King of the Teds, what I've heard," Jock said.

"Well, I appreciate that Jock, and we owe you one," Deano said.

"No problem, we'll catch up later."

Ricky watched them leave and head for the bar.

"Well, this has brightened up my day," Deano announced. "So, Clifford Tate is trying to build a super gang to take us on. You lot have got to keep this to yourselves alright and we'll talk about this later."

Lee put a large tray of beer down in the middle of the table.

"I'll just get the other one, shall I?" Lee sighed before stomping off back to the bar.

"Kenny, is that the Clifford Tate you mentioned at the party?"

"Yes mate. Clifford Tate is a psychopathic Skinhead and leader of the Bedford Boot Boys. If Deano is King of the Teds, then you can be sure that Clifford Tate is Prince of the Skins. They hate each other, and I mean proper hate each other. They have history, a complicated history."

"How do you know? I mean, can you say?" Ricky whispered.

"Look, you know that Melanie and Deano are like on and off?"

"Yeah?"

"Well, years ago, and I do mean years, after a night at a party she's only gone and got off with Clifford Tate."

"What, Melanie did?"

Kenny nodded.

"They have never been the same since. Deano goes hot and cold with her. It's like he wants everything to be alright and then he remembers the betrayal. Hey, Ricky, you don't get to repeat this. I do not want to be served up by Deano for sharing his private business," Kenny said cautiously.

"Yeah, of course mate. Not a word Kenny," Ricky as he ran his finger over his mouth.

"Have you been checking out the action here?" Kenny said as two girls dressed in short leather skirts and boots passed the table.

"You can't miss it mate," Ricky said. "There you go Kenny. Take a look at the blonde over there?"

Kenny turned and looked the girl up and down.

"Nah, she's all fur coat and no knickers."

"What about her mate then?"

"She's got high maintenance written all over her. I can see it now, five drinks in and she's like 'No, I never shag on the first date'.

"It's not like you to be fussy," Ricky said before taking a sip of his pint.

"Under normal circumstances a heartbeat or a pulse will do but I fancy something different tonight," Kenny said as he puffed out his chest.

"Well good luck with that mate. I'm going to take a look about. Michelle said she would be here," Ricky said.

"Is that the cracking little number from the party?"

"Might be?" Ricky said with a wry grin.

"Maybe she has a mate?"

"Well, if I find her and she has a mate who is desperate for anything with a pulse then I'll come and find you," Ricky said with a laugh.

"Oh, that was nasty. And there was me thinking we were friends," Kenny said, feigning disappointment "Go on, I'll catch you later mate."

Ricky walked through the dance hall. The DJ was playing 'Remember' by the Bay City Rollers with scores of girls dancing, while Teds, in small groups, stood around the edge of the dance floor smoking, drinking and chatting. Ricky made a point of nodding and acknowledging each group as he passed by. Michelle was not on the ground floor, so he walked up the stairway to the second floor. To his right was the VIP Bar. Ricky took a crafty look in as he passed. He had heard rumours and stories of the bar's reputation for being home to many of London's premier villains. The underworld faces dressed in tailored, handmade suits while the

107

young women wore expensive, glittery, short dresses in reds, black and blues with heels. Ricky caught a glimpse of Doreen by the bar. He continued his search around the second floor until he saw Michelle standing by the champagne bar with two friends. Ricky could feel his heart begin to race.

"Damn, Michelle is one damn good-looking girl," Ricky thought.

Michelle wore a dark blue blouse with an open butterfly collar and a matching pleated mini skirt, white knee length socks and crimson kitten heels. When she turned and faced Ricky, her face lit up.

"Hi Michelle," Ricky said

"Hello Ricky," Michelle said, looking him up and down in his new drape suit. "You look heavenly!"

Ricky felt himself blush.

"I'm pleased you're here," Ricky said.

"Me too," Michelle said, "I mean I'm pleased that you're here too."

They both laughed.

"Can I get you a drink?" Ricky said, "And your friends?"

"Thank you. I'll have a Pernod and blackcurrant. Don't worry about my friends. They have drinks and they both have boyfriends."

"So do you," Ricky said with a cautious smile, "If you'll have me."

Ricky couldn't help but notice that she began to glow.

"You're a bit on the cheeky side, you are," Michelle said.

Ricky motioned the barman over and ordered drinks. He thought he caught a glimpse of his friend Jackie the barmaid from the Arms by the stairway. When he looked again there was no one there.

"There you go," Ricky said as he handed Michelle her drink.

"Cheers."

"Can I have your autograph?"

Ricky turned to see two lads in Oxford, three button high waist baggies and short sleeved Brutus shirts. One wore black Doctor Marten Boots and a black leather bomber jacket. The other lad wore Ox-blood Doctor Marten shoes and a brown leather bomber jacket.

"You what?" Ricky said firmly.

The lads both laughed.

"Sorry mate, we thought you was Dave Bartram, you know, the lead singer of Showaddywaddy."

"Jokes like that can be a bit dangerous. Have you taken a look around here?" Ricky said.

"Ricky, this is Paul and Nick," Michelle said awkwardly.

"Hello mate," Paul said with a cheeky grin. "No offence, we were just having a laugh."

"No problem," Ricky said, before shaking each of them by the hand.

"I have to say Ricky, that is one hell of a suit! I love the music but don't aspire to be a Ted. If I did, I'd be wearing that," Paul said.

"Yeah, looks the dogs," Nick said as he stepped back and admired the drape suit.

"Cheers," Ricky said.

"Michelle told us that you saw off that twat Kevin the other night," Paul said.

"It was no big deal," Ricky said as he shrugged his shoulders.

"I never liked him," Paul said.

"You just don't like Old Bill," Nick said.

"Always asking questions, you know," Paul said with a sneer. "It's like he was always trying to get you to grass on your mates or get something on you."

"You should have nicked his motor," Nick said. "I'd love to have seen his face."

"Well, he's gone now," Michelle said with a sigh.

"I thought you said you caught a glimpse of him here earlier?" Paul said.

"No, I think I was mistaken," Michelle said, glancing around her, "Even Kevin wouldn't be stupid enough to come in here and cause a scene."

"Nah, I suppose so," Nick said.

"I wouldn't put it past him," Paul said. "Have you ever met someone that you'd like to buy an electric toaster for their bath? Well, I'd buy Kevin two!"

"Love it," Nick said.

"You boys are just incorrigible!" Michelle said before taking a sip from her drink.

"Seriously, Ricky, you might want to keep your eyes and ears open because I don't think Michelle has seen the last of him. That bloke ain't right in the head," Paul whispered.

"I'll deal with him as and when I have to," Ricky answered softly.

"Do you want a drink mate?" Paul said.

"No, I'm okay, but thanks. Michelle, do you fancy taking a walk to the dance floor?"

Michelle beamed and put her empty glass on the table. Ricky took her by the hand and led her over to the stairway, past the VIP Bar and down the stairs. *'Hey There Lonely Girl'* by Eddie Holman was playing. Ricky led Michelle onto the dance floor. She fell into his arms, and they began to sway as one to the music. Ricky could see Deano dancing with Melanie to his right, and Kenny slow dancing with a brunette wearing brown flared trousers and a mustard-coloured jumper. He winked at Ricky and lowered his hands so that they cupped her bottom cheeks.

"I've known Paul and Nick since school. They're a pair of rascals. Always in and out of trouble but they don't have a bad bone in their bodies," Michelle whispered.

"They seem like a couple of nice fellas," Ricky whispered back. "But I like you a whole lot more."

Michelle giggled and pulled Ricky in a little closer.

Ricky spent the rest of the evening with Michelle and at closing time they took a taxi down to the Ponds in Thornton Heath. It was a popular location for clubbers and late-night drinkers. The burger stall had been nicknamed 'The Acid Bath' by those that used it. The food was awful but at that time nowhere else was open.

Ricky ordered two cheeseburgers and coffee.

"I can't promise you'll like the food, but it will fill you up," Ricky chuckled.

"Here, I heard that," the owner said as he handed Ricky the food.

"You were supposed to," Ricky said, handing him the right money.

"Was it Kevin you saw earlier?" Ricky asked.

"I think it was. I can't be sure. I wish he'd just leave me alone," Michelle said.

Ricky took a bite of the burger, chewed several times and swallowed.

"I'm not sure what he's done, but this burger is better than usual. Not by much, but it is better, so I think you're reasonably safe to tuck in."

"Do you come down here often?" Michelle said.

"That's a bit of a cheesy chat up line," Ricky said, smiling.

"No, you know what I mean," Michelle giggled.

"I haven't been down here for a while. I do have a car, Michelle. She's a beauty but I'm afraid she's off the road at the moment and in need of a few repairs."

Just then everyone's attention was drawn to the mighty burble of highly tuned Ford V8's. Jeff Harris, in his Red Zephyr MK1 was the first to come into view closely followed by his brother Andy Harris in his black Zephyr. Both the modified cars stopped to the right of the burger van. The Black Zephyr lurched forward slightly and then the deafening roar echoed around the buildings as both the rear wheels spun with thick grey smoke belching from under the rear wheel arches. The black Zephyr inched forward with the rear of the car sliding sideways and leaving thick black rubber marks on the road. As Andy Harris steered the Zephyr sideways around the roundabout and past the burger van, the owner quickly closed the glass windows. Another raucous roar and the ground beneath Ricky and Michelle appeared to rumble and shake as the second Zephyr slid effortlessly around the Ponds roundabout with heavy tyre smoke gushing out from behind the car.

A blue Rover police car appeared and hit its siren and blue flashing lights. The Harris brothers, on hearing the siren, both blasted away side by side along the main road, with the mighty sounds of their engines echoing into the night.

"What the hell was that?"

Michelle was startled. She walked over to the burger van and threw her half-eaten burger into the bin.

"This evening's entertainment courtesy of The Harris's," Ricky said.

Chapter 11

Ricky rifled through his mum's collection of records and put *'All of My Life'* by Diana Ross on his parents' stereo. They had left earlier that morning for a week's holiday at a caravan park in Pagham in West Sussex. He looked over to the clock on the mantle-piece. It was just after 3.30am and he'd just arrived back from the Acid Bath at Thornton Heath. He had kissed Michelle goodnight and taken a taxicab home. He was buzzing with excitement thinking about how quickly he had been accepted by Deano, Kenny and the others in the Milton Road Teds. More importantly he had met up with Michelle and would be seeing her again. The kettle whistled in the kitchen, so Ricky turned off the stove and made a steaming hot mug of instant coffee. There was a knock at the door.

Ricky looked over at the time again. It was 3.40am.

"Who the hell is that?" Ricky thought.

Cautiously he walked up the hallway, undid the latch and opened the door.

"Jackie, what are you doing here? Is everything alright?" Ricky said.

"Can I come in Ricky?" Jackie asked as she stepped forward.

"Sure, do you want a coffee or something? I've just boiled the kettle," Ricky said as he showed her through to the living room. The record had finished.

Jackie shook her head.

"Are you okay? You don't seem right," Ricky said.

"Are your mum and dad in bed?"

"No, no, they've gone down to Pagham. You know them, proper creatures of habit. This time of the year, year in and year out they bugger off down to the caravan park in Sussex."

"Yeah, I remember that year your mum invited me down too. That was a great holiday," Jackie said.

"It was fun for sure," Ricky said. "You laughed your head off when that bloody horse kicked me. All I did was give it a friendly pat on the rear and the next thing I know I've been floored by a horse."

Ricky rubbed his leg.

Jackie laughed.

"Are you sure you don't want a coffee or something?" Ricky said as he took a sip of his.

"No, it's not a coffee I need."

"What's up Jackie?" Ricky said, putting his mug on the coffee table.

"Where did we go wrong Ricky?"

"I don't know what you mean," Ricky said, shrugging shoulders.

Jackie shook her head, closed her eyes and looked away.

"What?"

"I'm confused, Ricky, and believe me the pain I feel is very real. I just don't know what we are. It feels like it's always me that initiates any kind of conversation or makes the effort to maintain contact and then when you do make the slightest effort, I'm always left feeling like I'm not sure what is going on, you know? It's like mixed signals, and I find I'm spending all my time thinking about you and then, it's like the silent treatment and I think 'Well, what have I done wrong?'"

"Jackie, honestly, I'm not sure where this is coming from. We're friends. In fact, you are one of my oldest friends. If you think I've been toying with your emotions then I'm truly sorry because that was never my intention," Ricky said.

"It's this new girl, isn't it?"

"Pardon?"

"You heard me, Ricky. It's that girl I saw you with at the party and again tonight at the Cadillac Club. I saw the way you were looking at her. You're breaking my heart, Ricky. What is it she has that I don't?"

Ricky stood in silence.

"You can really annoy the shit out of me sometimes Ricky Turrell. You must have been walking around with your head stuck in the clouds if you couldn't see how I was feeling about you. I've been longing to just hold your hand, be held in your arms and be kissed by you. It's like you are the only thing that makes any sense of this miserable existence. I find myself in turmoil and now you're going all gooey eyed over this girl and I can feel you slipping further away," Jackie said as a single tear rolled down her cheek.

Ricky took a deep breath as a look of bewilderment panned across his face.

"Jackie, look, I'm really sorry you feel this way and you have to believe me when I say that all this is news to me."

Jackie started to undo her blouse buttons.

116

"What are you doing Jackie?"

Jackie took off her blouse off and let it drop to the floor.

"Let's go to bed Ricky," Jackie said lowering her voice and reaching around to undo her bra.

"Stop it Jackie, come on stop it."

Jackie removed her bra and stood facing Ricky, half naked.

"I want us to go to bed. This is the way things are supposed to be. Just you and I together, Ricky," Jackie said as she took a small step towards him.

Ricky held both his hands up and said, "This has to stop Jackie, now!"

Jackie stopped and wrapped her arms over her chest to cover her breasts.

Ricky leant down and picked up her blouse and bra.

"You and I are friends, Jackie, bloody good friends. I'm not this guy that you seem to think I am," Ricky said, shaking his head. "I'm full to the brim with faults, imperfections and vulnerabilities. You know that I've always liked you Jackie, and you mean the world to me but not in that way. I've always looked at us like a kind of brother and sister, you know?"

Jackie put her bra back on and slipped her arms through the blouse sleeves.

"So, what happens now Ricky? You go off with this new girl, what's her name?

"Michelle, her name is Michelle."

"So. You go off with your new Teddy Boy mates and this girl, Michelle and what... I just fade into the background and become yesterday's news with over ten years of friendship forgotten?"

"Don't be silly Jackie. We'll always be friends," Ricky said reassuringly.

"I can't imagine a life without you in it, Ricky," Jackie said with tears streaming down her face. "What will I do? My life will mean nothing, I'd be lost. I need you; you mean everything to me and... I love you, Ricky Turrell."

"Jackie, please. I don't want to lose you as a friend," Ricky pleaded.

The pair stood in silence for what seemed like an eternity.

"I've opened the deepest corners of my soul to you Ricky. I'm in pain and heartbroken and all you can do is stand there. I've embarrassed myself tonight and I promise that will never happen again. We're done!"

"Please, Jackie, have a coffee and let's sort this out. You're my friend and I care about you."

"No, no, you don't," Jackie said as she turned abruptly.

Jackie walked up the hallway, opened the front door and slammed it shut behind her.

"What the hell was all that about?" Ricky thought. *"Come on, you can't lie to yourself Ricky. You know that Jackie has been into you for years and you've encouraged it at times. You know that!"*

Chapter 12

Ricky was up and out of bed early, which was unusual for him on a Sunday. He had just poured boiling water into the tea pot and popped two slices of bread under the grill when there was a knock at the front door.

"Oh, shit," Ricky thought. *"I hope it's not Jackie."*

"Hold up," Ricky yelled out as he put on his dressing gown.

There was a second and then a third knock. Ricky opened the door.

"Ricky, hello mate," Kenny said with his usual winning smile.

"What, have you got a job as a paperboy or something?" Ricky asked before inviting him in.

"Very funny. I wouldn't give up the day job though if you plan on making it as a comedian."

"Do you fancy a cup of tea?" Ricky asked, leading him through to the kitchen

"Yes, mate and stick another couple of slices under the grill. I'm starving."

Ricky took the toast out and put two more slices under the grill. He put them on a plate with a teaspoon and a knife.

"Help yourself," Ricky said, pointing to the butter and marmalade.

"There is some pretty serious shit going down, Ricky!"

"What's up?"

"Well, you know Specs wasn't at the Cadillac Club last night."

"Yeah, you made out like he was under the thumb and not allowed out," Ricky said before taking a sip from his tea.

"If only it was just that," Kenny said before pushing the whole slice of toast and marmalade into his mouth.

Ricky waited while Kenny chewed and swallowed.

"It turns out that Specs was walking back through the estate yesterday after work and those mouthy builders that Deano spanked the other week spotted him and gave chase. They chased him through the flats, through the corridors and down the stairs, but these fuckers didn't give up. They brought him down, gave him a bit of a kicking and then bundled him into the back of their van and drove over to the back of the industrial estate."

"Jesus, you're joking."

Ricky was shocked.

"No mate. He was thrown out and the four of them gave him a right good hiding. I mean they beat the living shit out of him," Kenny said. "Some guy walking his dog found him and he was taken to the hospital last night."

"How bad is he?"

"Well, they stitched him up and plastered his arm, but his face is a mess. He was sent home in the early hours and Denise, his wife, called Deano."

"She must be beside herself," Ricky said with a concerned tone.

"Yeah, it's never good seeing someone you care about take a hiding and a bloody site worse when you hear that the bastards nicked all his money. I mean the rent money, bills… the lot. Listen, right, drink your tea and get dressed because Deano wants us all to go around and see Specs this morning at 11.00am."

Ricky looked up at the kitchen clock.

"I'll be ten minutes. Pour yourself another cuppa," Ricky said before racing out the door.

Ricky was washed, shaved and dressed in minutes. He wore his black drainpipes, red satin shirt, boot lace tie and leather bomber jacket. On his feet he wore his black brothel creepers with the silver buckle. He closed and locked the front door behind him.

"She can be a bit funny," Kenny said as he scratched his chin.

"Who?"

"Denise, Specs' other half. You know I can never understand how a bird can go out with a guy knowing who and what he is, marry him and then moan about what he does and try to change him. I mean if she had her way, Specs would be retiring his drape suit, go to work six days a week, pay bills and have fuck all to look forward to except a missionary jump at the end of the month if he's a good boy."

"That's a bit harsh ain't it?"

"Phew… you don't know her, like I do." Kenny said, shaking his head vehemently.

"What were you two?"

Kenny stopped unexpectedly and placed his finger on his nose and muttered 'Shush."

"What do mean 'Shush?'"

Kenny took out a pack of cigarettes, put a fag in his mouth and lit it.

"Keep it down Ricky."

"There's no one here," Ricky whispered.

"Well, you can't be too careful," Kenny said. "Yeah, I was going out with Denise for a while. Well not really going out with her, you know just getting round her place and slipping her a portion every so often and then she takes up with Specs. I'm blown out and they get married. She's a nice enough girl and Specs seems happy, but she always comes across as a bit miserable to me, you know?"

"Relationships and birds, eh?" Ricky said as he briefly reflected on the conversation with Jackie.

"Tell me about it. That's why I just stay foot loose and fancy free. I have no plans to become a slave to the system any time soon," Kenny said, taking a short bow.

***

The lads walked through the flats and then stopped outside a row of maisonettes in Porchester Close. Kenny knocked on the street level door. The door opened.

"I'm sorry to hear what happened, are you alright Denise?" Kenny said.

Denise stood a little over five foot tall. She had mousy blonde, shoulder length hair in tight curls. Her walnut brown eyes were red from being tired and crying. In her arms she held a little baby boy.

"Hello Kenny," Denise said.

Ricky noticed how the two of them looked at each other.

"Definitely history there," Ricky thought.

"Come in," Denise said, stepping back and opening the door.

"Cheers Denise. This is Ricky."

Denise nodded and smiled awkwardly.

"Deano and the others are in the bedroom," Denise said as she led them through the hallway.

Specs was laid up in bed with his right arm in plaster, his eyes were heavily bruised, and he had two thin strips of plaster across his nose. His lips were swollen and split. He was surrounded by Deano, Mick and Lee.

"Fuck me Specs, it looks like you've had a row with a steam roller," Kenny said as he peered through squinted eyes at Specs' injuries.

"Less of the jokes Kenny," Deano said sternly.

"Yeah, sure. Sorry Specs," Kenny said lowering his head.

Deano encouraged Specs to tell them how he was chased through his home turf by four geezers, bundled off into a van and then had the shit kicked out of him.

"They took his all money too, the bastards!" Denise said sharply as she rocked their little boy. "How are we supposed to get by with no money?"

"Don't worry about that Denise. We look after our own," Deano said. "Right, we're going to let you get on here Denise. You take it easy Specs, and I'll be back later."

Specs nodded his head.

As they left Ricky reached into his pocket and pulled out two ten-pound notes. He stuffed them into Denise's hand just before he left. Kenny stayed behind.

"Here Specs, are you able to get up out of bed?" Kenny whispered.

"Nah, not really," Specs said.

"Good, because I've got something for you," Kenny said, shooting Specs a dazzling smile.

Kenny's stomach began to rumble. He quickly undid his trousers, turned around and bent over. He let loose a long, killer, hissing ripper from his ass. The hot, potent, vile smell was intense and instant. Specs held his hand over his nose and mouth and began to gag and wretch loudly while trying desperately to wave the noxious stink away.

"I'll catch you later Specs," Kenny said as he pulled his trousers up.

Kenny closed the bedroom door and joined the lads in the hallway.

"Here Denise, I think Specs might need the toilet. It's really not very nice in there," Kenny said, waving his hand frantically in front of his face.

"Dirty bastard," Denise muttered as she stomped down the hallway.

Outside on the pathway Deano held court. "We need to talk about this. Let's grab a pint at the Arms."

Everyone understood this not to be an invitation but a command.

The Milton Arms was always packed on Sundays. Deano and the Milton Road Teds plotted up in their usual corner. Melanie had tried to get Deano's attention, but he would only say 'later'.

With pints all round, Deano lowered his voice and spoke.

"Right, these fuckers have taken liberties here and we need to spill some blood! Does anyone know where this lot usually drink?"

"I heard it was The Blue Anchor," Lee said softly.

"Nice one," Deano said.

"That's not just some everyday pub, Deano. The Blue Anchor is full of scaffolding teams, doormen and faces from around the manor. These are serious people," Lee said meekly.

"So fucking what!" Deano said firmly. "These people need to be hurt, because no one, anywhere, takes a pop at The Milton Road Teds. We let just one little mob get away with it and pretty soon it'll all be on us and I, for one, will not allow that to happen. So, Lee, if you're going to sit there shitting yourself you better fuck off out of my sight."

Deano glared hard at him before turning to face the others around the table.

"And that goes for anyone else," Deano said, looking straight at Ricky.

"I'm in," Ricky said as he sat upright and puffed out his chest.

"Fucking right I'm in," Ricky thought. *"This is the most exciting thing I've ever done. I'm getting drunk on the atmosphere!"*

"Good man!" Deano said, reaching over and patting him on the shoulder.

"I'm in," Kenny said.

"You know I'm there," Mick said.

They all looked at Lee.

"Yeah, of course I'm in. I was just saying, alright?" Lee said.

"Right, we're gonna need some proper numbers," Deano said as he rubbed his hands together. "Mick, can I leave that to you? Only those with plenty of bottle and proven in a tear up. No passengers or by-standers."

"Sorted Deano," Mick said with a broad grin. "It's been some time since we've had some aggro. I, for one, am looking forward to it."

"What about sussing the place out?" Ricky said cautiously.

"I was just coming to that," Deano said as he slid his pint closer to him. "We will need someone to go inside and check the place out before we hit it."

"Well, it can't be any of us," Kenny said. "I mean, being Teds, we don't exactly blend in."

"I'll speak to my mate Neil," Ricky said.

"Do you think he'd be up for it?" Deano asked.

"He's a good guy, we've been mates for years and I trust him. I'm pretty sure if I ask him to just go and check the place out and report back to us, he'd be in," Ricky said calmly.

"What about when it kicks off?" Mick said with an aggressive tone

"I can't speak for him. He ain't a Ted," Ricky answered.

"You weren't either a few weeks back, and now you're sitting here, bold as brass on the big table," Mick said forcefully.

"Leave it out Mick," Deano said sharply. "Being a proper, hard-core, Ted is not just about dressing in a smart drape suit or being able to bop around to some Rock 'n' Roll. A proper Ted is a state of mind and stepping up when your mates need you the most. Mick has it, you do, Kenny, and Lee is getting there. The drape is the adhesive that bonds us together, but your words and actions define you as a person. Ricky was the first to say he was in. Don't any of you forget that, and we'll all see how he takes care of business when we hit the Blue Anchor."

Ricky went to the bar to get a round of drinks. Kenny followed him.

"You didn't have to do that Ricky."

"What, step up?" Ricky said as he motioned the barman over.

"Nah, that's a given. I saw you give Denise some money."

"Specs is one of us and I'm flush at the moment, so I helped out. It's no big deal."

"He's right you know," Kenny said, putting the pints on the tray.

"Who?"

"Deano. Being a Ted is what sets us apart from all the bollocks that we're force fed into believing about how we are expected to live our lives. I know Deano and there is no way he'd let anyone get away with what those geezers did to Specs. He'd charge in there on his own if he had to and I'll tell you what... my money would still be on it being him that walked out on both feet."

Ricky spotted Neil enter the pub. He politely motioned Ronnie, the landlord, over and ordered another pint of bitter.

127

"No Jackie today, Ronnie?" Ricky said as he looked up and down the bar.

"Nah, she phoned in sick," Ronnie answered. "It's not like her, so it must serious."

"Kenny, give me a minute. I'm gonna have a quick word with Neil.

"Sure," Kenny said as he put the last of the pint jugs on the tray.

"Neil, mate. How you doing?" Ricky said as he handed him a pint of bitter.

"Alright, you know me. I was up early this morning to stock up," Neil said, lowering his voice. "There's another three motors around the garages.

"Nice one, Neil. I've got punters waiting on parts. Listen how do you fancy a challenge?"

"A challenge, what you on about?" Neil said with a chuckle.

"Listen, to cut a long story short, Specs has had the shit kicked out of him by those builders that were in here and Deano wants us to hit their pub."

"What do you mean hit their pub?"

"I mean he wants to cause carnage with bodies leaving on stretchers."

Neil looked stunned. "You're kidding right?"

"Nah, I'm asking you to go inside the pub, check the place out, you know, what kind of numbers are in there and where those geezers that were in here giving it the big one are plotted up."

"Fuck me Ricky, this is heavy shit ain't it?"

"Look mate if you don't want to do it then I understand and it's fine. I'd do it myself but look at me. I'm a Ted and they'll see me a mile off, but you, well you'll blend right in."

Neil took a large gulp from his jug and then a second.

"Alright, I'll do it," Neil said as he placed the empty beer glass on the bar.

"Really?"

"Yeah, I'm shitting myself, but I'll do it," Neil said with a broken grin.

"That's great Neil, cheers mate. Look, come and meet Deano and the lads," Ricky said as he pointed to the Teds at the end of the bar.

Ricky ordered another pint for Neil and the Teds before going back to Deano's table.

"Deano, this is Neil, the guy I was telling you about. He's in," Ricky said proudly.

Deano looked up with a broad smile, stood and shook Neil's hand.

"Good to meet you, Neil. Any mate of Ricky's is a friend of ours, right lads?"

Kenny moved his chair over, creating a space.

"Grab yourself a chair and take a seat," Kenny said.

Chapter 13

Ricky looked down and checked his watch. It was almost 8.00pm. He was standing with Kenny, Mick, Lee and fourteen lads that Mick had recruited from around the Milton Road Estate. These were not Teds, but a mob of no-nonsense game lads who were not afraid, and keen to make an impression on Deano the Dog and the Milton Road Teds.

"If you do the business tonight, Ricky, you'll go down in the annals of Milton Road history, mate," Kenny whispered smiling. "Either that or I'll be visiting you in hospital tomorrow."

Just then Neil pulled into the pub car park with a transit van, as he'd promised, closely followed by Deano in his PA Cresta.

Ricky could feel the tension as the lads hopped from one foot to another.

Deano wound down his window.

"Ricky, Kenny, Lee, you're with me," Deano said. "Mick, you lead the troops."

Mick nodded and walked around to the back of transit. He patted every lad as they entered the van. It was a squeeze, but they were all inside. Mick closed the van doors and strolled around to the passenger side.

Deano waved out of the window and then pulled slowly out of the car park.

"Is everyone tooled up?" Deano asked matter of factly.

Kenny held up a bicycle chain. Lee pulled out an eight-inch piece of rounded steel from his inside pocket.

"What about you Ricky?" Deano asked.

"Nah, nothing."

Deano took his left hand off the steering wheel, reached into his pocket, and threw a brass knuckle duster over to Ricky.

"Whatever you do, don't lose it."

Ricky looked down at the heavy brass knuckle duster. He had never seen one in the flesh before, only on television. He slipped his fingers inside and clenched his fist.

A smile crept across Ricky's face.

"Shit, this will do some serious damage," Ricky thought as he brushed the metal against the palm of his hand.

Deano pushed a cassette into the player and *'King of the Jive'* by Showaddywaddy boomed through the speakers.

Ricky could feel a strange sensation building up inside his stomach. It felt like a potent mixture of fear and excitement.

The car and van stopped just around the corner from the Blue Anchor pub.

Ricky watched as Deano closed his eyes, took a deep breath and slowly exhaled. His eyes were wide and alert. The lads all got out of the vehicles and huddled around the back of the van.

"Neil, you know what to do?" Deano said, looking for confirmation.

"Yeah, I'm shitting bricks, but no problem. I'm ready," Neil said.

131

Deano and the lads all laughed out loud.

"Good man, you get yourself in there," Deano said, patting his shoulder.

***

Neil walked around the corner and looked at the pub. It was positioned on a junction and looked as though it had originally been built as a large house in the 1930s. The large triangular front in the middle of the building, had a tall chimney stack on either side. Neil could feel his heart pounding against his chest. The small car park had two flat-bed transit vans and a small, white, Escort van with a sign on it saying Anchor Building Co. Neil wasn't sure, but he thought he recognised it from around the estate.

As he approached the front door, an enormous bouncer dressed in the usual black monkey suit, stepped out and stood by a crate of empty bottles. He was so large he had to duck down to get through the door. Neil could feel his legs urging him to stop, turn, and leg it down the road as fast as he could, but he didn't. He smiled and nodded at the bouncer before stepping through the doors and into the pub. He looked around at the smoke-filled room. There were maybe thirty men, mostly builder types, in scruffy jeans, work boots and oversized jumpers. The other drinkers looked like former convicts, petty thieves and back street villains. Neil ordered a pint of bitter at the bar. He noticed several older women huddled at the far end of the bar. When he heard a loud, raucous, laugh he looked over and recognised the largest of the builders he had seen at the Arms. He was being loud, brash and holding court with twelve men around him. Neil finished the pint and left the pub.

***

"Right, what's the score?" Deano asked excitedly.

132

Neil relayed what he'd seen, including the monster sized bouncer on the door.

Deano didn't flinch. He turned and faced the Milton Estate lads.

"You lot are here because you're amongst the hardest bastards on the estate and whilst you may not be Teds yet, we are all Milton Road and that makes us number fucking one. We don't take shit from anyone, anywhere, and our reputation is known and respected in all four corners of London and beyond. This lot," Deano said, pointing towards the Blue Anchor pub, "took liberties. It took four of them to bring down Specs. They didn't just have a go at a Ted or even the Milton Road Teds. No, no, they were having a pop at every fucking one of us on the estate and that cannot go unpunished."

The lads, with clenched fists and an arsenal of weapons bounced from their left feet to their right feet to build up adrenaline.

Deano looked over at two brothers, Steve and Terry Parker. They had just finished their time in the British army and had been active in Belfast for the last two years.

"I've been hearing good things about you lads. Show us what you can do!" Deano said.

An evil smile crept across their faces. Terry pulled out a short length of metal piping from inside his black Harrington jacket and Steve just rubbed his hands together.

Deano swung around and marched forward with the Milton Estate Lads following behind. Neil stayed back by the transit van. Once the lads turned the corner, he opened the door and climbed inside.

"I am buzzing," Ricky thought as the adrenaline raced through his body.

He gripped Deano's brass knuckle duster tight as they turned into the car park. The bouncer straightened up and took a step forward. Terry Parker raced forward, leapt into the air, and brought the metal pipe down hard on the bouncer's head. His legs crumpled beneath him as he slumped down to the ground, unconscious. Deano let out a demonic yell and ran forward. He kicked the door with such ferocity the hinges flew off and the door landed on an empty table sending it crashing to the floor. Deano, Mick, Kenny and Ricky led the lads through the door and into the pub. The women screamed in terror as the lads piled forward punching, kicking and bashing everyone in their way. Steve Parker had picked up the crate of bottles from outside and began to take aim and throw the empties across the pub. Ricky watched as one hit a guy in the head. The bottle shattered and the guy ran screaming towards the toilets with blood gushing from his face. The builders were game, with one of them picking up a chair, raising it above his head and smashing it down hard on one of their lads. Ricky raced forward and delivered a right hook that lifted the builder off his feet and over the table. Deano was piling in, firing powerful punch after powerful punch with one and then a second builder falling to the floor and curling up into a ball. Ricky watched as Deano shook his hands and then began to kick the guys. Their limp bodies rose and fell with each kick. Mick had dived on one guy and the two of them had landed on the floor. Quickly Mick scrambled on top of his victim, grabbed him firmly by the ears and began to smash his head against the floor. The women were still screaming as they clumsily bundled past the chaos and piled into the ladies' toilets. Steve Parker was still lobbing bottles across the bar. They hit their standing and floored targets with glass shattering across the floor. The largest of the builders was holding his own. He threw punch after punch but was no match for the hate filled Milton Estate Lads. It was Kenny that finally brought him down by swinging and launching his bicycle chain. His head jerked back as the chain tore into his flesh. He stumbled and fell, clutching his face.

Deano stood upright and proud as he soaked up the carnage he had initiated.

"Lee," Deano said.

"What?"

"Empty their pockets. I want all their notes as compensation for Specs," he ordered.

Lee scrambled around the floor amongst the bloody, beaten and unconscious men. He rifled through their pockets, emptied their wallets and stuffed the cash into his own.

Deano strode over to the bar where the landlord was cowered down. The Milton lads mobbed up behind him.

"Landlord, what you've witnessed here is retaliation from me, Deano the Dog and the Milton Road Estate Teds for mobbing up on one of our own and nicking his money. If anything, anything at all happens again, we'll be back. Only next time we won't take it so easy. Do you understand me?" Deano said menacingly.

The landlord nodded and muttered, "I don't want any trouble."

Deano led the lads out of the pub, past the smashed up bouncer and back to his car and the waiting transit van.

Ricky, Kenny and Lee got into Deano's PA Cresta.

135

"Now that is how you take care of business," Deano said with an excited chuckle as he slowly drove off the pavement and onto the road.

"That was the bollocks!" Kenny yelled out "And you, Ricky, were right in there. You did us proud my son!"

"You're one of us now," Deano said with a proud smile.

Ricky was still clenching the brass knuckle duster firmly in his fist. He could feel the adrenaline wearing off, the butterflies in his stomach were settling. Ricky slowly released his clenched fist and removed the knuckle duster. His palms were sweaty and a wave of tiredness washed over his body. He offered the knuckle duster back to Deano.

Deano grinned and shook his head.

"You can keep that Ricky, because being one of us means you'll never know when you need it," Deano said as he pushed Ricky's hand back.

Deano parked the PA Cresta outside the Milton Arms pub. The transit van, with Neil at the wheel, stopped behind him. All the lads bundled out onto pavement. They were still buzzing with excitement after the night's fracas.

"Neil, dump the van and come and have a beer with us," Deano said.

Neil nodded enthusiastically.

All the lads followed Deano into the pub. It was packed.

Ricky looked around to see if Jackie was behind the bar. She wasn't.

The lads ordered their beers while Kenny brought several tables together.

Deano wandered over to the jukebox, took a coin from his pocket, inserted it and selected a record.

"Ronnie," Deano called out. "Do us a favour and turn the juke box up mate."

The song began playing and Ronnie increased the volume. *'Trouble'* by Elvis Presley pounded out from the speakers. Kenny immediately shot up onto his feet, almost knocking his chair over, and with his legs wide apart began to bellow out the words to the song. Mick, Lee, Ricky, and one by one all the others joined in until almost everyone in the pub was standing with their arms apart, curling the corner of their lips, like Elvis, and screaming out the lyrics:

'If you're looking for trouble

You came to the right place

If you're looking for trouble

Just look right in my face'

Ricky was high on the night's excitement. He felt alive, and for the first time in his life experienced an overwhelming sense of real belonging.

'I never looked for trouble

But I never ran

I don't take no orders

From no kind of man

I'm only made up

Of flesh, blood and bone

But if you're going to start a rumble

Don't try it on alone'

When Neil entered the pub all the lads cheered and raised their glasses.

Lee emptied his pockets out onto the table and began to count up the money.

"Deano, there's three hundred and twenty-eight pounds."

Deano took the money and counted out one hundred pounds.

"Lee, go and stick that behind the bar. No one here pays for another pint tonight," Deano said as he raised his glass.

All the lads cheered and clinked their glasses

Melanie and the twins had been watching as the lads celebrated and finally she walked around to the back of the table. She put her arms around Deano's neck and kissed the side of his face.

"Speech, speech!" Deano shouted.

Lee stood up and everyone calmed down as he spoke.

"Well, I just wanted to say that I feel very proud to be a friend of Deano's and it's a privilege to wear the Drape suit and to hang out with the Milton Road Teds."

Deano began to clap, and everyone joined in, slapping Lee on the back and raising their glasses.

"What was that all about?" Ricky whispered.

"That always cracks me up," Kenny said with a giggle. "Deano starts shouting 'speech, speech' and Lee immediately just gets up and starts spouting off about how proud he is and stuff. Never fails to raise a smile."

"Oh, right," Ricky said, raising his glass to Lee.

Ricky sank the last of his drink and went over to the bar.

"You alright Ronnie?"

Ronnie leaned down, took out a glass, stood up and nodded. "It looks like you lot have been busy tonight."

"Yeah, just a bit of business," Ricky said with a grin.

"You've gotta be careful when you're out bashing people up," Ronnie said softly. "I had a mate, a good mate called Craig. We both used to work the doors for the Kray Twins and the Richardsons back in the day. Craig was one hard bastard and could have a proper row. Well, this little mob from East London started giving it the big one in the club and getting on everyone's tits. Finally the silly sod has only gone and touched up this bird and so he had to go. Craig dragged him through the club and then lobbed him out onto the road. Well, the twat has only gone and clumped his head on the kerb and the next thing you know the ambulance is there and the guy's brown bread, keeled over and turned up his toes from a minor knock on the kerb. The gavvers are all over Craig because he's got a bit of previous. The next thing I knew, Craig, my best mate and business partner, was weighed off and banged up at Her Majesty's with a ten stretch. I had to take stock of that and started looking for an alternative bit of work. That's when I met Alfie Kray."

"Alfie Kray?" Ricky said.

"Yeah, Alfie was uncle to Ron and Reggie. I remember meeting him at Esmeralda's Barn, the night club and casino in Knightsbridge. The Twins had just opened, and Alfie was running the place."

Ronnie smiled and rubbed his chin.

"There was nothing quite like that place back then and Alfie Kray ran it like clockwork," Ronnie said with a grin.

"So, did you run the doors, Ronnie?"

"Nah, nothing like that. Alfie was a clever, brilliant, businessman. He kept his head down and worked with firms from all over the UK, Europe and even as far away as America. Alfie could put a job together with the right people and then have the gear sold to waiting punters. If it was precious, Alfie was in, and those jobs went like a Swiss watch. Working with Alfie was the safest and easiest money I ever made."

"So, what happened?" Ricky said as he took a sip of his drink.

"Alfie went to the States on business and instead of waiting until he got back, I took another job, a wages snatch, and the rest is history. Someone had talked and the gavvers were all tooled up and waiting for us."

"You must have been gutted, Ronnie."

"Getting banged up and doing bird ain't no walk in the park and anyone who says different is a liar. When that cell doors slams shut the first time there ain't anyone anywhere that doesn't shed a tear or two. I was lucky enough to be on a wing with proper people, so everyone understood the rules. I did my bird and I've no intention of going back and I wouldn't wish it on anyone. So, take care when you're out there. Bad shit can happen at any time. Remember that."

"Cheers Ronnie," Ricky said as he picked up his pint and returned to the table.

Ricky, Deano, Neil and all the lads drank the night away. At closing time Deano and Ricky were chatting by the juke box when Ronnie approached them.

"Deano, I've just had a phone call. Frank Allen wants to see you tomorrow night at the Cadillac Club. He'll be in the VIP bar after 7.30pm."

Deano didn't flinch.

Everybody either knew or knew of Frank Allen. He was major face from the 1960's who did business with every major firm in London and never got caught, despite numerous attempts to nick him for things he did and didn't do. Frank was smart, and extremely well connected with the best barristers and political connections money could buy.

"I'll come with you," Ricky said.

"Nah, it's alright."

"I used to train at his boxing club until a few years back. I wouldn't say that we were great friends, but he did know me, so maybe, just maybe, that might help in some way," Ricky said.

Ronnie shook his head and walked away.

"Yeah alright, but keep this to yourself," Deano muttered.

"Of course, mate, mum's the word."

Ronnie called for the last orders.

Chapter 14

Ricky, Neil and Monkey were round the garages rapidly stripping down the stolen cars and placing the mechanical components into piles ready for when Ricky's growing list of contacts arrived to collect them. By 11.30 all the car shells were carted away on the back of a large low loader for scrap metal, and almost everything had gone, with some of the harder to shift stuff heavily discounted to make space for the next lot of cars. Ricky handed a bunch of notes to Monkey and a heavy wad to Neil. Ricky's Admiralty blue Rover P5B Coupe was almost ready with the new burgundy leather trim fitted throughout and the stolen 3.5 litre V8 engine and gearbox installed. Ricky and Monkey were fitting the battery and putting in water, fluids and oils. At 12.00 Ricky sat behind the steering wheel of his completed project and turned the ignition key and the crisp new engine roared into life.

Neil and Monkey decided to go to the Café down on the main road for a full English breakfast. However, Ricky, with a pocketful of money and brimming with self-confidence, had called Michelle at her home earlier that morning and arranged to meet her for lunch. He stripped off his overalls and washed his greasy hands thoroughly under the water tap at the top of the garages. Ricky got into the Rover, checked his reflection in the rear-view mirror, and slipped the automatic transmission shifter into Drive. The car lurched forward slightly. Ricky removed his right foot from the brake and let the car gently roll down the entrance. He checked to his left and then his right before pulling out onto the road. Ricky sat back in the comfy leather seat with both hands on the steering wheel. The car was everything he dreamed it would be when he first parted with his savings to buy it. Thanks to Neil and their new found business of stealing cars, breaking them up and selling the parts to trade, his Rover was finished a good year ahead of schedule. Ricky opened the glove box and pushed a homemade C90 tape he had made a few weeks back by recording the top twenty count down on the radio at 6.00pm on a Sunday night into the Sharp cassette player. He reached over and turned up the volume as *'The Cat Crept In'* by Mud played. Ricky rolled down his side window and placed his right arm on the door top. He pushed himself further back into the soft leather chair and held the steering wheel firm with his left hand. The sound of the throaty V8 and the glorious sounds of Mud had pedestrians turning to watch as he drove down the road.

Ricky came to a halt in the 'Rose and Crown' pub car park. A few days earlier Ricky had seen a sign outside saying that they did pub grub. He got out of the car and locked the door.

"Hello, you," Michelle said.

Ricky beamed.

"Hi Michelle. Wow, you look great!" Ricky said.

"Sure I do. I bet you say that to all the girls," Michelle giggled.

"What do you think of the motor?" Ricky said.

"Is this yours?" Michelle said, standing back and admiring the car.

"It is," Ricky said proudly.

"It's a beautiful colour and that red leather interior is fabulous. This must have cost you a fortune," Michelle said, still admiring the car.

"I'm an apprentice mechanic so when it came up for sale with a load of work that needed doing, I jumped at it and now she's all done," Ricky said confidently.

"Well done you," Michelle said before leaning forward and kissing him on the cheek.

"Shall we get something to eat? I'm starving," Ricky said as he rubbed his stomach.

Once inside the pub Ricky found a quiet table by the fireplace and ordered soft drinks for them both and a Ploughman's lunch each.

"I'm really pleased you came today," Ricky said.

"What can I say, I'm really pleased you called," Michelle answered with a giggle. "So, what do I know about Ricky Turrell other than he's a nice guy, works in a garage, is a Teddy Boy and can hold his own on the dance floor and…. is a great kisser!"

Ricky beamed.

"What do you want to know?"

"What are your plans? Your hopes and dreams," Michelle asked as she leant towards him.

"Okay then. It's only been during the last few months that I've started giving any of that some thought. I became a mechanic because I like cars and have never found solving their problems difficult. It's highly unlikely that I'll stay at Harrington's, that's where I work, once I'm qualified. I'm thinking that maybe I'll do something for myself. Actually, I've already made a start and being my own boss has become increasingly important to me. I don't want to have to answer to someone or to stand around taking orders from people I don't respect. Right now, I'm not sure exactly what it looks like, but the picture is taking shape. There is a lot of money to be made in the motor trade and to do the things I want to do, I need to be making a lot of money," Ricky said.

"What kind of things do you want to do?" Michelle persisted.

"I want to own my home. I do not want to live on a council estate. I want the choice of buying a home in an area that feels like home. Don't get me wrong, I'm not embarrassed or ashamed of where I live. It's just not a path I want to take. I suppose it's all about choices, Michelle, and it strikes me that the more money you make, the greater number of choices you have."

"What about being a Teddy Boy. How does that fit with a future you?" Michelle said, her eyes glistening as she leaned in further.

"I love being a Ted, Michelle, and everything that entails. It is me, right now. I don't know about the future but for right now it makes me feel like someone, you know?" Ricky said.

"Okay, now Ricky Turrell, tell me. Have you had lots of girlfriends?" Michelle said with a saucy grin.

"I've never measured my life by the number of girlfriends I've had Michelle. Sometimes you meet someone and you just kind of click and we'll spend time together and then that relationship runs its course and people move on. I do, or at least I did have a very good friend who is a girl. I thought we were just mates and then she sprung it on me. Told me that she loved me and stuff and that was kind of sad because ten years of friendship just disappeared after I told her I didn't feel the same way."

"That is sad, really sad. I would imagine that unrequited love has got to hurt."

"I suppose so. Anyway, that's enough about me. What about you? What is it that you do Michelle?" said Ricky with a sigh of relief.

"I am, or at least I was, a student at university," Michelle said as she leaned back into her chair.

"Well, well, I'm going out with a brain box. What were you studying?"

"I signed up for a three-year course in Architecture, Building and Planning. I've completed two years and then took some time out. It's a kind of gap year. My parents were not happy, especially my dad, because he had my future all planned out. He wants me to go back next year and finish my Bachelor's Degree, become certified by the Royal Institute of Architects and then go to work at his company where I'll spend twelve months under the direct supervision of a qualified architect."

"Okay, well it's great that your dad can help you, but is it what you want?"

Michelle hesitated and then took a small sip of her coke.

"To be brutally honest, and this is the first time I've heard myself say it out loud, I really don't know what it is I truly want which was why I had to take some time out."

"You'll know when the time is right and I'm sure your parents will understand and respect any decision you make," Ricky said reassuringly.

"I'd like to think so," Michelle said.

Michelle looked over at the large brass clock behind the bar.

"I'm meeting my mum shortly. I promised we would go shopping together so I'm going to have to leave."

"Oh, okay, no problem. Would you like a lift somewhere?"

"No, no, that's okay but thank you. I said I'd call her when I was ready and then she'd pick me up," Michelle said, pushing her glass into the middle of the table.

Ricky and Michelle left the pub and walked out into the sunshine and stood by Ricky's car. She leaned forward and the two kissed. Ricky held her in his arms and pulled her body close to his. As they pulled away, Michelle said, 'Oh no, not again."

"What's up?" Ricky said.

"It's Kevin. You know that Kevin from the party and the other night at the Cadillac Club?" Michelle whispered.

Ricky could see she was distressed.

"Where is he?"

"Over there, parked up in the police car," Michelle said. "I wish he'd just leave me alone."

Ricky turned and looked at Kevin sitting in the police car, staring at them both.

"Give me a minute," Ricky said.

"No, no I don't want you getting into trouble. He's a police officer and could cause all kinds of problems," Michelle pleaded.

Ricky turned, crossed the busy main road and walked briskly towards the police car. He stood by the driver's side door and tapped the window. Kevin slowly wound it down.

"What the fuck do you think you're playing at?" Ricky said as he peered in at Kevin.

"Listen here, sonny Jim, I'm a police officer and you cannot speak to me like that," Kevin said forcefully.

"Let's get it right matey. You're bothering Michelle by constantly harassing her and following her around, so don't go trying to hide behind that uniform. I told you before. Neither you nor it scares me," Ricky said bluntly. "So, I'm going to tell you one final time. Leave her alone!"

Kevin did his window up and started the police car up. As he pulled away, he put two fingers in front of his eyes and then pointed them back at Ricky.

Ricky silently mouthed "Fuck Off!" and crossed back to Michelle.

Ricky had a flashback to being a young kiddie growing up on the Milton Road Estate. A few of Ricky's friends would talk to a guy they had all named Santa because of his long grey beard. They would engage him in talks about London's King Pins in the 1950s and 1960s. It was Santa that had introduced them all to the alternative 'slang' names for the police: Gavvers, Cozzers, Rozzers, Old Bill and The Filth. It was also Santa that installed the unwritten rules: Never, ever grass - even on your worst enemy. If you're pulled by the police, you say absolutely nothing because they can and will turn your own words against you. He was taught not to be afraid or intimidated by any man in a uniform because it is just that – a uniform.

"Are you okay?" Michelle asked, clearly sounding concerned.

"Yeah, sure. I told him to bugger off. If he bothers you again let me know and we'll have another chat," Ricky said.

"He scares me," Michelle said.

"He's nothing. Just a bloke hiding behind the police uniform."

"No, I mean he proper scares me. I should never have gone out with him."

"I kind of figured that he must have been an ex-boyfriend."

"It was a mistake. The whole thing was a mistake. He seemed so nice at first but then he became very possessive and began telling me what I should and should not be wearing. He would turn up at my friend's home even though he wasn't invited and then when I finally summoned the courage to dump him, he threatened to arrest my dad for something and ruin his reputation," Michelle said with a heavy sigh.

"You're kidding me."

Ricky was shocked.

"No, so I carried on going out with him. I hated every second of being in his company and then, when I summoned up enough courage, I told him he could do whatever he wanted because I was not going to go out with him anymore. It was just after that that he turned up at the party where you and I met. That was the first time I had ever seen him back down from anything."

"Scum. The bloke is scum," Ricky said angrily. "People like that are all big and brave with those that don't or can't stand up for themselves. I've seen it scores of times and you learn very quickly. He's a bully and uses the uniform and his position to get what he wants but it stops today, okay? If he tries to bother you again, Michelle, you call me, promise?"

Michelle nodded.

"Thank you, Ricky," Michelle said as she leant forward and kissed him gently on the lips.

"Are you going to be okay now?" Ricky said as he looked around him. "The offer of a lift is still there if you want it."

Michelle shook her head and smiled.

"No, I'm sure everything will be okay now. I'll call Mum and she can pick me up. Home is not even five minutes in the car from here," Michelle said.

"As long as you're sure," Ricky said.

The couple kissed again, and Ricky drove away in his Rover.

Chapter 15

Ricky went home, washed and changed and then drove down to the Arms where he had arranged to meet Deano.

"Nice motor," Deano said, admiring the bodywork. "I could do with something that doesn't break down every ten minutes."

"Cheers," Ricky said.

"I've been around to see Specs and Denise and I gave them the money we took. There was well over two hundred quid there, so they should be sorted. Specs wanted me to thank you for slipping Denise a few quid. That was a pretty decent thing to do."

"He's a mate, so happy to help," Ricky said. "What do you reckon Frank Allen wants to see you for?"

"I don't know, and I don't care too much either," Deano said, shrugging his shoulders. "He's a proper villain with plenty of clout so it's better that I turn up than just ignore him."

"I've heard all kinds of stories about him," Ricky said. "You've gotta be pretty damn smart to make the kind of money he's made and never do a spell inside."

"Yeah, yeah," Deano said with an exaggerated sigh, "But if it came down to a right good tear up on the cobbles, one on one, then I'd fucking give Frank Allen a hiding he'd never forget."

"I think we both know, Deano, that all he'd do is make a few phone calls," Ricky said cautiously.

"Exactly and that's why I'm even bothering to turn up," Deano replied firmly.

"Shit, I hope he isn't going to be like this around Frank Allen or we'll both wind up dead and buried under some motorway bridge out in the sticks," Ricky thought.

Ricky parked the Rover outside the club. He checked his watch. It was dead on 7.30pm. Ricky and Deano walked up the stairway and were met by two bouncers.

"Can we help you?" one of the bouncers asked.

Ricky estimated that he must have been a good six foot four inches tall with a forty-six-inch chest.

"We're here to see Frank Allen," Deano said. "He's expecting us."

Ricky could feel the butterflies in his stomach again and a strange sense of excitement. It felt just as it had before they hit the Blue Anchor pub only days before.

The bouncer led them through the nightclub, up the stairs to the second floor to the doorway of the VIP Bar.

"Mr Allen, there's two men here who say you're expecting them," the bouncer said.

Frank Allen looked up from the paperwork on his table. Everything about Frank Allen oozed power and imminent danger.

"Thank you, Cookie. Can you get the motor brought around to the front? We need to be out of here and in Islington by 9.00pm."

Cookie was Frank Allen's enforcer and personal bodyguard. He had been with Frank throughout the late 1950s and swinging sixties. After a business disagreement with a Soho Maltese gang, Cookie, during the violent outbreak, took a cutthroat razor and cut the face of Elias, the head of the Baldacchino family. Seeing Elias scarred up and hospitalised, one of the family broke all the underworld rules by calling in the police. As a consequence, the Baldacchino's were hounded out of London and with Frank Allen's persuasion, most of their business interests fell into the hands of the Kray family. Cookie didn't utter a single word throughout the investigation and the Old Bailey trial. He was imprisoned for five years. Frank made sure that his family were well provided for and visited Cookie every month until his release.

Frank beckoned them over.

The VIP Bar was decorated in pastel blues with thick buttoned velour stools at the bar and matching chairs around highly polished oak tables. The lighting was soft, creating an upmarket, select and prestigious atmosphere that could only be sampled and enjoyed by those who were chosen.

Frank Allen was in his mid-forties. He had thick brown hair that had been styled into a side parting and regularly trimmed. He wore a blue pin stripe suit that looked as though it had been tailor made in Saville Row. His crisp white shirt had two open buttons and his black and blue chequered tie was folded neatly on the corner of his table. When he looked up, Deano and Ricky were struck by his piercing blue eyes. Frank carried a formidable presence; he oozed power like the presiding judge at the Old Bailey. Amongst the London criminal fraternity, Frank Allen was judge, jury and executioner.

"Sit down," Frank said firmly as he motioned them to the chairs opposite his.

"Deano Derenzie, right?"

Deano nodded.

"And who is your friend?"

"Ricky, Ricky Turrell," interrupted Ricky. "I used to box at your club, the Regal."

Frank looked Ricky up and down.

"Hmm, I remember you. Not a bad boxer as I remember. You should have kept it up. Maybe you should have come and worked for me" Frank said.

There was a moment's silence.

"I knew that we'd meet sooner or later, Deano Derenzie, or is it Deano the Dog?" smirked Frank. "I know you to be a man with a fearsome reputation and so I'll afford you the appropriate respect as I'm sure you will me."

Frank took a deep breath and sat back into his chair.

"We both have a problem and I'm hoping that together we can resolve it amicably. Your problem," Frank said leaning forward, "Is that you and your boys smashed up a pub that falls under my protection. Now my customer will be expecting retribution in return for the payments he's been making for well over ten years. Can you see my problem?"

"They kicked the shit out of one of my guys and so we hit back. No big deal," Deano said adamantly.

"Well, that's your reasoning and I applaud your loyalty to each other but that doesn't solve our mutual problem."

Deano remained quiet.

"Would anybody mind if I offer a suggestion?" Ricky said

Deano shrugged.

"It was Ricky, wasn't it?" Frank said

Ricky nodded.

"Let us hear your suggestion," Frank said, motioning Cookie to join them at the table.

"Okay," Ricky said before coughing to clear his throat. "I think we all agree that we must stand resolute by our friends and when necessary, go the extra mile for them even if that includes the use of violence. Deano is spot on when he said that they ganged up with numbers and bashed up our friend, but Frank, they went one step further and stole his wages. They took every penny out of his pocket. For that to happen to a Milton Road Ted or a resident of the Milton Road Estate, just cannot go unpunished. So we did what we believed to be right. We administered retribution and by way of compensation we took their money and gave it to our injured friend. Sadly, the pub we hit was damaged and I'm thinking in the spirit of mutual co-operation that compensation should be made to the landlord of the Blue Anchor."

Frank nodded. "What did you have in mind?"

"One hundred pounds," Ricky said.

Deano's eyes widened.

"I was thinking more like two hundred pounds," Frank said.

Ricky reached into his pocket and pulled out a roll of notes. He peeled off two hundred pounds in ten-pound notes and placed it on the table.

"Are you happy with this solution, Deano?" Frank said.

"Sure," Deano nodded.

"Good," Frank said as he picked up the money.

He then reached over and shook them both by the hand.

"This is the way business should be conducted. Now in the future, if you have a need to conduct confrontational pursuits can I suggest that you call me or speak to Cookie first... to avoid any potential conflict of interests," Frank said.

Ricky looked at Deano. He nodded.

"Who knows," Frank said as leant back in his chair. "Maybe there's some kind of enterprise we can do together in the future."

Frank smiled and rose from his table.

"Thank you, Mr Allen," Ricky said.

Deano stood and nodded.

"Stand up people like you, Ricky Turrell, get to call me Frank. I have a feeling that you and I will get to talk again."

"What does Frank mean by that? Did I impress him or piss him off? Nah, don't be silly, Ricky, he said that stand up people get to call him 'Frank'. You did the right thing. Just as Deano has his reputation so does Frank Allen, and it could have easily got very nasty. Maybe, just maybe, neither Deano nor I would be making it home tonight. What's to say that Cookie didn't have a shooter inside that jacket of his and one word and we'd be both be dead and buried in the foundations of some future London landmark," Ricky thought.

Cookie showed Deano and Ricky back through the club out to the entrance. Outside, parked with the back door open, was an immaculate, slate grey, Bentley S3.

"Nice motor," Ricky thought.

With Deano in the car, Ricky turned the ignition key and the V8 motor roared into life.

"I can't take the money back from Specs," Deano said.

"We don't have to Deano," Ricky said. "Look, I've got a good thing going with my motor spares business and given the situation I think it was money well spent. I don't want the money back and no one needs to know about it either."

Deano turned and faced Ricky.

"I don't like caving in for any man. That includes Frank Allen, Cookie his sidekick, or anyone else," Deano said.

"I know that mate. Everyone knows that you, Deano, led a great victory for the lads on the estate. For one night they all felt a part of something special and that doesn't need to change. This was nothing more than the cost of putting things right and managing the balance of power. So, as far as anyone is concerned, you and Frank had a chat and that was it. Nothing more and nothing less," Ricky said as he shifted the lever into gear.

"That works," Deano said, "but if you say anything..."

"Hey," Ricky said, "You have my loyalty and my friendship Deano."

"I always knew you were alright," Deano said with a half-smile.

Chapter 16

Ricky and Neil were visiting Dingwall Motor auctions. Ricky had bought a Cortina 1500GT earlier that week. It was a non-runner and out of MOT. Ricky had told the owner that he needed the car for spares and paid him ten pounds. Once Ricky had removed the Vehicle Identification Number (VIN) from under the bonnet, he called the scrap man and had it removed from where he bought it. With the vehicle registration, VIN plate and a new MOT that he paid Monkey to write for him at his work, he had Neil steal an identical car but in excellent condition. It took just minutes to swop over the VIN. Then they took it down to the Dingwall auctions to have it sold - ideally to a motor trader. Dingwall held auctions twice a week. Ricky saw a few people that looked as though they were private buyers, but most had the appearance of the typical shady car dealer that would take over plots of land overnight and hang red, white and blue bunting above a stock of second-hand cars with the price clearly displayed in the window.

"What do you think we'll get for it?" Neil said.

"I've no idea, but anything over a hundred and fifty quid, bearing in mind this lot need to make a profit too, has got to be good," Ricky said.

"Easy money," Neil said.

"This is our trial run. We can watch and learn. If it all goes to plan, we can start to up our game and push through more, newer motors," Ricky said. "Anyway, how are you getting on with Doreen?"

"Mate, Doreen is something else. I mean it just keeps getting and better. She says that men of her own age are obnoxious, controlling and sexually well past their peak. She says that what makes us most compatible is our age difference. She reckons that she's at her sexual peak and so am I. To be honest when she starts rattling on about that stuff, I do kind of gloss over and just want to watch her slip out of her clothes. You've got to keep this to yourself but Ricky, she always wears these black stockings and suspenders. It's difficult to explain but just knowing that under her skirt are these black nylons and a hint of soft flesh at the top is just irresistible. No sooner does she open her front door than I'm thinking about what she has on under her skirt. And Ricky, she always smells so good. Kind of expensive," Neil said with a chuckle.

"You sound smitten Neil. Look, I ain't one to judge but don't you think it's just a tad bit strange that you're banging a bird that's old enough to be your mum?" Ricky said.

"Nah, not really. No messing about with childish drama, it's just full on rampant, adventurous sex and Ricky, I'm loving it," Neil said.

"Good for you mate. So, do you guys go out and stuff?"

"No, I have asked on more than one occasion, but she has made it quite clear how she wants it to work between us. Rule number one is that I am not to tell anyone. Number two is that anything sexual happens on her terms and her terms only. It doesn't matter how horny I am because if she's not wanting it then it doesn't happen," Neil said.

"That sounds like most married couples," Ricky said with a chuckle.

"For right now it works for us both and believe me I have zero interest in girls my own age. What about you and Michelle?" Neil said as he took a sip from his paper cup of tea.

"Yeah, it's good. She's different, smart and funny. I like that. I'm actually picking her up later. We're going to the pictures," Ricky said.

"You're not going to take her to the Arms then?"

"Not a chance," Ricky said. "That said I might drop in for last orders if you're about."

"Nah, not tonight. I'm with Doreen."

"Here look, the Cortina's coming through."

Ricky and Neil watched as their car was driven in front of the auctioneer's stage. With his gavel in hand, he described the car and then opened with who would give him thirty pounds. Hands shot up from around the crowd that circled the car. It reached one hundred pounds very quickly. There were now just three men actively bidding in ten-pound increments. One looked like a private buyer. He was a young guy in his mid-twenties. No sooner had the motor trader upped the bid than his hand shot up. At two hundred pounds there were just two bidders. The motor trader upped his bid by twenty pounds, much to Ricky and Neil's shock. The trader was trying to frighten off the private buyer. However, caught up in the excitement of the process, he responded immediately with a further ten-pound bid. The auctioneer slammed his gavel down at two hundred and thirty pounds. The private bidder won the auction.

"Over two hundred quid clear profit," Ricky said. "We need more cars, lots more cars."

"Let me know as soon as you're ready and I'll go to work," Neil said.

"Monkey was telling me about this salvage yard that took in insurance write-offs in Mitcham. I'll get myself over there in the next day or so. I'm thinking we should stick with Fords, you know, Escorts, Cortina's and Granada's," Ricky said.

"Mate, I can nick anything, but Fords are a piece of piss and as we've seen here today, they sell like hot cakes."

***

Ricky drove Neil back to the estate before driving over to Michelle's house. She lived in an expensive, tree lined, road. Ricky felt a little out of place but his car, the Rover P5B, fitted in perfectly. Each of the semi and detached homes had its own drive with a mix of Jaguars, Ford Granada's and Rover P6's. Ricky spotted Michelle's father's Jaguar. It was parked in the driveway of a huge, Tudor style, double fronted, detached house. Ricky parked the Rover, checked his reflection in the rear-view mirror and got out of the car. He walked gingerly down the driveway. The hardwood front door had a large, brass, lion's head knocker. Just as he reached up to knock, the door opened.

"You must be Ricky?" Michelle's father said.

"Err, yes," Ricky said awkwardly. "Is Michelle at home?"

Michelle's father stepped out of the front door and onto the drive. He looked Ricky up and down.

Ricky felt a little uncomfortable with his scrutinising stare.

"That's a very colourful pair of shoes. Are you going to a fancy-dress party?" Michelle's father said finally with a sarcastic laugh.

"No," Ricky said shaking his head. "These are my brothel creepers. They go with my outfit. I like Rock 'n' Roll music and so I like to dress as a Teddy Boy."

"Interesting," Michelle's father said. "So, are you in a Rock 'n' Roll band?"

"No, I'm an apprentice motor mechanic. I work at Harrington's Garage," Ricky said.

"Oh yes, I know Harrington's, and the owner Robin. We attend the same Lodge."

"I've only seen Mr Harrington a couple of times. He rarely comes down into the workshop," Ricky said.

"Yes, I can believe that. So, tell me, do you live locally?"

Ricky was becoming agitated by the constant, sarcastic, questioning.

"What you want to know is do my parents own their home, where they live and what my prospects are, so you can make up your mind if I'm good enough for your daughter, correct?"

Michelle's father was a little taken aback. He took a short step back and crossed his arms.

"I live on the Milton Road Estate with my parents Arthur and Caroline. My dad is a miserable sod that works on the shop floor in a factory, and my mum works part time at the local school as a dinner lady. They are good, hardworking people. I became an apprentice mechanic because I wanted a trade. People will always have cars and they will always break down, so I figured I'd always be able to make money and get by. What are my prospects? Well, I'm still a young man with plenty of drive and ambition. In the fullness of time, I will work for myself and own my own business. And now the big one. Michelle and I have only recently met. I think she is beautiful, intelligent and great company and I have to pinch myself sometimes because frankly, sir, I can't believe that she likes me too. Does that answer all your questions?"

"Well I say, that was quite aggressive, Ricky, considering it's the first time you've met one of your girlfriend's parents."

"I wouldn't call it aggressive," Ricky said calmly. "I'm being assertive by letting you know that I'm not ashamed of where I come from or my working-class roots."

"Hello Ricky, I thought I heard your voice," Michelle said. "Dad, why didn't you tell me Ricky was here?"

"Sorry sweetheart, we were just chatting, you know, men's stuff," Michelle's father said.

"Wow, you look great," Ricky said.

"Thank you." Michelle beamed.

"Where are you both off to?" Michelle's father asked.

"We're going to the pictures," Ricky said.

"Are we?" Michelle said.

"Sure, there are two great movies at the Odeon to choose from. First is James Bond in The Man with the Golden Gun or the new David Essex movie, Stardust. It's the sequel to the brilliant 'That'll Be the Day."

"They both sound great. I'll leave it to you to choose," Michelle said.

"Well, it was nice meeting you," Ricky said as he held out his hand for Michelle's.

"It was interesting to meet you too Ricky. Now Michelle, don't be too late," Michelle's father said.

"I thought you and Mum were going to your Lodge dinner tonight," Michelle said.

"We are."

"Well, have a nice evening," Michelle said.

Ricky raced around and opened the passenger side door for Michelle and closed it once she was settled and comfortable. Michelle's father watched Ricky's every move.

***

"I think my dad likes you," Michelle said.

"Really? What makes you think that?" Ricky said with a wry smile.

Ricky started the car, slipped the gear shifter into gear and let the Rover slowly pull away with just a burble from the rear exhaust.

"I don't know, I just think he does," Michelle said.

"There could be a bit of wishful thinking there," chuckled Ricky. "What is that thing your parents are going to tonight?"

"It's a Ladies' Night. Daddy's Lodge has one very year. I remember," Michelle said with a giggle, "them both coming home from the last one in the early hours. They literally fell through the front door because they had so much to drink. My dad was laughing as my mum tried to help him up the stairs. It was lovely to see them enjoying themselves. They can both be so serious sometimes."

"Is a Lodge one of those Freemason things?" Ricky asked.

"Yes, Daddy is a Freemason. It's something he takes quite seriously. As a child I remember hearing him reciting the words from a small blue book he kept with his regalia in a black briefcase."

"Isn't Freemasonry a secret society?"

"Daddy says that it's not so much a secret society but a society with secrets. I know that they do a lot for charity and it's something he's very proud to be a part of," Michelle said.

Ricky pushed the homemade C90 cassette tape into the player. *'Rocket'* by Mud boomed out of the speakers. Ricky quickly reached out and turned the volume down.

"Sorry about that. I can get a bit carried away sometimes when I'm playing music," Ricky said.

***

Ricky drove to the Odeon cinema and parked just around the corner. They checked out the posters outside. The James Bond movie poster had Roger Moore holding a gun across his chest and various scantily clad women around him.

"What do you think of Roger Moore as James Bond?" Michelle said.

"I suppose because I grew up with Sean Connery, for me he is still James Bond. Don't get me wrong, I thought 'Live and let Die' was brilliant, but with Connery as Bond I think it would have been better. What about you?"

"My dad loved Roger Moore as The Saint. He would stop whatever he was doing and just turn up the volume and watch the show from beginning to end. Even Mum knew not to interrupt him and so I look at Roger Moore and still think of Simon Templar," Michelle said.

"Funny that, my dad and your dad are a million miles apart and yet, like you, I can still see him settling down to watch The Saint with my mum. What about David Essex?"

"Phew me!" Michelle said with a giggle. "He is just so handsome and cool. I still have a poster of him on my bedroom wall."

"Well that's good to know," Ricky said, rolling his eyes. "I thought 'That'll Be the Day' was a brilliant movie on so many levels. The music opened my eyes and ears to Rock 'n' Roll music and that Jim McClaine had to be more than what those around him expected. He knew life had more in store for him than running the family corner shop. I can completely understand how he just threw his schoolbooks in the river and ran off to the coast in search of his true self and direction."

"I think that settles it then," Michelle said.

"Settles what?"

"We both agree that Sean Connery was the better Bond. I fancy David Essex and you admired the part he played in the movie so... let's go and see Stardust," Michelle said.

***

It was dark when the movie finished. As they left the cinema, Ricky slipped his arm around Michelle's shoulders.

"What did you think?" Ricky said.

"I still fancy David Essex, but he turned into a complete, self-obsessed, arse in the movie. I hated the part where he drugged

Adam Faith's dog out of jealousy. I can imagine the music business being a dog-eat-dog world where the artists are just commodities to be used and exploited by big business," Michelle said. "What about you?"

"It was like most sequels for me, disappointing. I felt myself almost willing Jim McClaine on, but it was like he was set on a path of self-destruction. That'll Be the Day was a great movie, but 'Stardust' was just okay."

"I agree," Michelle said. "Would you like to come to my place for a coffee?"

Ricky smiled. "I'd love to have a coffee at your place."

***

Ricky parked outside Michelle's home.

"Are you sure you parents will be okay with this?" Ricky said.

"Of course they will. Besides, it's only just after ten and they won't be home for hours yet," Michelle said with a glint in her eye.

Michelle opened the front door and led Ricky through to the lounge. The suite was finished in a dark red leather with two armchairs and a buttoned Chesterfield couch. At either end of the room were crimson velvet curtains styled into swags and tails. The shag pile carpet was so thick that Ricky felt himself sink into it the moment he stepped into the room.

"I'll just put the kettle on," Michelle said.

Ricky walked over to a sideboard with a stereo turntable. It was a Bang and Olufsen. He reached down and pulled out three albums from a rack. They were Beethoven, Mozart and Tchaikovsky.

Shaking his head, he put them back in the rack and sat down on the couch.

"Coffee is ready," Michelle said as she entered the room wearing a white silk knee length dressing gown.

With each step Ricky couldn't help but notice a momentary glimpse of her upper thigh.

"How do you take it?" Michelle said as she put the tray on the coffee table in front of the couch.

Ricky was finding it increasingly difficult to avert his eyes as the dressing gown rose up when she sat down beside him. He coughed to clear his throat.

"Milk and two sugars please," Ricky said.

Michelle leant forward and spooned in two sugar lumps, some milk from a small jug and stirred their coffees.

"Thank you."

"Would you like to hear some music?" Michelle said, glancing over at the stereo system.

"I did take a quick look at your parent's collection and to be honest classical music just doesn't do it for me," Ricky said with a chuckle.

"I know what you mean," Michelle replied as she leapt up and crouched down in front of the sideboard. She opened the door revealing several albums.

"These are Mum's," Michelle said with a wry grin.

She removed a black vinyl from a cover that Ricky couldn't make out. Michelle turned the stereo on and placed the vinyl on the record deck. She moved the switch around to 33 RPM, lifted the stylus and placed it on the vinyl.

"I love this album," Michelle said with a half-smile. "I think I must have played it more times than Mum over the years.

Michelle skipped back to the couch just as *'I'm Still in Love with You'* by Al Green played. The sound was crisp and clear and unlike anything Ricky had experienced from a stereo before.

Ricky took a sip of his coffee.

"Michelle, what coffee is this? It's really good!"

"I'm not sure which coffee beans I used. Daddy is a bit of a coffee buff and will only have percolated coffee in the house. He says that instant coffee doesn't contain any of the real coffee beans and is created by either freeze drying or spray drying brewed coffee that then removes all the water from the coffee which is why it's so lightweight. Then, when hot water is added it's rehydrated, hence instant coffee. Personally, I like all types of coffee."

Ricky smiled weakly and swallowed a second sip.

"I like you Ricky Turrell," Michelle said, leaning towards him.

"I like you too," Ricky said with a faint smile.

"You've kind of caught me off guard," Michelle said. "I'd just managed to get shot of that loser, Kevin, and then you came into my life. I know this probably sounds a little lame, but I was a little scared at first and then, the more time we spent together and watching how you dealt with Trevor, well, I just found myself falling for you Ricky."

There was a moment's silence as the tension in the room rose between them.

"I'm not the kind of girl that goes out with lots of boys, but I like you a lot," Michelle said, moving closer.

Ricky and Michelle edged slowly closer to each other, and their eyes closed as their lips met. Michelle began to stroke his chest and shoulders as they kissed. Ricky moved his hand cautiously and placed it beneath her dressing gown and onto her thigh. Their kiss broke momentarily as Michelle groaned and bit her lower lip. She lowered her hand and began to stroke Ricky's inner thigh while kissing his neck and ear.

"Ricky let's go to my room," Michelle whispered passionately.

Chapter 17

R icky had been over to the salvage yard in Mitcham where he bought two Cortina Mk3's and two Ford Granada's. All four had been written off by their insurance companies for extensive accident damage and a burnt out engine bay. Ricky had arranged for them to be delivered to his garages where he planned to strip down what was resalable, remove the VIN plates so the car could be rung with freshly stolen, identical, cars. Ricky had paid just over six hundred pounds including delivery. He expected to get at least that back with part sales and make over two thousand pounds clear after selling all four cars at Dingwall car auctions.

Ricky parked outside the community centre. He spotted Doreen standing by the wall with two of her girls. They had scores of bags between them and a queue of customers picking up stolen school uniforms being sold at half price. Double Bubble stood close by handing out cash to woman from the estate. As he wrote the transactions into his book, the women crossed over and gave the money to Doreen in return for the stolen uniforms.

Ricky paused and looked at Doreen with her long platinum blonde hair. He could see that she was an attractive woman and better understood Neil's attraction to her.

"Ricky, Ricky, have you got a minute?" Trudy called out as she crossed the road with her pushchair.

"Yeah, sure. How are you, Trudy?" Ricky said.

"You know, things can always be better but I'm not complaining," Trudy said.

"Listen," Trudy said, lowering her voice, "I've had this police guy knock on my door. I've not seen him around the estate before, but he was asking questions about you."

"What kind of questions, Trudy?" Ricky asked.

"He wanted to know what kind of stuff you were involved in. He was digging. I told him Ricky, told him straight, that yes, I knew you, but that was about it. You lived on the estate and occasionally we saw each other in the pub but as far as I knew you worked in a garage," Trudy said.

"Did he ask which one?" Ricky said.

"He did, but I told him I didn't know," Trudy said. "I didn't like him, Ricky. I mean all Old Bills are slimy gits but this one was different. He looked, well kind of mean, determined and full of hate. He asked me the same questions four different ways. Don't worry he got the same answers, but I just wanted to let you know."

"Thanks for putting me in the picture Trudy, Ricky said, reaching into his pocket and sliding her two ten pound notes.

"You don't have to do that Ricky, we're friends," Trudy said.

"I know that Trudy, but I appreciate you letting me know. I know the copper you're talking about and he's a nasty piece of work. He likes to bully young girls. We've had a little run in and he's obviously trying to get something on me. If you see him again..." Ricky said.

"Yeah, of course. Are you sure about this?" Trudy said, holding the notes firmly.

"Get you and the little one something special," Ricky said with a wink.

"Thanks Ricky," Trudy said.

Ricky watched as she handed one of the notes to Double Bubble.

"That copper, Kevin, is really getting on my wick," Ricky thought. *"I can't afford to have him prying about while I'm knocking out ringers. One way or another he'll have to be sorted."*

Ricky pushed open the doors to the Milton Arms pub. The usual crowd were there who he acknowledged as he walked down and joined Deano at his usual table at the far end of the bar.

"Hello Deano, how are you mate?" Ricky said.

"I'd be a bloody sight better if my motor didn't keep breaking down. I'm supposed to meet some people tonight. I've got a bit of business to get sorted."

"I've got my motor outside. I can run you about if that helps," Ricky said.

Deano was silent for a moment.

"Are you sure?"

"Yeah course, that's what mates do," Ricky said.

"Look, whatever you see or hear has to stay quiet. Do you understand?" Deano said firmly.

"Yeah, goes without saying Deano. Not a word to a living soul."

Deano reached over for his pint and swallowed it all back in one gulp. He wiped his mouth and smiled.

"Well come on then Ricky, let's get out of here."

The two Teds climbed into the Rover.

"Where to?" Ricky asked.

"Do you know The Adam and Eve pub in Battersea?" Deano said, fastening his seat belt.

"I know Battersea. It's just the other side of Clapham Common."

"That's close enough. I can give you directions from there," Deano said as he patted the dashboard.

"Have you got any proper music we can play?" Deano said, scanning the car for tapes.

"What like?" Ricky said.

"Rock 'n' Roll, what else?" Deano said with a grin.

Ricky reached into his glove box and produced a 'That'll Be the Day' soundtrack tape from the movie. He put it into the Sharp stereo and *'Runaround Sue'* by Dion and the Belmonts played.

"That will work," Deano said as he pushed himself back into the deep, comfortable, leather seat.

One track merged into another as they drove across London to Clapham Common. Once Ricky pointed out that they were there, Deano gave Ricky directions to the Adam and Eve pub. Ricky drove past the pub slowly. Every outside table was taken with Teddy Boys in their full drape suits. Ricky watched as Deano began to rub his hands together. A car pulled out just ahead, which gave Ricky a space to park. They were just a few car lengths from the pub.

Ricky opened his glove box and took out the brass knuckle duster that Deano had given him.

Deano chuckled. "Ricky, you won't be needing that mate!"

Ricky locked the car and the two Teds swaggered towards the pub. Immediately the Teddy Boys began to look up and acknowledge Deano.

"Alright Deano?" one Ted called out.

"Good to see you mate," another called out.

Deano smiled and nodded back to each and every one of them.

They walked into the pub and towards the bar. The landlord, an older guy dressed in a dark grey waistcoat, white shirt and bootlace tie looked up and smiled.

"Hello Deano, the boys are upstairs. Go on up," the landlord said as he pointed towards the staircase.

Ricky followed Deano to the end of the bar, through a bare wooden door and up a tight stairway. At the top of the stairs was a closed door with a 'Private' notice screwed on to it. Deano marched over and opened the door. Ricky followed him in and closed the door. Inside there was a large table with ten Teddy boys sat around it. The chair at the end of the table was empty.

"Alright boys," Deano said as he strode around to his place. "Ricky, grab yourself a chair."

Ricky took a chair with a threadbare seat from the window and placed it by the table. He recognised Jock Addie, leader of the Croydon Teds.

"I appreciate all of you coming together like this at short notice. Around this table are the leaders of some of the biggest, most brutal and vicious gangs of Teds in London. In the past, when necessary, one or two of our gangs have come together under the united banner of being Teds and taken out rival gangs. Over the years the Milton Road Teds have stood side by side with each and every one of your gangs at some time. Thanks to our friend, Jock Addie from the Croydon Teds, we have information that a bunch of Skinheads are putting together some kind of super gang. I've heard that step one is to try and take us on at the Milton Arms and then one by one Clifford Tate wants to smash seven sorts out of everyone here. Make no mistake, he wants to stamp his name down as number one and his Skinheads over and above us Teddy Boys."

Deano looked around the room making eye contact with each of the leaders.

"That cannot happen, because as Teddy Boys we will not allow it to happen. United under one single banner we will crush their audacity, their cheek and their ambitions."

Ricky watched as Deano controlled and manipulated the atmosphere and tension in the room with his words.

"It's time for us to move beyond a minor tear up here and there and hit these racist, Nazi inspired, Skinheads hard and where they live," Deano announced.

"I'm in," Jock Addie said, holding up a clenched fist.

"Me too," Nelson hissed.

One by one every gang leader confirmed that they were in and the boys around the table began to cheer and punch the air.

"We will need numbers, but more importantly I want Teds that can stand up and have a proper fight. None of us need the ones, and we all know who they are, that don't have the bottle or will have it on their toes when it really kicks off. Our Ted army will pulverize everyone that stands in our way. We do unto others as they would do unto us, only we do it first!"

"Are we going tooled up?" Jock said enthusiastically.

"Chains, dusters, pickaxe handles, cricket bats, coshes - you can all take your pick - but no knives. We'll be inflicting severe, bloody, punishment but we're not killing anyone. Is that clear?" Deano said firmly.

The leader of each Ted gang nodded and agreed. They would each pick only the hardest, toughest and most fearless members to come together. Deano and the Teds spent the next hour making their plans.

Deano and Ricky left just after 9.30pm. The Teds had tried to get Deano to stay and drink with them, but he declined saying that he had another meeting. Ricky and Deano got into the car and headed back.

"Where to next?" Ricky asked.

"Back to the Arms mate. We should be back in time to get a couple of beers in."

"Sounds good to me," Ricky said.

"You did alright tonight, Ricky. There are many that would have been intimidated by that group, but you weren't. I'm proud of you mate and I liked the way you embedded yourself, like you belonged amongst the best of the best," Deano said.

"Cheers Deano," Ricky said. "That means a lot."

"Alright, let's not get soppy. You can get me a pint when we get back," Deano said with a laugh.

"Clifford Tate must be some kind of delusional nutter wanting to take on every Ted in London," said Ricky.

Deano smiled and began to shake his head slowly.

"I told them what they wanted to hear and gave them a cause that was worth fighting for. We have a united Ted Army now that can be called upon when needed. Some days you're the dog and others you're the tree it's pissing on. Today I'm the dog," Deano said.

"Deano the Dog," Ricky said.

"King of the Teds," Deano said.

***

Back at the Arms, Mick, Kenny and Lee were sitting at the far end of the bar with Steve and Terry Parker. Deano caught Ronnie's eye and mouthed 'same again all round'.

"Deano, what, you went with him?" Mick said with a sneer pointing at Ricky. "He ain't been here ten minutes and you go with him?"

"Give it a rest Mick. My motor broke down, again, and so Ricky took me. Is that alright with you?" Deano said in a forceful tone.

"I don't believe it," Mick said shaking his head.

Deano took two steps forward.

"I do not explain myself to anyone... ever. Now drink your beer and sort yourself out because we have the biggest ruck in history coming soon and I need you on the front line. You're my number two Micky Deacon!" Deano said.

Deano turned to the brothers, Terry and Steve Parker.

"You boys were dynamite the other week when he hit the Blue Anchor. I was impressed. I think you lads are Milton Road Ted material. We would all be proud to have you both among our ranks," Deano said as he handed each of them a pint.

The brothers clinked glasses with all the Milton Road Teds and confirmed that they were in.

"We have a big bit of business coming off soon and I mean epic. I want you down the front with my number two, Mick. Is that okay for you?"

The brothers both shrugged their shoulders. "Sure, we're in," Terry said.

Deano took up his usual seat and shared his plans for Clifford Tate and the Bedford Boot Boys.

"Ronnie, have you seen Jackie about?" Ricky said as he scanned behind the bar.

"The last I heard she teamed up with Doreen," Ronnie said.

"What, she's out there hoisting?" Ricky asked.

He was shocked.

"What do you think?" Ronnie said as reached down for a glass.

Chapter 18

Ricky had spent the morning around the estate garages with Monkey. They had agreed on an early start. By lunch time all four cars were successfully rung and were ready for the auction. The insurance write-off motors were stripped down to the shells and the car parts stored. The scrap man had arrived on time, just as he promised, and carted away the shells.

"Mum, I need to make a few phone calls. I'll leave a few bob on the side. Is that alright?" Ricky said.

"Of course you can," Caroline said, handing him a cup of steaming hot coffee.

"Thanks Mum," Ricky said, taking a sip from the mug. "Have you ever tried percolated coffee?"

"No, I don't think I have," Caroline said.

"Would you like to?" Ricky said as he put his mug on the table.

"Hmm, sounds nice," Caroline said with a warm smile.

Ricky watched as she carried a tray with two cups through to the front room. Ricky closed the door and picked up the telephone receiver. He called three back street garages that had bought parts from him before. He lumped goods together with an attractive price and had sold everything.

"This is money for old rope," Ricky thought. *"That's well over two grand clear profit by the time the motors are sold at auction."*

Ricky telephoned Michelle.

Ricky: Hello, is Michelle there please? It's Ricky.

Michelle's Father: Oh, it's you.

There was a short silence.

Michelle's Father: Michelle, there's someone on the phone for you.

Michelle: Hello.

Ricky: Hello Michelle, how are you?

Michelle: Much better now that I'm talking to you.

Ricky: I've been thinking about you.

Michelle: I've been thinking about you too.

Ricky: Are you able to get out later?

Michelle: No, sorry, my grandparents are visiting.

Ricky: Oh, okay another time then.

Michelle: Good. My dad has finally left the room.

Ricky: Why, what's up?

Michelle: It's that Kevin.

Ricky: What's he done now?

Michelle: When I got out of the shower this morning, I found an envelope on my bed.

Ricky: An envelope? I don't understand.

Michelle: When I opened it there were photos of you and I standing outside the Odeon. Then another of us getting into your car and the final one must have been taken through our lounge window because it's you and I kissing on the couch. It's a bit blurred but you can see it's us. Ricky I'm scared. If my parents saw these photos, they would go up the wall.

Ricky: I can't believe this. What kind of nutter would do something like that?

Michelle: It's worse than that Ricky.

Ricky: Why? What do you mean?

Michelle: It means that he must have broken into our home while I was alone in the shower and put that envelope on my bed. I can't help thinking what if... you know?

Ricky: That doesn't bear thinking about. Do you have Kevin's address?

Michelle: Why, what are you going to do?

Ricky: I need to make this stop. It isn't right.

Michelle: Is it worth me speaking to my dad but without mentioning the photos? Maybe he can put a stop to all this by speaking to the family solicitor.

Ricky: I wouldn't do that Michelle. Let me have the address and I'll have one last go at putting a stop to this.

Michelle gave him Kevin, the police officer's, address.

Michelle: Don't go doing anything that will get you into trouble Ricky.

Ricky: No, I won't, don't worry.

Michelle: You promise?

Ricky: I promise to do my best to make all this stop.

Michelle: Thank you. I miss you, Ricky.

Ricky: I miss you too. I'll call you tomorrow, okay?

Michelle: Okay. Goodbye, Ricky.

Ricky put the receiver back on the phone.

"What kind of bloody nutcase would break into someone's house and leave photographs," thought Ricky, *"and run around the estate trying to get something on me. This mad bastard needs sorting and sorting quickly!"*

"Thanks Mum, I've left a quid on the side for the phone," Ricky called out as he headed towards the front door. "See you later."

***

Ricky found Neil outside the chip shop and between them they drove the cars back and forth to the auction. Ricky had tried to instigate a conversation about Kevin, the copper, and what he was up to, but he didn't want to risk his new business and frighten Neil off. Big money was now beginning to flow through the door and Ricky wasn't about to risk that. Money provided choices - what you wear, what you drive and where you go. Those four ringed motors and the sale of parts was more than he would earn as an apprentice mechanic in a year. Ricky had the taste of money, and he didn't want Neil to bottle it now. It all confirmed that Kevin would need to be visited sooner rather than later.

Chapter 19

Michelle was at home. Her parents had gone out for the day. Ricky would be telephoning later and then they would be going out. She got out of the shower and dried herself before wrapping the bath towel around her slender frame. She looked up at her David Essex poster and smiled. Michelle put several vinyl singles onto her stereo and smiled before sitting down at her dressing table. The first single to play was *'Love Me for a Reason'* by The Osmonds.

Michelle sang along to the song as she took her make up from the drawers. From the corner of her eye, she thought she caught a glimpse of something. She turned around quickly and there stood Kevin, in his police uniform, by the doorway.

"What the…?" Michelle cried out.

Kevin rushed forward and grabbed her. He put his hand over her mouth before she could scream.

"Oh, Michelle I am so disappointed in you," Kevin hissed into her ear.

Michelle struggled but was firmly in his grip.

"You know we were destined to be together. I understand you needed your space because a love like ours can be so consuming. I know you feel the same way I do. It grates with me that you had sex with that low life Teddy Boy from the Milton Road Estate. I can only imagine that you must have been momentarily confused and he took advantage of you, but don't worry, Michelle, I will forgive you. I'm looking at the bigger picture. Together we will get over this misdemeanour. We can work through it and get our love back on track," Kevin whispered, squeezing Michelle tighter. "I did think at first you needed to be punished for cheating and betraying me like I was just some worthless nobody but something inside said all I needed to do was to save you from yourself. We both know that the day will come when we will be married and who knows, maybe have children? I've often thought that I'd like to have a baby with you, Michelle, my soulmate. Destiny has brought us together and I know that you also know we are destined to be together for all time."

Michelle stopped struggling. She could see Kevin's reflection in the mirror. His eyes were glazed over, his grip tightened.

"If I take my hand away, do you promise not to scream?"

Michelle nodded her head.

"Don't make me hurt you Michelle," Kevin hissed. "You wouldn't want me to hurt you, would you?"

With Kevin's hand still covering her mouth she shook her head. Kevin slowly released his powerful grip. Michelle took a deep breath.

"You shouldn't be here Kevin," Michelle said.

"What do you mean?" Kevin shrieked through gritted teeth.

His face was contorted by hate and jealousy.

"I just meant that my parents will be back soon, and my dad would not be happy if he found someone in my room," Michelle pleaded.

"Well, it's a shame that you didn't think about that when that Ricky Turrell was here. I saw you both on the settee. I watched you through the window as you kissed him. I thought 'you disgusting slut' and nearly, very nearly, came into the house to punish you both as you had sex in that bed there!" Kevin said, pointing to the bed. "It would have served you both right!"

Sensing that Kevin was becoming increasingly agitated Michelle tried to calm the situation.

"That was a mistake. I know that now. I hope that you can forgive me, Kevin, because you'll have to for us to get back together."

"Tell me you love me Michelle," Kevin said.

"I love you Kevin," Michelle said softly.

"No, no, no!" Kevin yelled, slamming his fist down onto the dressing table, sending makeup all over the carpet. "Say it with meaning!"

"You're frightening me Kevin," Michelle implored.

"Say it, say it, say it!" Kevin screeched.

"I love you, Kevin. You mean everything to me, and I know that we are meant to be together forever," Michelle said as a single tear trickled down her cheek.

Kevin smiled.

"Now doesn't that feel better, sharing your feelings with your soul mate?" Kevin said as he kissed her forehead. "Come on, let's cuddle together on the bed."

"I can't Kevin. My parents will be home anytime," Michelle pleaded.

Kevin took her firmly by the hand and led her to the bed.

"Please, please, if you feel anything for me don't do this," Michelle sobbed.

"I'm just going to cuddle you," Kevin muttered as he positioned Michelle on the bed. He then walked around to the other side and slid in next to her. He put his arm around her shoulder.

"Doesn't this feel just so right," Kevin whispered.

"Please don't do this," Michelle whimpered.

"It's wonderful to just lie here with the love of my life," Kevin whispered.

Kevin shot up when he heard the sound of the front door opening downstairs. He put his finger to his lips, indicating that Michelle was to stay quiet.

"Hello Michelle, we're home," her dad called out. "Mum's just putting the percolator on. Do you fancy one of my new coffees?"

Kevin stood by her bedroom door wide eyed with his fists clenched. He shot her a stare that sent shivers through Michelle's body.

"Michelle?" her dad called out for the second time.

Kevin motioned for her to respond.

"Hi dad, I'd love a coffee. I'll be down in a minute," Michelle replied as she wiped the tears from her eyes.

"Are you okay?"

"Yes, I'm fine," Michelle called back firmly.

"Oh, okay," her dad said as he walked through to the kitchen.

Kevin slid out of her doorway into the hallway with his finger still against his lips. Michelle stood by her bedroom door and watched as Kevin crept down the stairs, across the lobby and out of the front door.

***

Later that day Michelle took a taxi to Harrington's Garage and met with Ricky as he left work. Once they were alone in the car, she told Ricky everything that had happened. Ricky drove her home and then drove back to the estate and called on Kenny.

"Hello mate, what are you doing here?" Kenny said as he stepped out the front door and looked up and down the road.

"I'm going to need your help, mate, but there can't be any questions," Ricky said, holding out a black woolly hat with two slots cut out for the eyes.

Kenny smiled. "Do I need any tools?"

Ricky nodded.

Kenny ran through the hall and bounded up the stairs. He returned seconds later carrying a baseball bat. "Will this do?" Kenny said.

"Perfect," Ricky hissed.

"I take it this is not Ted's business," Kenny said as they walked towards Ricky's car.

"No mate. And the less you know, the better," Ricky said.

"Okay, no problem. You'd do this for me, wouldn't you?" Kenny said.

"In a heartbeat mate," Ricky said.

Ricky started the car and drove slowly through the estate.

"Is it far?" Kenny asked as he rubbed his stomach. "I haven't eaten yet."

Ricky shook his head. "Once we've taken care of business here, I'll get us both some fish and chips, alright?"

"Sounds good to me Ricky. What are the chances of you throwing in a couple of pickled onions and a bottle of lemonade?"

"You've got it," Ricky said, reaching over and turning the stereo on. The 'That'll Be the Day' movie soundtrack cassette was still in the player. 'Red River Rock' by Johnny and the Hurricanes played.

"I love this track," Kenny said, reaching over and turning up the volume.

Ricky could feel his heart pounding furiously against his chest. The adrenaline was racing through his body as he recalled Michelle telling him what Kevin had done.

Ricky drove through Morden and came to a halt just around the corner from the underground tube station.

"Is this it?" Kenny said.

"Yeah, the target lives there," Ricky said as he slid the brass knuckle duster onto his right hand. "Right, let's do this."

Ricky and Kenny got out of the car. As they walked up the pathway to Kevin's front door, they both pulled the black woolly hats with the holes cut out so they could see, over their heads. Ricky clenched his fist and then rang the bell with his left hand. The hallway light came on and he could see an outline coming towards them through the two rectangular frosted glass panels in the door.

The door opened, and as soon as Kevin caught a glimpse of the two masked men he yelled out and tried to slam the front door closed. Ricky managed to get his foot jammed between the door and the frame and Kenny gave the door an almighty kick. It flung open, almost sending Kevin to the floor. Ricky and Kenny were inside and the front door was closed. Kevin tried desperately to get back onto his feet as he scampered awkwardly down the hallway. Ricky raced up behind him, grabbed him by the shoulder and swung him around. He fired a right hook, taking the wind out of him. Kevin bent forward and was gasping for air. Ricky raised his knee with such ferocity that Kevin's nose cracked as his body was sent sprawling to the floor. Ricky kicked him over and over again while Kenny stood by the door holding the baseball bat.

"Leave it out, leave it out!" Kevin screamed, holding his bleeding nose.

Ricky stood over his body and then slammed down with his knees, pinning Kevin's shoulders down. With his left hand holding Kevin by the throat, he took aim and fired three punches, causing torn flesh, blood and broken teeth. After the last punch Kevin was motionless but Ricky could hear him whimpering and spitting out blood.

Ricky leant down and whispered into Kevin's ear.

"If you ever contact or go near Michelle again, I will fucking kill you! Do I make myself clear?"

Kevin remained silent but Ricky could see that he was still conscious. He got off Kevin's limp body, turned to Kenny and lowered his voice.

"I'll see you back in the motor in two minutes, alright?"

Kenny nodded and left the room.

Ricky turned back to Kevin as he lay on the floor. He stepped over him and clenched his right fist with the blood-stained brass knuckle duster.

"Okay, I get it," Kevin whimpered.

Ricky launched one final kick hard into Kevin's limp body.

***

Both lads had removed their masks before they left Kevin's house.

Once inside the car Kenny spoke.

"You are one very vicious young man."

"It had to be done," Ricky said.

"I'm not sure you needed me," Kenny said.

"I had to be sure that he got the message, and I couldn't take a risk on it being a one-on-one fair fight," Ricky said as he steered the car out onto the main road by the station.

"Will there be some kind of come back after this?" Kenny asked.

"No mate, it was all taken care of," Ricky said confidently.

Once Kenny had left the house, and Kevin received his final kicking, Ricky took a small tin of red spray paint from his jacket pocket. He wrote on the living room wall in four-foot letters 'POOF!' and 'SKINS RULE!' before calling 999 and reporting the incident to the emergency services. Ricky requested the police and an ambulance. He knew that homosexuals were being preyed on by right wing Skinheads and the incident would look like another case of 'queer bashing'. By calling the police it would ensure that Kevin's own kind, no matter how hard he tried to convince his fellow officers otherwise, would believe that he was a homosexual and the largest gang in the UK, the police force, would not be coming to the aid of a suspected homosexual police officer.

"Not a word to anyone about this, okay?" Ricky said.

"Yeah, of course, Ricky. It was just a warmup for what's to come," Kenny said through his maniacal smile.

Once back at the Milton Arms, Ricky called Michelle from the payphone and told her that he and Kevin had worked things out and that she wouldn't be hearing from him again.

Chapter 20

Deano had arranged for all the Milton Road Teds to meet outside the train station. With lads from the estate, surrounding areas and the addition of Steve and Terry Parker, they totalled twenty-six. Ricky was buzzing. He had dressed up in his favourite powder blue drape suit. He looked around at the Teds who were all dressed in drainpipe trousers, brothel creepers, waistcoats or drape jackets. Deano had called together only the hardest, toughest and most fearless in their ranks.

"Specs, it's bloody good to have you here!" Deano said with a grin that spanned the width of his face.

The lads rallied around, patting him on the shoulders. He was back amongst friends.

"I wouldn't miss it for the world," Specs said.

"Bloody right you wouldn't," Deano said before turning to the Teds, "This man is a maniac when he gets going. Mick, are you ready for this?"

Mick pulled out a rubber cosh from his inside pocket and pounded it onto his open palm. "Those Skinheads are gonna get a right taste of this."

"That's why you're my number two, Mick. You're brave, loyal, and a force that's definitely not to be messed with."

The lads all cheered.

"Lee," Deano said.

The crowd of Teds went silent.

"By rights you shouldn't be here but that said, I am into giving second chances. When we invade those jug-headed bellends I expect to see you smashing seven shades out of everyone that moves. Can you do that?"

"I'm there Deano," Lee said as he pounded his fist against his palm.

"Good man, that's the spirit. I want them Skinheads to take one look in your eyes and want to run for their lives," Deano said firmly.

"I'm on it!" growled Lee.

"Ricky, you sorted?"

Ricky raised his right hand with the brass knuckle duster.

"I never doubted it," Deano said with a wink.

Deano looked down at his watch. "Right, we're on the next train. The Milton Road Teds surged forward and into the station.

"Twenty-six returns to Sutton," Kenny said as he handed a small bundle of notes through the ticket vendor's glass window.

The old woman looked startled when she saw the large number of Teddy Boys milling around her station.

"Err, yes," the vendor replied.

Kenny watched as her nervous hands shook while she gathered up the tickets and passed them through the glass screen.

"Cheers," Kenny said as he folded the tickets and placed them into his inside jacket pocket.

The train rolled into the station on time and the Teds climbed into the carriages.

Ricky could almost feel the adrenaline rushing through the Milton Road Teds. Everything around him felt heightened, clearer, and sharper. Even the air he breathed tasted different.

"This is what it's all about Ricky," Deano declared in an ardent, fervent, tone. "A right proper mob of Teds."

"Ted Army!" Mick yelled out.

TED ARMY... TED ARMY... TED ARMY! The Teds chanted together.

"Can you feel it?" Deano said as he faced Ricky. "That feeling of excitement. The anticipation of what's about to happen surging up from the pit of your stomach. Everyone here is feeling it. We're going into battle as Teds, a united force under one banner."

"I'm buzzing Deano."

"Good man. You get in there today and make us all proud!" Deano said as he held up his clenched fist.

Some of the Teds had opened the windows and were hanging out of them as the train rolled into the next station.

"Deano, its Jock Addie and the Croydon Teds," Lee said.

"What kind of numbers?" Deano asked.

Lee started shaking his head. "Deano, the platform is jam packed! There have got to be thirty if not forty Teds.

"Excellent," Deano said as a crazed grin spread across his face.

The train came to a halt and all the Milton Road Teds cheered as Jock Addie and the Croydon Teds climbed aboard the train. Jock passed through the carriage shaking hands and patting his fellow Teds on the back. He stopped in front of Deano.

"Budge up," Deano said to Lee.

Lee, reluctantly, got up and made a space for Jock.

"Looks like I brought a few more lads than you, Deano," Jock said as he sat down.

"With the Milton Road Teds it's quality over quantity. We don't take just anyone, but all that said, it was me that has brought us all together," Deano growled.

"Yes, you did, Deano the Dog, King of the Teds!" Jock yelled out.

All the Teds cheered as one.

DEANO... DEANO... DEANO!

Deano leant forward while the lads continued cheering his name. "Jock, yes, I am and it's best that no one forgets that."

"I didn't mean any disrespect," Jock replied. "I was just pushing the envelope, you know, having a laugh."

"Are you tooled up?" Deano asked.

Jock opened his drape jacket revealing a heavy, three link, bicycle chain he'd threaded through as a trouser belt.

"Very nice," Deano said, nodding his head. "I'm impressed. When all this is over, I want to see that dripping in flesh and blood."

"We ain't taking no prisoners," Jock said. "Deano mate, loving the creepers!"

Deano was wearing a new pair of blue suede crepe soled brothel creepers. Attached to each of the lace eyelets was a chromed knuckle duster with the shoelaces running through them.

"I have to got to get me a pair of those. Where did you get them?" Jock said leaning forward to get a better view of Deano's shoes.

"I had them specially made."

"Mate I love them. Who made them for you?"

"These are a one-off. The only pair in existence and exclusive to me, Jock."

Jock began to nod his head back and forth slowly. "Class, King of the Teds, absolute class."

Ricky could sense a little rivalry between Deano and Jock. He looked Jock up and down and then looked at his friend Deano.

"Jock Addie, you wouldn't stand a snowball's chance in hell against Deano," Ricky thought.

The train came to a halt and Deano stood up and led the Ted Army out of the carriages and onto the platform. They moved as one through to the stairways and out into the street outside. On the opposite side of the road was another mob of thirty plus Teds.

"Good, they're all here," Deano said.

"Deano," said Mick, "with this lot we could take on the bloody world. They ain't going to know what's hit them!"

All the Teds from Clapham, Balham and Streatham had come together as Deano had planned.

Deano led the Teds across the road. They moved as one, with cars coming to a screeching halt. One driver began to hoot his horn and wave his fist at the Teds. Terry Parker bolted towards the car. He grabbed the windscreen wipers, pulled them off and threw them to the ground. The driver opened his door and began waving his fists and shouting out threats. Terry produced his metal cosh and smacked the driver hard across the side of the head. He collapsed over the top of the door before tumbling to the ground, unconscious. Terry strode around to the front of the car and smashed both headlights before joining the rest of the Ted Army.

A traffic warden was writing out a ticket while a young mother with her pushchair was trying desperately to explain how sorry she was for being late. As the lads approached, Ricky tapped the traffic warden on the shoulder. He turned to see scores of Teds moving towards him. Ricky grabbed the ticket and his book. He tore it up and threw it down on the ground.

"I hate bullies that hide behind a uniform," Ricky said. "You get yourself away from here, sweetheart, because it's about to get nasty."

The traffic warden stood motionless while the Teds filed past. Some of them slapped him around the head as they passed by. Ricky and Kenny helped the woman put her pushchair into the boot of the car.

"Thank you," the woman said as she hurried to get into her car and drive away.

"Shame she's got a sprog," Kenny said, "I could get right down and dirty with a bird like that."

"Would having a little one really make that much difference?" Ricky asked.

"Nah, married birds are the best. Just all the good stuff without any of the drama that goes with taking them out," Kenny said.

The Army of angry young men followed Deano through the side roads. Shoppers crossed the road or dived into shop doorways to avoid the moving force. Cars came to a complete halt with many drivers leaning down over the passenger seat with their heads down.

Deano led the Army of Teddy Boys down the High Street. With a single movement from his hand, the group broke into three. One led by Micky Deacon and the second by Jock Addie. The 'Beverley' pub came into view. All the tables outside were littered with Bedford Boot Boys, the Cambridge Flats lot and the Chandler Drive Mob. There were Skinheads, Soulboys and Glam Rockers in their wedged shoes and brightly coloured tank tops. Deano started the chant:

TEDS... TEDS ... TEDS...

Almost as one the group outside the pub rose to their feet as over one hundred, hard-core, Teddy Boys came into view.

TEDS... TEDS ... TEDS...

Deano pointed as several of the boys outside the pub clambered to their feet and scarpered away. The Teddy Boys jeered and began chanting again.

TEDS... TEDS ... TEDS...

Micky Deacon watched as Terry and Steve Parker broke ranks and ran towards a parked HGV truck unloading bricks outside a building site. Terry took out a metal cosh and whacked the driver sending him to the ground. The brothers quickly pulled down the sides of the truck exposing the pallets of house bricks. Mick understood and led the lads over to the truck. Terry was the first to throw a house brick. It landed a little shy of its target, knocking over a table full of drinks. Mick's group began to lob the bricks across the street. The gangs dodged as best they could. One lad was hit face on, and he fell to his knees, cupping his face. Another brick hit the windscreen of a passing car. The driver hit the brakes and screeched to a halt on the pavement after knocking over a motorcyclist on a moped. A second brick smashed the side window in. The driver dived across the passenger seat, below the dashboard and out of sight. Scores of bricks rained down on the enemy. The motorcyclist curled up into a ball protecting his face as the house bricks rained down. The first brick found its way through the pub window with glass shattering out onto the tables. The pub doors burst open, and a thick stream of furious thugs stormed out onto the street. They bounced from left to right in their ten-hole Doctor Marten boots, and waved their fists, taunting the Teds on.

TEDS... TEDS ... TEDS!

"Teds forever!" Deano shouted, as he broke into a jog towards the pub. The army of Teds charged forward with brothel creepers kicking, fists flying and bicycle chains swinging. The sheer number of battling Teds and the bombardment of house bricks drove the Clifford Tate super gang of Boot Boys and Skinheads backwards.

Ricky steamed forward and threw a right hook that sent the Skinhead sprawling to the ground. As Skinhead after Skinhead was brought down with chains, knuckle dusters and metal coshes, some of the opposing gang broke away and legged it away from the pub. Ricky watched as a huge Skinhead dressed in tight blue jeans, white

Ben Sherman shirt and red braces kicked tables out of the way to get into the fight. With fists the size of a bunch of bananas he clobbered and clumped Teddy Boy after Teddy Boy. As they fell, he barked out orders for his troops to regroup. Ricky knew that he must have been Clifford Tate.

Ricky caught a smack to the side of his face that shook him off balance. Instinctively he turned swiftly and fired a lethal right hook. The knuckle duster caught the Boot Boy clean on the chin. The lad yelled out as broken teeth and blood shot out from his mouth. Ricky stepped back, took aim and kicked the lad straight between the legs before charging past and pulling off a lad that was kicking a Teddy Boy he'd seen on the ground. As the lad fell backwards, he saw it was his friend Kenny. Ricky, in a fit of fury and rage, began to frantically kick and punch at all those around him before reaching down and helping Kenny back onto his feet. To his right he saw Deano and a dozen or so Teds piling through a bunch of Glam Rocker lads in their coloured vest tops and wedge shoes. Steve and Terry Parker were kicking wildly at a Skinhead on the ground. As each boot connected, his body rose up from the concrete. The brothers were relentless in their mission to administer pain. As the battered Skinhead tried to wrap his beaten body around the centre leg of the table they pulled and pushed at it to finish him.

Ricky caught a glimpse of Jock Addie as he and two of his Teds surged forward to get at Clifford Tate. There was a deafening war cry as Clifford Tate took one punch after another but still kicked and punched back while moving slowly forward. Jock Addie swung his bicycle chain and narrowly missed Clifford Tate. Another Ted ran forward but was met with the full force of Clifford Tate's fist as it smashed him straight in the stomach. The Ted bent forwards struggling to catch his breath while Clifford Tate grabbed him by the hair and sent his knee hurtling skywards. The Teds legs gave way and Clifford Tate slung him effortlessly by the hair to one side.

"You alright Kenny?" Ricky called.

"Yeah, yeah, I'm fine. Cheers," Kenny said before homing in on his next target.

Deano was surrounded by Teds and all around him Clifford Tate's super gang was falling, with the weaker lads scurrying away and making a run for it. Ricky felt an incredible, electrifying, shock surge through his body and an overwhelming need for greater violence and to get at Clifford Tate. He wanted to fight with the Prince of the Boot Boys.

Deano, with his fists still tightly clenched, took a deep breath and yelled:

TEDS...TEDS... TEDS!

Half beaten Skinheads and Boot Boys clambered awkwardly to their feet and began to run and scarper as the Army of Teds chanted in ever increasing numbers. The Teds that still stood helped those that had fallen or had taken a beating, back onto their feet. Their victorious chant drowned out everything around them. Ricky watched as Clifford Tate, along with the last of his hardened Boot Boys raced away, narrowly avoiding frightened and stunned motorists and cowering members of the public.

TEDS...TEDS...TEDS!

"We did them Deano!" Mick cried out victoriously. "We sorted those jug-headed bellends well and good!"

Deano stood like a victorious general surveying the bloody carnage he had brought down on those that would dare to question his position as King of the Teds or threaten the violent reputation of the Milton Road Estate as number one.

"Deano, shouldn't we be away from here before the gavvers turn up?" Ricky said as he peered up and down the road.

Deano looked down at him. His eyes full of hate and still blazing from the battle.

"Make sure we have everyone and let's move!" Deano ordered.

The army of Teds fell back into their ranks and followed Deano back up through the High Street, down the back roads and into the train station. In the distance they could hear the sounds of police and ambulance sirens.

Chapter 21

Deano the Dog led his victorious army of flamboyantly dressed Teds from the train station, through the town and onto the Milton Road Estate. As they passed the hand painted 'Turn Back or Die' written under the Milton Road Estate sign the Teds let out an almighty roar and began to punch the air. Deano yelled out:

TEDS…TEDS…TEDS!

The army passed by the community centre where Double Bubble was conducting his money lending business and Doreen and two of her girls were surrounded by a mountain of carrier bags full of freshly stolen goods. Residents on the estate watched as the Army passed by the chip shop, the Chinese and the bookies before passing through the doors of the Milton Arms pub. Ronnie had never adhered to the licensing laws and kept the pub open all day right through to the early hours and Thursday right through to Saturday. The pub had its usual mix of youngsters and old timers supping on pint jugs of bitter and girls with their gin and tonics. Ricky spotted Melanie, Kaz and Donna down by the jukebox. Ronnie stood watching in amazement as Ted after Ted filed through his doors

"Alright Ronnie," Deano said.

"What's all this then?" Ronnie asked, looking around at his pub half full of Teddy Boys with split lips and blood-stained noses.

"I thought I'd bring a few friends in for a drink," Deano said as he placed a wad of notes on the bar.

"Right then lads," Ronnie said, holding up an empty pint glass, "Who's first?"

The Teds clambered around the bar barking out their orders to Ronnie and the two barmaids

Ricky sensed the excitement spreading around the pub, with old timers from around the estate raising their glasses out of respect to Deano and the Milton Road Teds. Melanie slipped a coin into the slot of the Jukebox. *"Rock 'n' Roll Lady'* by Showaddywaddy pounded out through the speakers. Immediately the Teds, as one, began, with a jug of beer in one hand, to sing out loud to the song. Melanie turned and faced the hordes of Teds. She looked magnificent in her short red pleated skirt, white Bay City Roller top with red tartan embroidered onto the seams. In her knee-high red leather platform boots she strutted slowly towards the bar. At that moment every male in the pub wanted her and every woman secretly wanted to be her. The record played and the Teds, arms around each other's shoulders, sang along.

Deano, surrounded knee deep in Teddy Boys yelling from the top of their voices 'She's a Rock 'n' Roll Lady' turned to face her. The lads parted as Melanie passed amongst them until she was face to face with the King of the Teds. She placed a pair of red silk panties into Deano's hand, leant forward slowly, placed her arms around his neck, pushed herself onto the ball of her feet and kissed him passionately with her luscious lips. As her left boot rose into the air, the Teds let out a raucous cheer.

Beer was spilt onto the stained and threadbare carpet while Ronnie and the two barmaids furiously poured pint after pint.

"You alright Kenny?" Ricky asked.

"Yes mate. I caught one on the back of the head and I lost it for a few seconds and the next thing I know I've got all these Skinheads kicking seven sorts of shit out of me. Thanks Ricky, I appreciate your help mate," Kenny said.

"It was nothing mate. It's what we do for each other, right?" Ricky said before sinking down the last of his pint.

"That's what being a Ted is all about for me, Ricky. We stand by our own. It doesn't matter if you're a Ted from London, Manchester or Birmingham we stand together as rock 'n' roll brothers against all enemies. I think Deano has really started something by bringing all this lot together."

"I think you're right," Ricky agreed while motioning one of the barmaids to pour him another pint.

"Speech, Speech," Deano called. The other lads from the MRT joined in, calling for Lee to make a speech.

Ricky and Kenny helped Lee up onto the table, so he stood above everyone in the pub. Lee coughed a couple of times to clear his throat.

"I just wanted to say how proud I felt today standing alongside Deano, King of the Teds, Mick, Ricky, Kenny, the MRT, and to every one of our friends and allies from all over London. We fought as one incredible fighting force and walked away as the victors. I want to pay homage to Jock Addie and the Croydon Teds, the Clapham and Streatham Teds, and to all those who rose bravely to the call to arms," Lee said, scanning the sea of drape wearing Teddy Boys.

The pub went quiet for a few moments.

"Lee, that was probably the best speech you've ever made," Kenny called out. "Somebody get this man a pint!"

The Teds all cheered. The girls kept the music playing with 'Rave On' by Buddy Holly and the Crickets.

"Here Ricky," Deano said, gulping down the last drops of his fourth pint.

"Yes mate."

"You did bloody good today. I was proud to see you in action and have you as part of my inner circle," Deano said as he patted Ricky on the shoulder. "Mick was his usual animal self and Lee, especially after that last speech, is now firmly back in my good books."

"Cheers Deano," Ricky said as he raised is glass. "Do you think that's it?"

"What do you mean?" Deano said, motioning Lee to get him another pint.

"Is it over or will they come back at us?"

Deano shook his head.

"I can't see that happening. I watched the so-called Bedford Boot Boys, Cambridge Flats and the Chandler mob have some of their boys run for the hills when we charged in. Clifford Tate knew that it would take serious numbers to bring us down and he failed. We gave them a proper good kicking in their own back yard. We not only reinforced our reputations but also as a consolidated Teddy Boy army. No one, anywhere, would dare mess with us," Deano said as he puffed out his chest.

"I don't know Clifford Tate, but those around him stood and fought despite our overwhelming numbers," Ricky said.

"Here Mick," Deano called.

"Yes mate?" Mick slurred.

"You're my number two, right?"

"Yes I am, and some people around here might need to remember that," Mick said, lowering his tone and glaring directly at Ricky.

"Ricky seems to think that Clifford Tate and his lot could come back at us. What do you think?"

"Not a chance. They took a damn good hiding today. We ain't gonna be hearing from them anytime soon," Mick said defiantly.

"I was just saying..." Ricky said before he was interrupted.

"Well don't just go saying. You ain't been part of the MRT ten minutes, so don't go thinking because you've slapped a few Skinheads about that you can question Deano or me!" Mick said with a glare.

Ricky held his composure.

"One of these days," Ricky thought as he held Mick's stare, *"I'm going to really hurt you Mickey Deacon"*

"He didn't mean anything by it, did you Ricky?" Deano said as Lee placed the pint on the table.

Ricky shook his head. "I was just asking your opinion, nothing else."

"What the...?" Mick cried out as he turned to see two old timers with red and white road cones on their heads dancing around in the middle of the pub. The larger and drunker of the two men lost his balance, tripped, recovered and then fell across a table sending drinks onto the laps of the women. Each of the women, with wild, taut, facial expressions began to slap and kick the man as he tried to pull himself up from the floor.

"Alright, alright, that's enough," Ronnie warned.

"Look what this stupid old geezer has done," one of the women shrieked, pointing to the stain on her blouse.

"He's going to replace your drinks, isn't that right?" Ronnie said as the old man pulled himself up.

"Yes, of course ladies. I'm very sorry" he muttered.

"I'll stick it on your tab," Ronnie said, waving to one of the barmaids.

As the day passed, the visiting Teddy Boys left the Arms. Melanie had taken Deano firmly by the hand and left, leaving just Ricky, Specs and Kenny at their usual table. The lads had consumed several pints and each of them was feeling quite merry. Specs began to slur his words.

"You know I love you Ricky," Specs slurred.

"Yeah, course you do," Ricky said with laugh.

"Not you though, Kenny," Specs said seriously.

"Why not me?" Kenny chuckled.

"You know why!" Specs said, slamming his pint jug down on the table.

"I've no idea what you're talking about," Kenny said with a confused expression. "I thought we were mates."

"I tolerate you, that's about it," Specs said, wiping beer froth from his mouth.

"Come on, leave it out," Ricky said calmly, sensing that the conversation was taking a serious turn.

"No, sod him Ricky. If he has something to say then he should just say it," Kenny said before slamming his pint glass down on the table.

Specs took a long swig from his pint.

"I know about you and Denise," Specs said, screwing up his face aggressively.

"I don't know what you're talking about Specs. You're drunk and talking bollocks," Kenny said.

"Denise is my wife, Kenny, and Tommy is my son and don't you ever forget it!"

"You need to get yourself home Specs," Ricky suggested.

"Don't think that I don't know!" Specs said through gritted teeth.

"Come on Specs, you've had one too many. We've all been there, mate. Best to call it a day, get yourself home and sleep it off," Ricky said with a friendly wink.

"I know!" Specs shouted, jumping to his feet and pointing wildly at Kenny. "They're my family, not yours!"

Ronnie came out from behind the bar. "Okay, Specs it's closing time now, mate. I'll see you to the door."

Ronnie led Specs towards the exit. He patted him on the shoulder, walked him outside into the night air and then returned, closing the door behind him.

"What the hell was that all about?" Ricky said as he shrugged his shoulders.

"No idea," Kenny said, pushing his glass to the middle of the table. "He's just had too much to drink."

Chapter 22

Deano and the lads had met in the Arms for a few drinks and to talk about traveling over to a Woolwich pub to see Crazy Cavan and The Rhythm Rockers in the New Year. Deano was making arrangements to meet with the leaders of Teddy Boy gangs from Plumstead, Greenwich, Peckham, New Cross and a gang with a growing reputation from the Nightingale Estate in Hackney. They were to meet at McDonalds, a new American Burger restaurant in Woolwich.

"Sound great," Ricky said cheerfully. "I'll go."

"We'll all be there Deano," Mick said, "won't we boys?"

The lads all nodded.

"There will be Teds from all over London going. This is a chance for us to meet and build bridges with other mobs and gangs. I've got this vision of a fearsome, well disciplined, Ted Army several hundred deep with just the toughest that London has to offer in its ranks. Can you imagine that?" Deano said looking skywards, "Wall to wall Teddy Boys all standing behind the Milton Road Teds?"

Earlier that morning Ricky had been with Neil swapping number plates and VIN numbers on six stolen cars ready for the auction. Monkey had been busy stripping the cars down before the scrap man came to remove all the incriminating evidence. Ricky and Neil had built their operation to delivering between two and three thousand pounds, after all expenses, each, a week. He had asked Neil to join them in the pub later, but he declined saying that he had a hot date that evening and didn't want to spoil it by drinking in the afternoon. Ricky had asked if it was Doreen, but Neil had just smiled and shook his head saying that she had been fun but was now firmly in the rear-view mirror. He had moved on to someone a bit special. Ricky pressed him for a name, but Neil wouldn't give anything away.

SMASH!!!!

"What the…?" Ricky said, looking up as the pub window came crashing down and sprayed broken glass across the tables and the floor. The woman directly under the window threw her hands into the air and let out a spine-tingling shriek as thick crimson blood streamed down her face

The pub doors flew open, crashing against the wall with a swarm of Skinheads with gritted teeth and veins bulging from their heads and necks waving pickaxe handles. They raced forward swinging the weapons. An old timer by the far end of the bar caught a smack in the back. He yelled out and fell to his knees. The Skinhead then sank his Doc Marten boots into his side.

Deano, Ricky and the rest of the Milton Road Teds rose to their feet. Ricky reached into his pocket for his knuckleduster and quickly slipped it on. The Skinheads raced forward kicking over tables and battering the pub's customers as they left their seats and tried running towards the back of the pub. Ronnie, the landlord, leapt clean over the bar and smashed a pint jug around one of the Boot Boys before grabbing another by the hair and bringing his head down onto the bar. Deano spotted Eddy Boyce and, remembering him from the Wimpy Bar incident, raced forward, fired a punch and missed his target. Eddy ducked down and then swung his home-made cosh. It caught Deano on the side of the head. He shuddered and shook his head from the furious impact. His knees buckled and Ricky thought he was going down. Ricky slung the table out of his way and charged forward, punching and kicking until he reached Eddy Boyce who had lifted the cosh high above his head and was about to bring it down on Deano who was now down on one knee. Ricky leapt into the air and smacked Eddy on the side of the head. He fell against a table and then down on to the floor. Ten, fifteen and now twenty plus skinheads were inside the pub. Deano was back on his feet with rage in his eyes. He grabbed Eddy by the scruff of his shirt and began to pound his face with punch after punch until the front of his white shirt was soaked in blood. Mick had thrown a chair at Clifford Tate and followed it through with several jabs. His fists bounced off the big man. Clifford seized him by his jacket and threw him several feet. He landed in a heap on the floor by the bar.

"Why you long streak of piss!" Ronnie shouted when he spotted a Skinhead holding a coke bottle with a rag hanging out its top. Ronnie knew that it was a homemade petrol bomb. The Skinhead put it between his legs and pulled a box of matches out of his pocket. Before he could light the match, Ronnie had stormed over. He caught a clump from a pickaxe handle as he passed one wild Skinhead whose job it was to make sure that no one escaped through the exit. Ronnie threw himself on top of the Skinhead with the petrol bomb and head butted the lad before receiving a smack across the back that left him gasping for air.

In a wild, hate-fuelled frenzy, several Skinheads were kicking Kenny, Lee, Specs and Mick across the floor. Only Deano and Ricky were left standing. A lad ran forward and tried to swipe Ricky around the head with his pickaxe handle. He missed him by just inches. Before the skinhead could recover his position, Ricky kicked him hard between the legs and fired a punch that put the lad on the floor. Ricky grabbed the lad's weapon, turned to Deano, now surrounded, and threw him the weapon.

Wah Wah… Wah Wah… it was the sound of several police cars.

"It's the old bill. Let's get out of here!" Clifford Tate ordered, and he sunk his Doc Marten boot one last time into the Milton Road Ted's number two, Mickey Deacon.

The Skinheads piled back out of the door, carrying their injured, as quickly as they had arrived.

Ricky helped Kenny back onto his feet, then Specs and Lee. Mick was having none of it. He pushed Ricky's hand away then reached out for the nearby table and pulled himself back up.

"Are you alright Ronnie?" Ricky asked, offering him his hand.

"Yeah, yeah, been in much worse than this," Ronnie said, still trying to catch his breath.

"They beat us. I can't believe it, those jug-headed bellends turned us over on our own manor! We are the Milton Road Teds and they done us!"

"We've got to get out of here Deano, all of us, before the gavvers start nicking everyone in sight," Ricky said.

"You said this might happen," Deano said as he turned to Ricky.

Ricky could see that he was furious with himself and by what had just happened.

"No one saw it coming," Ricky said as he pointed to pub door. "We have got to get out of here now."

Deano and the MRT left by the front door. On the wall and painted in tall black lettering read:

Bedford Boot Boys Rule!

"They are going to pay for this!" Deano snapped.

"Bloody right," Mick said as he punched the palm of his hand.

Deano and the MRT slipped into the bookies. They picked up pencils and betting slips pretending that they were customers. Several police cars came to a screeching halt outside. Uniformed officers, with truncheons drawn, ran towards the pub door.

"That was a close shave," Ricky said as he glanced outside at the uniformed officers.

"You said this might happen, Ricky, and I didn't listen," Deano said as he slowly shook his head.

"We have to hit them back Deano," Mick said with a snarl, "And I mean today!"

"They are going to pay; you can believe that. This is a war they'll never win," Deano said as he regained his composure.

"We need a plan," Ricky said calmly.

"What are you talking about? Who do you think you are telling us what to do?" Mick said, shooting Ricky a menacing glare.

"I'll tell you who I am Mick. I'm one of just two who were still standing, mate. I agree completely that we have to hit back but just not as some unruly pack. We have to have a plan and then we can hurt them," Ricky said with clear, calm, clarity.

Before Mick could retort Deano spoke.

"You're right Ricky. We're all pretty pissed off right now but to do this properly we need a plan. We'll give it half an hour for the old bill to bugger off, and then we'll get over to my place. We'll make some calls, get the numbers and find out where they are. Mick, get

216

yourself round to Steve and Terry Parker's place and put them in the picture"

Chapter 23

"Ricky, do want a cup of tea and a sandwich or something?" Caroline called from the kitchen

"No thanks, mum, I'll grab something out, cheers," Ricky replied.

Ricky had put on his favourite powder blue Drape Suit and had used the suede brush to clean his brothel creepers. He combed his hair back with a smidgen of Brylcreem and checked his reflection in the mirror.

"Mum, I need to use the phone, okay? I'll leave a few bob in the jar," Ricky said as he reached into his pocket.

"Of course you can," Caroline said before placing two hot mugs of tea and a large plate of sandwiches on a tray. "Your dad and I are going to watch the James Bond movie tonight."

"What one is that then mum?"

"Oh, I don't know but it does have that nice Sean Connery in it," Caroline said with a cheeky grin.

"Your eye looks a bit bruised Ricky, is it alright?" Caroline said as she stopped by the kitchen door.

"Yeah, I was working on my car earlier and trying to undo this really tight nut when the spanner slipped off and caught my eye. It's no big deal though mum," Ricky lied.

"Oh, okay darling. You have a nice time tonight."

"Cheers Mum," Ricky said before picking up the phone. He dialled the number that Frank Allen had given him. It rang three times.

Unknown: Hello.

Ricky: Hello, can I speak to Frank Allen please.

Unknown: Who shall I say is calling?

Ricky: Tell him it's Ricky Turrell. He knows me.

Unknown: Hold a minute.

Ricky: Okay.

The phone went dead for several seconds.

Frank: Hello Ricky, Frank Allen here.

Ricky: Hi Frank. There is going to a bit of a commotion tonight at the Bedford Working Men's Club. Does it fall under your protection?

Frank: You boys are certainly putting yourselves about. The Beverley last week and now this.

Ricky: Bad blood Frank. This should be the last one.

Frank: I heard that some Skinhead gang tried to take the Milton Arms. Is that right?

Ricky: Like I said, Frank, it's bad blood but it will be sorted.

Frank: Well for what it's worth you have my blessing. Violence does have its place Ricky but turning a pound note should always be a wise man's priority.

Ricky: Thank you Frank.

The phone went dead.

Ricky checked himself in the mirror again and felt inside his jacket pocket for his brass knuckle duster. He felt the rush of excitement as his fingers slipped so easily inside the cold metal. He clenched his fist and smiled.

"I'm out now. See you later," Ricky called out as he closed the front door.

Earlier at Deano's flat on the estate, they discovered that the Bedford Working Men's Club was the usual haunt for Clifford Tate and the Bedford Boot Boys on a Saturday. With its bingo, pie and mash, cheap beer, snooker, one arm bandits and weekend entertainment, it was, like the Milton Arms, the adhesive that bonded the local community together. Call after call rallied Teds from all over London.

Ricky got inside his Rover P5B. He ran his hands around the steering wheel and took a deep breath. The engine roared to life and he slipped the shifter into gear. He reached over and pushed the cassette into the player. *'Hell Raiser'* by Sweet began to pay. Ricky turned up the volume.

"It might not be Rock 'n' Roll but it's just what I need to hear to get me ready for what's coming," Ricky thought.

Ricky wound down the driver's side window and placed his arm on the pillar. He breathed in the cold night air and pulled into the layby outside the Milton Arms. Despite it being dark he could still clearly see the spray painted 'Bedford Boot Boys Rule!' graffiti on the wall outside the pub. Somebody had painted an NF symbol next to it in bright red paint.

"That has got to come off," Ricky thought.

Deano, Mick, Kenny and Lee got into his car.

"Alright Ricky, are you ready for this?" Deano with an evil glint in his eye.

"I'm ready, willing, and more than able."

"Good because we are going to serve this lot up big time," Deano said defiantly. "Can you believe the bloody audacity of it? I mean who do they think they are? Well, now they're going to pay."

"Bloody right," Mick cried out. "We'll kick their heads in good and proper!"

"Are you alright Kenny?" Ricky said.

"He's fine," Deano said. "I've known this man since we were kids, and he can dish out a right beating when necessary. Ain't that right Kenny?"

"Yeah, I'm good, just psyching myself up," Kenny said, shooting Ricky a wink.

"What about you Lee?" Ricky said.

"Yeah, I'm fighting fit," Lee said.

Ricky caught a glimpse of the worried expression on Lee's face in the rear-view mirror.

"What about numbers?" Ricky asked.

"Don't you go worrying yourself about all that," Mick hissed. "You leave all the general stuff to me and Deano. You just keep your head down and soldier!"

"If you keep talking to me like that Mick then you and I are going to fall out," Ricky said firmly.

"So what, I never liked you anyway!" Mick retorted.

"When all this is done and dusted you and I can meet up one on one for a straightener," Ricky said bluntly.

"I'll kick seven sorts of shit out you!" Mick yelled.

"Yeah, yeah, we'll see," Ricky said in a self-assured tone.

"You, Ricky Turrell, couldn't knock out a wank!" Mick said aggressively.

"That's enough Mick," Deano commanded, "and you Ricky. We've got some serious work to do and there's no time for all this old bollocks right now."

"I'm going to hurt you Mickey Deacon, and knock that sarcastic smirk right off your ugly mug," Ricky thought.

"Ricky, stop down by the bus garages. That's where I've arranged to meet the others and our reinforcements," Deano said.

Ricky pulled in behind a line of parked cars. He looked over to the bus garage entrance where he spotted a group of thirty, maybe forty Teds.

Deano got out of the car and led the lads over to the Teds. He greeted them all warmly with firm handshakes.

"Is Jock Addie and his Croydon lot coming?" one of the Clapham Teds asked

Deano looked down at his watch. "Yeah, shortly."

Just then a stream of Zodiacs, Crestas and Consuls drove slowly up the road. Each parked by the other and turned their lights off. The doors opened and swarms of Teddy boys clambered out and onto the road.

"There's got to be fifty plus Teds," Ricky thought.

Jock Addie led the group to Deano. The two Teds shook hands.

"I hope you don't mind Deano, but I brought along a few friends from South Norwood and Tulse Hill," Jock said with a broad grin.

"Nice one Jock," Deano said before swivelling on his heels to face the mob of Teds. "Are you lads tooled up?"

The Teds produced a mix of chains, coshes, knuckledusters, cricket bats and one Ted held a metal tyre lever.

"Good because there can be no prisoners. If they move... you hit them. If they fall... you hit them again and if they run then you turn around and hit anything that is still standing," Deano commanded.

"What about you Deano?" Jock said. "Are you tooled up?"

Deano held up both his fists. On each one he wore a thick brass knuckle duster.

"The streets of Bedford will run with blood by the time we've finished," Deano roared.

Ricky could feel the pent-up tension and electricity in the air.

"This is going to get nasty," Ricky thought. *"But this had to happen."*

"We're the United Ted Army," Deano shouted proudly. "Let's do this!"

Deano led the Teds through the dimly lit back streets until they were just around the corner from the Bedford Working Men's Club.

Deano peered around the corner.

"Steve, Terry, can you go check the place out."

The two brothers, dressed in matching drainpipe trousers, brothel creepers and powder blue shirts nodded. Ricky watched as they walked slowly down the path and passed the club. Seconds later they crossed over the road and walked back.

"The placing is heaving," Terry said.

"Yeah, and there's a salad dodger on the door. I think he must be eating the troublemakers rather than throwing them out," Steve said with a sarcastic laugh.

"That must be Fat Pat," Mick said.

Fat Pat was a South London Doorman come enforcer during the mid-sixties. It was rumoured that he had once hit a guy so hard that he wound up in hospital with brain damage.

Deano led the Army of Teds out and onto the road. They marched seven across and ten deep. The sounds of *'Born with a Smile on My Face'* by Stephanie De Sykes and Rain got louder the closer the Ted Army got to the club.

Fat Pat straightened up when he caught sight of the hoard of Teds.

He held his hand up in a stop gesture.

"Alright lads we don't want any trouble," Fat Pat said calmly.

Steve Parker bolted forward with his cosh in his right hand. Fat Pat threw a left hook, but Steve ducked and then turned and hit the

224

doorman with an almighty smack to the side of his canister. Terry steamed forward and launched a kick between his legs. Fat Pat collapsed onto one knee. He had blood streaming out from between his fingers as he cradled his head. Two more of the Teds ran forward and began to launch a succession of kicks until Fat Pat was on the ground. Deano held both his armed fists up in the air and kicked the swing door to the club open with such force, it barely hung on with a single hinge.

Inside the club was rammed with working class people from all over the estate. There were Skinheads, Boot Boys, working men and their wives and girlfriends out drinking in their local. An overweight guy dressed in ill-fitting jeans and an off- white vest shirt stood up. Deano hit him first with a body shot and then a rapid right upper cut that sent him, the table, and all the drinks on it to the floor. The whole club erupted into an orgy of extreme bloody violence with men and young adults racing forward to meet the heavy surge of tooled up Teddy Boys. Terry Parker leapt over the bar and hit a barman with his cosh. The second barman threw himself down onto the beer-soaked floor and cowered under his arms. Terry grabbed a bottle of Bells Whiskey and threw it into the crowd. It smashed and an almighty yell was heard as a Boot Boy, with blood pouring from his face, tried to run in the opposite direction. Terry picked up a second and then a third bottle and lobbed them relentlessly into the chaos. A Skinhead made a swipe at Ricky with a broken light ale bottle. It narrowly missed his face but nipped the side of his forearm. The jagged glass had ripped clean through his shirt and cut his flesh. Ricky grabbed a chair and brought it in front of him as the Skinhead tried to cut his face a second time. Ricky yelled out and ran forward with the chair knocking the Skinhead off balance and making him fall backwards. Ricky quickly raised the chair and brought it down hard onto his attacker's head. Instinctively he did it again and then again. The Skinhead had released the broken bottle and was clambering clumsily for the protection of a table. Ricky saw his target and launched a kick, right smack bang between the Skinhead's legs. He was done. Ricky turned to see Terry still throwing bottles and Mick sat on top of a lad with his hands on his ears smashing his head on the carpeted floor. Ricky caught a clump to the side of his mouth. He turned in time to miss the follow up. Ricky kicked out and then fired off a right hander with his knuckleduster. His opponent cupped his face. Blood pumped out in erratic spurts from his nose.

"Oh my God, help me, help!" the lad cried with a blood curdling shriek.

Ricky kicked him over and looked around the room for his next target.

Deano was moving forward, firing a relentless succession of punches. Bodies collapsed around him as the two heavy brass knuckledusters splintered bones and tore into flesh. Seeing his friends from around the Bedford estate fall, one guy bricked it and scurried off to the toilets. Jock Addie, Kenny and four of the Croydon Teds rocked the pool table back and forth and until it turned over. While they swung the pool cues, Steve Parker scrambled around the floor collecting up the pool balls and throwing them at anything that moved that had a shaven head or was wearing a butterfly collar shirt. The panic-stricken wives and girlfriends screamed and ran to the back of the hall and into the ladies' toilets. A half bottle of vodka caught one of the escaping women on back of the head. She stumbled forward and lay motionless, face down. A second and third bottle smashed and shattered against the toilet door as the last of the women slammed it closed behind them.

Tables were being turned over, chairs thrown, and flying bottles were still being thrown relentlessly at all those other than Teds. It was utter carnage.

The last of the Bedford Boot Boys around him had fallen and Deano stood just a few feet from his nemesis, Clifford Tate. He watched momentarily as Clifford floored one of the Clapham Teds with his mighty fists and booted another to the floor.

Clifford spotted Deano and let out a spine-tingling yell. He tossed over a table of drinks to his right and stormed forward. He leapt into the air with his right steel toe capped Doctor Marten boot outstretched. Deano spun to his right as Clifford landed on both feet and then like a tightly tensed spring swung back round at an incredible pace. His left fist connected. There was a sickening crack as teeth shot out onto the threadbare, beet stained, carpet. The right fist almost knocked his shaven head clean off his shoulders. Deano hit him again and then again. The skin headed giant of a man swayed back and forth, spitting broken teeth. The blood poured from his mouth, down his chin and onto his blue and white chequered short-sleeved Ben Sherman shirt. Deano squared up, his fists were ready to fire when Clifford Tate's eyes rolled back inside his head and closed. He slumped over a bar stool and fell into an unconscious heap on the floor.

"YES!" Deano screamed out as he stood with clenched fists and gritted teeth over his arch nemesis.

Ricky looked around him. The fight was over. The Bedford Boot Boys and all those that lived on the estate were beaten. He was surrounded by the whimpers of those nursing their wounds. The song 'This Town Ain't Big Enough For Both Of Us' by Sparks was playing from the coin operated jukebox.

"How bloody appropriate is that?" Ricky thought, as he rubbed his bleeding arm.

"How bloody right was that!" Deano said, patting Ricky on the shoulder. "Rightful retribution and it served as a crystal-clear message as to who the Milton Road Teds are and the real guvnors!"

While Teds helped their fallen friends and allies back onto their feet the oncoming sound of multiple police sirens got closer and closer.

"We gotta go Deano," Ricky warned.

"Let's do one!" Deano shouted.

As the Teds filed back out of the club there were scores of angry men stood in the street. Some held large chunks of wood while others stood pounding their tightly clenched fists into their open palms. These were not Bedford Boot Boys. These were residents who had come out of their homes to defend their home area. Deano was the first to swing a punch. It was an older man in his mid-thirties. He looked like a construction worker in his faded blue jeans and open check shirt. Before he had enough time to throw a punch Deano had decked him with one single blow and then moved calmly onto the next. Jock Addie led the charge as his Teds stampeded forward with brothel creepers kicking and bicycle chains swinging. One of the Clapham Teds was lifted off his feet and thrown clean across a parked Ford Anglia. As the man turned, he was met with a dull thud as Terry Parker's cosh brought him down. Three blue Rover P5 Police cars came to a screeching halt, closely followed by a white HA Viva with a red stripe. A Black Maria police van pulled into view. Hordes of uniformed policemen waving their truncheons charged towards the raw brutal violence.

"FIGHT THE FILTH!" Mick yelled as he stormed forward throwing punches and kicks. The first police officer was head-butted, booted and then knocked over, while a second officer picked his spot carefully and took Mick down with a single clump from his truncheon. Mick lay unconscious on the tarmac road while two officers clamped him in handcuffs and dragged him away to the waiting Black Maria police van. Lee, from out of nowhere, ran forward, leant down, and grabbed a police helmet from the ground and ran back to the invincible wall of Teds.

"Deano, we gotta have it on our toes," Ricky said as the adrenaline raced through his veins.

Deano smacked one last guy to the ground and then stamped his right foot hard down on his head. He stopped, and with his hate filled manic grin surveyed the carnage and violence around him. In the distance more police cars were on their way.

TEDS...TEDS...TEDS...! Deano yelled, with the Ted Army quickly joining him. Their collective chant drowned out all the noise. Together as one they backed away leaving the police to mop up the blood, carnage and chaos. As they turned the street corner, the Teds broke into a run back to their waiting cars all parked up by the bus garage. Car doors were flung open, and the army of Teds climbed inside and drove away into the night.

"Did you see Mick?" Kenny asked.

"Sure did," Deano replied. "Fight the filth...what a nutter... he knocked that pint sized copper spark out... brilliant!"

Ricky drove away smoothly, not wanting to bring any attention from the old bill.

"And you, Lee," Deano said as he pointed to the police helmet, "Are a legend mate!"

"I've got to hand it to you, Lee, that was some quick thinking there, mate. That helmet is going to look the dogs nuts on show in the Arms," Kenny said with a broad grin.

"Is everybody alright?" Ricky asked.

"Your arm is bleeding Ricky. Do you need to go the hospital or something?" Kenny said.

"No mate, it's just a nick from a broken bottle, that's all. It looks much worse than it is," Ricky said as he slowed down at the traffic lights.

"You were savage my son," Deano said as he patted Ricky's shoulder. "Bloody proud of you!"

"Do you think he'll be alright?" Kenny said as he wound down his window to let the cool night air in.

"Who?" Deano said with an exaggerated laugh.

"Clifford Tate," Kenny replied coyly. "I think you really hurt him Deano, done him up like a kipper. I mean he just keeled over and, well, he wasn't moving. Do you think he's dead?"

"Listen, right, that no good skin headed slag must have known that this was coming! No one tries it on with the Milton Road Teds. He took liberties and paid the price. Alright, so I might have knocked most of his teeth out, but he can get a new set of Hampstead's on the national health. Besides, now he'll have stories to tell his children about the day he came face to face with the King of the Teds!"

Everyone in the car went quiet. Ricky looked down and at his petrol gauge. It was in the red, so he pulled into a Shell garage. He stopped the car and began to fill up when a Gold Cortina 1600E pulled up behind him. Inside sat four lads. *'One and One is One'* by Medicine Head boomed out from the passenger side window. Ricky went inside and paid for his petrol but as he returned to his car, the driver hooted his horn three times. Ricky stopped and looked over at the driver. He was moving his cupped right hand back and forth and mouthing 'wanker'. The other lads in the car were all laughing. Ricky slipped his hand inside his pocket as he walked towards the Cortina. He slipped his fingers inside the brass knuckleduster and slowly removed his hand from his pocket. Ricky stopped just a few inches away from the driver's side door. He looked down at the driver and then fired his armed and loaded fist. The might of his thrust and the solidity of the brass knuckle duster shattered the driver's side window sending broken segments of shattered glass over all over the driver and his passengers.

"You wanna shut your big gob?" Ricky said calmly.

"Yeah, yeah, sorry mate. I didn't mean nothing by it, honest" the driver pleaded. "I was just being a bit of a prat. I'm really sorry."

Ricky turned slowly and walked back to his car.

"Do we have a problem?" Deano asked, reaching for the door handle.

"No, no just a few mummies' boys out in the family motor and giving it the big one. It's sorted," Ricky said.

Ricky drove the Teds back to the estate and parked up outside the Milton Arms.

Chapter 24

During his lunch time Ricky had popped out and bought his mum a new coffee percolator along with several different types of coffee beans. That morning he had received two cheques from the car auction totalling just over five thousand pounds. With another six cars waiting to be rung, the money was coming in thick and fast. He wanted to do something special for his mum. She had got excited by the thought of trying percolated coffee.

Ricky parked outside his home and carried the box through the concrete hallway and into his home.

"Hello Mum!" Ricky shouted. "I've got you a present."

There was no reply. Ricky walked into the front room where his dad was standing in front of the gas fire holding a newspaper.

"Alright," Ricky said with a grin. "I've got you a present Mum."

Caroline smiled back awkwardly.

"Have you bloody seen this!" Arthur screeched, waving the newspaper.

Ricky shrugged his shoulders "No, should I have?"

"Look at that on the front page!" Arthur yelled stabbing his finger against the headlines.

The headline read:

TEENAGE RAMPAGE!

The subheading read:

POLICE OFFICERS INJURED IN VIOLENT STREET BATTLES!

"What's that then?" Ricky said innocently.

"Don't you come all that with me Ricky. What, do you think I was born yesterday? That was you and those yobbos you've been calling friends. I knew that nothing good would come of all this the moment I clapped eyes on you in all that Teddy Boy get up."

Ricky placed his mum's present on the dining table.

"What's this, the cat got your tongue?" Arthur said angrily. "Our son has turned into a good for nothing thug, Caroline! To make things worse he doesn't even try and deny that it was him."

"Was it you, Ricky?"

Ricky half smiled and shrugged his shoulders again.

"Right, well that's it then. I'm now taking back control of this family. From here on in you can damn well get rid of all that Teddy Boy get up and stop drinking in the Milton Arms pub. I've told you plenty of times before that it's nothing but trouble," Arthur said belligerently.

"He's just fallen in with the wrong crowd, that's all," Caroline said.

"Well that won't be happening again because he will not be going out. I want him home indoors by 9.00pm and that's it," Arthur said belligerently.

"Sorry, Dad, but that's not happening," Ricky said calmly.

"What do you mean that's not happening? You listen here, my boy, it's my money that pays the rent and it's my name on the rent book so you will do as you're bloody well told!"

"Dad, I'm almost twenty years of age. I'm a grown man with my own mind and I can tell you now, I will not stop being a Ted. It's a part of who and what I am, and I will not stop using the Arms because that is where my friends get together, and I will not give them up for anyone. I'm sorry, Dad, but that includes you. Your name may be on the rent book but I pay my way so you have no right at all deciding what I should or shouldn't be doing."

"Well, that's it then," Arthur said rolling his eyes.

"No, please, Arthur," Caroline beseeched.

"I cannot and will not have someone capable of this," Arthur yelled, waving the newspaper, "Living under my roof. I've told you before that I will not have you bringing the police to my front door!"

"Please Arthur," Caroline pleaded.

"No Caroline. I was prepared to give your son another chance but only under my strict terms and conditions. He's made his bed and now he has to lie in it. Ricky, you are no longer welcome in this house. I want you out!" Arthur said pointing to the door.

"Bollocks to you then!" Ricky said.

"What did you say?" Arthur shrieked before throwing the newspaper to the floor.

"You heard me," Ricky said calmly. "You might bully Mum by telling her what she can and can't do but that ain't happening with me. In this house you might think you're the kingpin but out there in that big wide world you're nothing, a nobody that scrimps by with no

234

ambition beyond paying the rent and watching the bloody television."

"Why, you...!" Arthur bellowed, clenching his fists and stepping forward.

Ricky stood firm.

"Take another step and I'll show you what I'm really capable of," Ricky warned.

"Ricky, don't talk to your father like that. Come on now, let's try to work this out," Caroline wailed.

"Sorry Mum, but we're at the point of no return. It's time for me to break away and make my own way in the world. I hope you enjoy the present and I'll be back during the day tomorrow to collect my things."

"They'll be packed up and on the doorstep!" Arthur said.

"You, old man, don't push your luck," Ricky said before turning to Caroline. "I'll see you tomorrow, Mum."

Ricky closed the front door firmly behind him.

"Who does he thinking he's talking to?" Ricky thought. *"No, I'm pleased this has happened. It's what I needed to move on. It's a blessing in disguise. No one is controlling my life. I'll show him what I can do, and I can't wait to see the look on the old git's face when he sees me in own my home and in a nice area. I'll show him what I can achieve. Now I'm going to really up the ringing operation, you'll see. I'm not changing me for anyone."*

Ricky walked back to his car and drove it the short distance to the Milton Arms.

"Hello Ronnie," Ricky said as he sat on the stool by the bar, "Can I have pint please, mate?"

"Yeah sure. This is a bit early for you, isn't it?" Ronnie said, glancing up at the clock above the bar.

"Bit of a domestic at home," Ricky said, shrugging his shoulders.

"Is everything alright?" Ronnie asked as he placed a freshly poured pint on the bar.

"My old man has booted me out. It's not a problem though. I'm not short of money and it's about time I got my own place, you know how it is?"

"Look, I have a room upstairs. It's not the Hilton or nothing but you can use it until you get yourself sorted," Ronnie said.

"Are you sure?"

"I wouldn't say if I wasn't. See me later and I'll sort you some keys."

"Thank you, Ronnie. I really do appreciate you helping me out like this."

Ricky handed Ronnie a pound note as payment for the pint.

"Ronnie, can I have some change for the phone, please mate?"

Ronnie nodded and handed him back a handful of coins.

"Cheers."

Ricky took the pint, walked to the end of the bar and placed it on the table by the pay phone. He placed a ten pence piece by the slot and dialled the number that Michelle had given him. It rang and he pushed the coin in.

Ricky: Hello, is Michelle there please?

Michelle: Hello Ricky, how are you?

Ricky: I'm fine. Listen I've managed to have a few words with Kevin, and you will not be hearing from him again.

Michelle: Really?

Ricky: Trust me Michelle. He will never contact you again. You can be sure of that.

Michelle: What did you say? Or was it something you did?

Ricky: We came to an understanding. The most important thing is that you're safe and that nutcase will not be bothering you again.

There was a muffled noise and an exchange of words. Ricky thought that Michelle must have placed her hand over the phone so he couldn't hear.

Ricky: Hello Michelle, are you okay?

Michelle's Father: Hello Ricky this is Michelle's father. I've read the local newspaper and I'm telling you now that you will not be seeing my daughter again. I knew that you were trouble the very first time I set eyes on you.

Ricky: Will you allow me to explain?

Michelle's Father: I'm not interested in what you have to say. You and all your Teddy Boy thugs do not scare me, Ricky Turrell. Yes, I know who you are! My daughter will be going back to finish her studies at University and I'm warning you that if you call on this house or attempt to contact Michelle, I will use all my significant influence with the local police to keep you away. Do we understand each other?

Ricky: Can I least say goodbye to Michelle?

Michelle's Father: No!

The phone line went dead.

"Oh, bloody great. Lobbed out my home and the first girl I've ever truly liked has been taken from me. What's next?" Ricky thought.

Ricky took the remains of his pint and sat alone at the end of the bar. As time passed the bar began to fill up. It was just after 7.30pm when Ricky spotted Cookie enter the bar followed by Frank Allen. He walked straight over to Ronnie and the two men shook hands. Ronnie then pointed towards Ricky.

Ricky could feel his heart rate go faster and his mouth go dry as Frank looked his way and then slowly walked towards him.

"Can I take a seat?" Frank asked, as he pulled out a chair.

"Yes, of course, please do."

Frank sat down and then made a gesture to Ronnie who immediately picked up a tumbler from the bar.

"I was in the area and thought I'd take a chance and stop to see if you were here," Frank said as he unwrapped a cigar.

"Really? What is it I can help you with Frank?" Ricky said.

"I wanted to thank you personally for giving me the heads up on that fracas at the Beverley pub. It could have been very embarrassing for us all had the pub fallen under my protection," Frank said as he rolled the cigar between his fingers

"We agreed that we would when we last met, Frank."

"It did have me wondering if that heads up came from you or Deano Derenzie," Frank said before placing the cigar into his mouth and lighting it with a solid gold cigarette lighter.

Ronnie placed a large whiskey and ginger ale on the table along with a pint for Ricky.

"Thank you, Ronnie," Frank said with a gracious nod.

Ricky remained quiet.

"I thought as much," Frank said before drawing on the cigar and blowing the smoke towards the ceiling. "You seem like the kind of person that I could do business with."

"What kind of business?" Ricky said, trying to hide his excitement.

"My sources tell me that you dabble in the motor trade."

"How did you know that?" Ricky said, looking a little concerned.

"There isn't much that I cannot find out Ricky, and don't worry, your little ringing operation is completely safe and if we agree to work together then it would also be protected," Frank said before taking a second long draw on his cigar.

"What is it you want me to do?"

"Well, until recently a friend of mine was importing cars into Cyprus, but since Turkey invaded the island, his business went quiet, so he has moved over to South Africa. I'm not sure if you know, but there are a great many African countries that drive on the right-hand side of the road like us. My friend has been scuttling around building contacts right across the continent and is now looking for a business partner to supply him with high end motor cars like Jaguars, Ford Capris, well, you know the kind of stuff. Part of my role is putting good people together and so he has asked me to connect him with a reliable business partner and I thought of you, Ricky. Are you that person and can you obtain those kinds of cars and get them safely delivered to the docks?"

Ricky found himself nodding before he'd even had a chance to think through Frank's proposal.

"Good," Frank said, putting his cigar in the ashtray and reaching across the table to shake Ricky's hand. I trust my instincts, Ricky, and something tells me that we will be doing a lot of business together in the future. We can have another chat at the Cadillac Club and go through the final details. Cookie has added you to the list of VIP guests. You may like to visit alone and enjoy the company of one our special hostesses or with friends. The choice is yours, but I would ask you to be selective with your guests as the VIP bar is renowned as a safe place for sensible people to talk comfortably about business. I'm sure you understand me."

"I understand completely," Ricky said before clearing his throat.

"Good. Now, is there anything that I can help you with Ricky?"

Ricky paused for a couple of seconds.

"There is, actually. I want to buy my own apartment. It needs to be something special in a nice part of town. It has to have at least two good sized bedrooms and fitted out with a smart kitchen, bathroom and stuff."

"Okay," Frank said.

"I have money for a deposit but will need a mortgage. Can you help?"

Frank rubbed his chin and then smiled.

"Actually, I have a builder friend who has just finished building a nice block of apartments. I think it could be just what you're looking for. I will make the phone call. As for the mortgage, providing you can stump up at least twenty per-cent of the asking price, then I have a man that will arrange that for you. It will cost five hundred pounds with no questions asked. Is that a problem?"

"Not a problem at all Frank, and thank you," Ricky said as a smile began to spread across his face.

"Right, well I'm pleased that we've had this conversation and I look forward to seeing you at the Cadillac Club soon.

Ricky stood and shook Frank's hand again. Frank turned and walked back to the bar where he exchanged a few words with Ronnie and then left, with Cookie opening the door for him.

Moments later Neil entered the bar and waved over to Ricky.

"Here did you see that smart looking Bentley outside?" Neil said as he pointed to the window.

"No."

"I'm sure that's Frank Allen's motor," Neil said.

"Oh yeah, he was just in having a chat with Ronnie," Ricky said dismissively. "Listen I'll be able to sort your next lot of money out for you shortly as I got the cheque from the auction this morning. Give it a couple of days to clear and I'll wedge you out."

"No rush, mate."

"We've got six more motors to sort out, are you okay?" Ricky whispered.

"Sweet, no problem, Ricky. I've found some and the rest will be hunted down, mate. This time tomorrow night we'll have all six motors ready to go."

"Nice one," Ricky said. "Do you want a drink?"

"I thought you'd never ask," Neil chuckled.

Ricky stood up and before he left the table to go to the bar, he lowered his voice again. "Here Neil, what are you like with Jags and up market stuff?"

"No problem. I can take a Jag as easily as I can a Granada," Neil said with a crafty wink.

"Excellent!"

Chapter 25

Ronnie placed a cup of coffee on the table in front of Ricky.

"It seemed a bit early for a pint," Ronnie said as he sat on the chair, placed his hand between his legs, and pulled the chair towards the table

"Thanks Ronnie, yeah I'm not really in the mood for a drink just yet," Ricky said.

"I was sorry to hear about young Mickey Deacon being nicked. It sounds like they have him bang to rights. He will go down for that, you know." Ronnie said.

Ricky nodded.

"All this having a row with other council estates, mobs and gangs is alright for a bit of fun and a tear up on a Saturday night when there's nothing else to do but there's no money in it, Ricky, which is why I was pleased when Frank said that he was going to put a bit of work your way," Ronnie said as he raised his coffee mug.

"He told you that?" Ricky said as he raised to head to look at Ronnie.

"Where else do you think he would have got the inside info on whether you could be trusted or not?" Ronnie said with a half chuckle. "Frank Allen is quite something Ricky. There were not too many people who could move so easily between Britain's most notorious and feared gangs- the Krays and the Richardson - during the sixties. Frank was unique and a man of honour and respect. He had this uncanny ability to build trust, recognise raw talent and nurture it into something special. I'd seen it and heard about his exploits before I finally met him. Career villains from all over the country, will actively seek his help to find that rare talent that could make or break some criminal enterprise. Frank Allen is a shrewd, cautious businessman first and foremost, but he's never, ever to be underestimated. His reach, and believe me I know, is far and wide."

"I want to amount to more than living on a council estate, Ronnie, and doing a nine to five that just about pays enough to cover the bills," Ricky said. "I have to amount to more than my old man. I want better than that."

"I completely understand that Ricky. Get this right and move up so you fall under Frank's protection and then you'll see doors really open. Other than my friend, Alfie Kray, I've rarely seen that kind of power before. We're talking lawyers, barristers, judges, politicians and the very senior old bill. You don't get to stay on top for as long as he has without some kind of serious power," Ronnie said before taking a sip from his steaming mug.

"We're going to have a chat at the Cadillac Club in a few days to just iron out the final details," Ricky said.

"Give him loyalty and the respect he richly deserves, and you'll get it back tenfold."

"Thanks for the heads up, Ronnie. I appreciate it," said Ricky. "There's something I think I need to do. If Deano and the others come in, can you tell them I'll be back later?"

Ronnie nodded.

Ricky left the pub and drove his car to where Michelle lived. He drove up and down the road twice before finally coming to a halt under a streetlight just a few houses down from Michelle's home.

He turned the ignition key off and left the cassette on. It was an old blank C90 tape that he had used to record the top twenty chart hits on a Sunday night the previous year. *'Ghetto Child'* by The Detroit Spinners was playing. Ricky turned it down and stared at Michelle's home. He held the vinyl single *'When Will I See You Again'* by The Three Degrees in his hand. Earlier Ricky had sat in his rented room, taken a pair of scissors and cut out two pieces of white card. He then glued them to the centre of the record so that the song title couldn't be read. On the A-side, he wrote, with a thick felt tipped pen, the words: 'PLAY ME LOUD!'

"This seemed like a good idea earlier," Ricky thought. *"I feel like a bloody fool now. I don't want to lose you, Michelle. It can't end now because we've barely just begun and probably for the first time in my life a person has come along and just turned my world upside down and inside out. Okay, sure, I know I had a thing for Jackie when we were kids but that was just it. We were kids, and now, when I least expect it, you came into my life. I told you things that I've never told anyone. I shared my hopes and dreams and I know that you did too. Being with you Michelle was just so incredibly special. Just holding your hand in mine made me feel like I was walking on air, like I was ten foot tall and nothing in the world mattered, just you and me."*

Ricky shook his head several times and gripped the steering wheel with both hands.

"To think I was stupid enough to think that meeting your parents would be okay and that they could see how happy we were, but oh no, the minute your dad clapped eyes on me, he bloody hated me. I was never going to be good enough for you. All he could see was some kid off the council estate that would never amount to anything and that would never be good enough for you, well, not in

his eyes anyway. I don't know what to do Michelle. Should I knock on the door and try to reason with your dad? If that failed then maybe I should just batter down the door, knock him spark out and then carry you off into the sunset with me. I'm at a loss Michelle. All I know is that I want you and I miss you and I've never felt this strongly about anyone ever before," Ricky thought.

Ricky stared up at the front window. The light was on and he saw a figure move back and forth. He wanted to believe it was Michelle looking out for him, but he knew that it wasn't.

Ricky felt several tears stream down his cheek. He wiped them away. Suddenly a figure appeared at the window and closed the curtains. Ricky wiped the tears away with his forearm, picked up the vinyl record and opened the car door. He stood motionless for several seconds just inhaling the cold night air before slamming the door shut and taking several steps towards Michelle's house. Ricky stopped at the end of their driveway. He looked down at the vinyl record and then rubbed his head.

"This is just stupid Michelle," thought Ricky. *"If I come marching down your drive then your old man will be on to the Gavvers in seconds and nothing good can come from that. I'm breaking up inside, but I know that I'm going to have you to let you go for now Michelle. We will have our time, I promise you that, but it's just not today."*

Ricky threw the vinyl record into their hedge, turned, and walked back to his car. He started the engine and fast forwarded to the next track on his cassette. The intro to *'Cum on Feel the Noize'* by Slade started. Ricky immediately turned up the volume, wound down his window and sang along.

Chapter 26

___

"**D**id you hear about the old bill kicking down doors on the estate yesterday?" Neil said before taking a sip of his tea in Doreen's kitchen.

"No, what was that all about?" Doreen asked, checking her reflection in the mirror by the door.

"I heard it was a blag on a building society that went wrong and the gavvers somehow knew it was them," Neil said.

"Someone's grassed then," Doreen hissed.

"Probably."

"I hate grasses," Doreen growled. "Bloody interfering busy bodies with no right to God's clean air!"

"The only good grass is a dead grass!" Neil shouted.

"Neil, why are you still sitting there in your underpants? I told you I have some people coming around this morning and you need to be gone."

"Yeah, no problem. I'll just finish this tea and I'll be up and out."

Their conversation was interrupted by three knocks at the front door.

Doreen looked down at her watch.

"Damn Neil, my bloody watch has stopped and you're still here. Quick grab your tea, disappear into the bedroom and close the door!" Doreen said patting herself down and taking one last look in the mirror before walking slowly up the hallway and opening the front door. Neil bolted down the hallway in the opposite direction, went into Doreen's bedroom and carefully closed the door.

"Hello Melanie, Kaz, Donna. Come on in girls," Doreen said warmly.

"Hi Doreen," Melanie said, "I'm sorry we're early. We can come back later if you like."

"No, no, I wouldn't hear of it," Doreen smiled. "Come on through to the lounge."

The girls followed Doreen into the front room.

"Take a seat and get yourselves comfortable," Doreen said as she motioned for them to sit down.

All three girls sat down. Doreen stood in the centre of the room so she could easily address them all.

"I'm really pleased that you reached out, Melanie. I've had my eye on all three of you girls for some time and you all have potential," Doreen said.

"Everyone knows that you are the go-to person on the estate for cut price goods. My mum has been buying stuff from you for years," Melanie said with a broad smile.

"Ours too," Kaz said.

"We saw Jackie the other day and she told us how she was making a lot of money working with you and that we could do the same," Melanie said coyly.

"Ah, Jackie, she is my brightest star. She took to hoisting like a fish to water. Within just a few weeks Jackie was making more money in a week than most working stiffs will make in two months, and come Christmas, that girl will be clearing well over a thousand pounds a week," Doreen said proudly

All three girls perked up.

"Can you tell us more about what it involves?" Donna asked.

"Donna!" Kaz muttered.

"No, no it's alright. Donna is right to ask what's she's getting involved in. I operate a team of professional shoplifters and there are openings for just three more. Stealing goods from stores and then trying to sell it on afterwards is for amateurs. My list of contacts expands right across the South of London. We shoplift goods to order. I have hundreds of customers across South London who call me with their specific needs. I break that down into shopping lists and then take my girls out in the minibus to locations both in London and the suburbs. I have enough work to keep all my girls working six days a week, week in and week out. Each and every one of you will be clearing at least five hundred pounds a week in no time.

"That sounds fantastic but what about store detectives and shop assistants?"

"Good question. You girls will be expected to dress, do your hair and manicure yourselves like you belong in the upmarket shops that we steal from. That way no one will be looking at you. The store detectives are looking at people who clearly do not belong. You will move around the store with complete ease because you will look well off, and the shop assistants see and sense that. I do have two store detectives on the payroll. By that, I mean I get a daily call from each of them telling me where they are operating. Neither one knows about the other. That way I can double check that my team are safe, and my customers will get what they've ordered. These store detectives are moved around from place to place and are given a specific number of collars they are expected to make in a day. This will shock some of you, but it can be as much as one every two hours. That's sounds a lot, right?" Doreen said.

The girls all nodded.

"It is, but what they do to keep those numbers high is patrol places like Brixton, Stockwell and Peckham where the amateurs work, and I'm told they can reel them in every half an hour. Ladies, we will be on the other side of town dining out like bandits," Doreen said with a giggle.

The girls all joined in the laughter.

"Doreen, other than a few pick 'n' mix sweets out of Woolworths in the town, I've never nicked a thing in my life," Melanie admitted.

"We have," Donna said with a glint in her eye.

"Yeah, we used to nick Paper Mate and Parker pens out of WH Smiths and give them away as presents at Christmas," Kaz said as she rubbed her hands together.

"You girls have absolutely nothing to worry about. I will train you all to become professional shoplifters. I will give you a trade that will make you more money than you'll ever make going to work in a shop or serving fish and chips. All you girls, in time, will have your own flats off the estate, a wardrobe full of expensive clothes, the best perfumes and make up, money in your pocket, a car outside and you'll never be reliant on any man to keep you. I will liberate you and give you financial independence."

The girls all looked at each other with excitement.

"There are conditions attached to this. First is how the split works. I'll use round numbers to keep this simple. If I have a shopping list that has one hundred pounds worth of retail goods, then my client pays me half price. That's fifty pounds. I will then split that with you. I get twenty-five pounds as management, and you get twenty-five pounds. When you're ready you will be making that every few minutes. Just last week Jackie earned over nine hundred pounds in four days! That's right, let that sink in, nine hundred pounds. A lot of money, right?" Doreen said, extending her arms and nodding her head.

"That's fantastic," Melanie said, "and you'll train us?"

"I will train you girls to avoid security cameras, overcome sensor tags and how to deal with a jobs-worth shop assistant with just a few words. Yes, that's right, you did hear me correctly. I said words. You have to remember that the outfits you'll be wearing will have cost more than their entire month's wages. This is where psychology comes in and just a few well-chosen words in most cases, will send the assistant away with a flea in her ear. Believe me I've had them falling over themselves with apologies and all the while I've got several hundred pounds worth of dresses, shoes and boots in my bag. It can be done, and I will show you how," Doreen said.

Doreen looked around the room, enjoying their excitement.

"What are the other conditions?" Donna asked.

"What I'll be giving you is very powerful and in no time you will all look on this as a job. It's how you make your money and support the lifestyle that you all so richly deserve. Trust me, after a few weeks, with a purse stuffed full of money, you won't even feel like what you're doing is wrong. It's about this time that, in the past, some girls have decided that they want more and try to cut out the management, that's me, and that... I will not tolerate. Don't get me wrong, if you want to nick a few luxury items for friends and families as gifts, then that's fine but if a pound note changes hands, then half of that is mine and I do expect to be paid," Doreen said firmly.

"That sounds fair enough to me," Melanie agreed.

"Yeah, sure, why bite the hand that feeds you," Kaz said.

"I only look to recruit girls with potential," Doreen said. "I have no time for adrenaline junkies looking for some kind of rush for nicking a few quid's worth of stuff. I want girls who will seize the opportunity with both hands and carve out a life for themselves that others can only dream about."

"What if we're caught?" Donna asked.

"Doreen's already told you. We learn how to talk our way out of it," Melanie asked.

"But what if they won't have it and they search you and you're caught with a bag full of nicked gear?" Donna said.

The room went quiet.

"There are pros and cons to every opportunity and so it becomes risk versus reward. If a shop assistant becomes persistent, I'd most likely give her a good shove and run for my life. Yeah, I have been there and done that. If they catch you and there's no escape, you are on your own. There will be no cavalry to save you. The first time, and I'll pull no punches here because it most probably will happen, you sit still, apologise and the chances are you'll get a telling off, a slap on the wrist and that's it. The second or third time you get caught you will be nicked, carted off to the police station and formally charged. At court the very most they'll give you is a two month sentence which means you'll probably do four weeks. Think about that for a moment. If you are making over five hundred pounds a week, that's twenty-five thousand pounds a year, tax free, in your hand. It's the price of a nice house in a good part of town and if all you have to do is serve four weeks then, in my view, it's a no brainer.

First and foremost, I take every precaution to limit my chances of being caught, but if I am, then, so be it, it's four weeks away and then straight back to work and pulling in that easy money. For me and the team I run, the rewards far outweigh the risks," Doreen said.

"I wouldn't want to go prison, but when you put it like that, it's nothing, is it? I mean what is a few weeks locked away when you can earn so much life changing money?" Melanie said.

"I can see that you are definitely cut out for this Melanie," Doreen said.

"You bet! For five hundred quid a week I am definitely in!" Melanie said.

"What about you, Kaz? Donna?" Doreen asked.

"Yeah, I'm in," Kaz said.

"Me too," Donna said.

"One final thing. I have no time for grasses," Doreen said bluntly.

"I would never say anything," Melanie said

"I'm sure all three of you girls are staunch, but if a girl squeals when she gets caught, make no mistake, I will cut her," Doreen said.

"Cut her?" Donna said.

"I will take a blade and cut her face," Doreen said calmly. "The grass will be marked for all time. No one will work with them again and people, our kind of people, will know that they are a grass and therefore untrustworthy," Doreen said.

"I would never grass," Melanie said.

"Me either," Kaz said.

"Have you ever cut anyone Doreen?" Donna asked.

Doreen paused for a moment.

"In all my years, and believe me I've been doing this for a long time, I have only ever had to mark someone once. It wasn't nice and it did leave her face in a state, but she grassed on our whole team. We were all banged up in Holloway for two months and out in one. The woman was marked, and no one gave her the time of day in there. She did her time alone in her cell while the rest of us had our Christmas dinner served by the screws. The team came back together again, and we went right back to work. That low life grass had to move away. The last I heard was she was living up in Norfolk or something. Can you imagine all that unnecessary drama just because she didn't keep her big mouth shut and do the time?"

"I would never grass," Donna said.

"I don't expect any of you ever will. You're all from good stock and live here on the estate. I have some errands to run today but I would like you all to come back here at 7.00pm, okay? I'll order us some Chinese food and we'll have a few drinks together before I begin to teach you your new trade as professional shoplifters," Doreen said.

"That's brilliant," Melanie said. "Is there anything you'd like us to bring?"

"No, just yourselves and open minds," Doreen said.

"Thank you for this opportunity," Kaz said with a beaming smile.

"Yeah, thank you Doreen," Donna muttered.

Doreen saw the girls to the front door and then called out to Neil.

"That was a close one," Neil chuckled.

"Too close," Doreen said with a hint of impatience. "How much of that did you hear?"

"Nothing really. I just got back into bed and smoked a couple of your cigarettes."

"Oh, really."

"Yeah, I was thinking about us and what a great couple we are together," Neil said with puppy dog eyes.

"Okay," Doreen replied cautiously.

Neil stood upright and took a deep breath.

"Doreen, how would you like to go out one night? You know just you and me and a fancy restaurant somewhere. We can get dressed up and maybe share a bottle of French wine or something. What do you think?" Neil said.

"No, I don't think so Neil," Doreen said, lighting a Dunhill International cigarette.

Neil looked a little shocked and disappointed by her answer.

"Why not?"

"I like the way things are," Doreen answered before drawing hard on her cigarette.

"But we don't do anything," Neil said, shrugging his shoulders. "I mean something together like a real couple, a proper boyfriend and girlfriend thing.

"Don't spoil things Neil," Doreen said firmly, stubbing out the half-finished cigarette.

"How can I be spoiling things? All I want is for us to go and spend time together outside of your flat."

"Neil, I like things the way they are," Doreen said bluntly.

"What is it we do then, other than have sex? Please tell me because I'm at a loss," Neil said, taking a deep breath and putting his hands on his hips.

"You've had to spoil it, haven't you? What we had worked for me. I don't want or need any man to take a role in my life, Neil. I make my own money and I make my own way but every now and again I want some male company. I do not want to be wined and dined or brought flowers. What I want and what I need is what we have been doing. I like to have no strings sex with none of the emotional baggage that goes with it. I don't want any of the pretence of make-believe love and holding hands while walking through the park. That rubbish is for the made-up television shows or those silly romance novels that young girls believe in," Doreen said.

"Is that all I am to you Doreen? Just some guy that that you can turn on and off when it suits you?"

"You're a nice, sweet, guy and you've been fun."

"What about how I feel Doreen? I think I've fallen in love with you. I've even thought about asking you about us living together."

"Don't be so bloody ridiculous Neil. You have no idea what love is, and I can tell you straight that what we do here in the bedroom is not love. Its lust. It's me meeting a need that I have and as for asking me about living together, that's just downright barmy!" Doreen shrieked.

"You're breaking my heart here Doreen. I thought we were more than that."

"Well, wake up and smell the coffee, Neil, and stop day dreaming! I am a strong, independent woman and I have no intention of running around after you, cooking your meals, washing and ironing your clothes or running your bath at night when you get home from whatever kind of work you do. We sleep together and for most men that should be enough, but you've spoilt it now. I don't want to lose you as a friend but whatever you think we might have had is over," Doreen said firmly.

"Come on, you can't mean that," Neil whimpered.

"Yes I do, and I think it's best for both of us if you leave now," Doreen said, pointing to the door.

"Can't we talk about this, please Doreen?" Neil pleaded.

He looked stunned, hurt and a tear rolled down his cheek.

"There's nothing else to say Neil, and I would like you, please, to respect my wishes and leave my home," Doreen said adamantly.

"So, this is it?"

Doreen folded her arms and nodded.

Neil picked up his jacket and looked one last time in Doreen's direction.

"Goodbye Neil."

Slowly Neil walked towards the kitchen door, down the hallway and out of the front door onto the landing. As he closed Doreen's front door, he felt the tears of rejection streaming down his face. As he stood on the pathway outside the block of flats the feelings of being dumped struck his self-esteem like a hammer. He hadn't seen it coming and wanted to believe that what they shared was so much more.

A few minutes passed as Neil tried to make sense of what had just happened.

"Is that you Neil?"

Neil turned and saw Jackie.

"Hi, Jackie," Neil said, trying to compose himself.

"Are you okay?" Jackie said, patting his shoulder.

"Yeah, yeah I just heard some bad news about my Nan and it kind of got the better of me," Neil said. "How are you, Jackie? I haven't seen you around in ages."

"I'm sorry to hear about your Nan. I lost mine last year. We take having them around for granted and then one day they're gone. So I completely understand and I'm sorry for your loss. Since leaving my job at the Arms I've been keeping myself to myself."

"I had heard you were doing a little work with Doreen," Neil said as he stepped back and looked her up and down. "I have to say you look great!"

Jackie blushed and ran her hands over her jacket.

"I didn't think me working with Doreen would become common knowledge," Jackie said. "But, yeah, I'm a part of the hoisting crew and frankly I don't give two hoots what anyone thinks or says. I make more money in one week than most people do in two or three months. I've got a wardrobe full of good clothes, I get my hair styled at a hairdresser and my nails manicured. I'm looking for my own flat, you know, and I've been taking driving lessons. Once I pass my test, I'm going to treat myself to a Triumph Stag sports car."

"Good for you," Neil said, lowering his voice. "Between you and me I've been doing a bit of business with motors, and I've got nearly four thousand quid saved up. I've been thinking about moving out from my mum and dad's and getting my own place too."

"How things change eh, Neil? It doesn't seem that long ago that you, me and Ricky were all at school and messing about in the playground and now here we are both making our own way in the world with money in the bank. How is Ricky?"

"Yeah, he's okay. We do still see each other, you know, good mates and that, but since he became a Ted, he's somehow different. I suppose I'm not the priority I once was. Don't get me wrong we're alright, it's just that we don't see each other as much as we once did and he's pretty serious about some of the stuff the Milton Road Teds get up to," Neil said. "I'm a game guy, as you know Jackie, but I'm not in that league. To be honest I didn't think that was Ricky,

259

but he's right at home alongside Deano and the others. He's changed."

"I suppose I always thought he would become something like that, Neil. Ricky has always wanted to be so much more. We used to talk about loads of stuff when we were younger and if it wasn't a Ted then it could just as easily have been a Skinhead or a Boot Boy. He'll need to be careful though, because Deano is the real deal. He isn't just talk. I've seen him take out two six-foot bouncers outside a club in seconds. I mean they were proper beaten up, on the floor and still he was kicking the, well, you know what, out of them. They don't call him Deano the Dog for nothing," Jackie said, raising her eyebrows.

"Believe me that is tame compared to what the Milton Road Teds are up to now and Ricky, alongside Deano and the rest of them are up to their high necks in it," Neil said, shaking his head.

Neil looked up towards the sky when he felt a couple of raindrops fall on his face.

"I was just about to go and grab a coffee and sandwich at the cafe. Do you fancy joining me?"

Jackie looked down at her watch and then smiled.

"Yeah, why not. I will have to be back here in an hour as I've got a meeting with Doreen," Jackie said with a warm smile.

"Sure, no problem," Neil said excitedly. "I've got a motor parked over there."

Neil pointed to a blue Ford Granada GXL that he had stolen the night before and had planned to drop it around to the garages to be rung later that day and then moved on to the auction for sale.

"Jackie, if you see Ricky don't mention what I said alright?"

"I doubt very much if I'll be bumping into Ricky and even if I did anything that you and I say is between friends," Jackie said.

"Good friends," Neil replied as he opened the car door for her.

Chapter 27

Ricky took a taxi up to the Cadillac Club. He had moved the few possessions he had from his parents' home into Ronnie, the landlord's, spare room. It was basic but comfortable and Ricky was grateful for the lodging with such short notice. That morning he banked another large cheque from the motor auction. There was no shortage of cars at the insurance salvage yard and Neil was true to his word and delivered identical motors for ringing within just days. Business was good.

As the taxi left the estate, he thought he caught a glimpse of Jackie. He smiled and waved but she turned away.

"Did she just blank me or what?" thought Ricky. *"Maybe it wasn't her. Yeah, that was her alright. What did she blank me for? I know, maybe she just didn't see me. I mean it's not like I'm in my own motor or anything. Nah, we're friends, Jackie wouldn't blank me... would she?"*

As Ricky entered the Cadillac Club he could hear *'Like Sister and Brother'* by The Drifters. He immediately began to think of Michelle and how they had chatted for hours that night in the Cadillac Club. Ricky decided that he would walk around the dance floor and check out the downstairs bars before venturing upstairs to the VIP Bar. He circled the dance floor and bars twice just in case, but there was no sign of her. He concluded that Michelle must have already been shipped off back to university to finish her degree.

Cookie stood on the door of the VIP Bar.

"Hi Cookie, Frank is expecting me."

"Come in," Cookie said, ushering him through to the exclusive bar.

Ricky looked around him. It was packed with villains, thieves, some serious faces and pretty, single girls with an appetite for bad boys and lounge lizards pretending to be someone they're not in the hope of bedding one of the young girls.

"Hello Ricky, what are you doing here?"

Ricky turned to see Doreen.

"Are you alright Doreen?" Ricky said.

"I'm fine," smiled Doreen, "and business couldn't be better."

"I might have something to put your way if everything goes to plan. How are you with things like towels, cutlery sets, curtains and the like? I only want good gear though," Ricky said.

"What, is it a present for your mum or something?" Doreen said.

"No, it's for me. I'm looking at my own place and need it fitted out with, well, everything I suppose," said Ricky.

"Oh, you'll be wanting a kettle, cooking pans the whole nine yards," Doreen said with a grin.

"Yeah, I've got the just the clothes in my wardrobe," Ricky said.

"Just let me know when you're ready and I'll make you up a list of everything you'll need for your first home. It'll be just good gear and half the retail price, okay?" Doreen said.

"Sounds perfect," Ricky said. "I've got to see Frank. I'll catch you a little later."

"He's sitting over there," Doreen said, pointing towards Frank's usual table.

"Cheers," Ricky said.

Ricky approached the table tentatively and kept a distance as Frank was engaged in a conversation with two men. He looked up, smiled, and waved Ricky over.

"Ricky, take a seat," Frank said.

"Thanks," Ricky said as he sat down.

Frank looked over towards the bar and motioned one of the barmen over.

"You want a drink?" Frank asked.

"Yes, thanks Frank," Ricky said.

"Here's the information I promised," Frank said, reaching down to the side of the table and then placing a folder in front of Ricky. "There are just a couple of two-bedroom flats remaining. I asked my friend, the developer, to hold the best one for you until Sunday. That should give you enough time to view it and say yes or no. There is no pressure. The mortgage is no problem. All you'll need to do is sign and pay him his bit of scratch. You should be out of Ronnie's place and into your new home within a few weeks."

Ricky was thumbing through the apartment's specification. It had a fitted modern kitchen and a fully tiled bathroom with a bath and a separate shower. Ricky was impressed.

"Thank you, Frank. I feel it should be me buying you a drink," Ricky said.

"Let me introduce you to Daniel and Sean, my two friends from across the water," Frank said.

Ricky shook their hands as the barman placed a tray of four double malt whiskeys on Frank's table.

"Daniel and Sean are very professional, high end thieves Ricky, and I can assure you that despite their Irish descent neither had anything to do with either the Guildford or Birmingham pub bombings," Frank said.

The two men gave a false laugh.

"I asked them to join me tonight as you will no doubt be needing a complete furniture package for your new apartment, should you decide to go ahead, and Daniel and Sean are just the men for the job," Frank said.

"That's not a problem," Daniel said in a broad Irish accent. "We can get you a television, stereo system, double beds, cabinets, and wardrobes and don't worry, it'll all be brand new and straight from the showrooms. Sean and I can get you everything you need."

"Sounds great. How do I get hold of you?" Ricky said.

"Pop in to see us here on Sunday night after you've seen the apartment. Two weeks is plenty of time for Sean and I to scope a few places out and have your new furniture ready for moving in. As a friend of Frank's, we'll look after you on price," Daniel said.

"Cheers, I appreciate that," Ricky said.

"Now this is the way good business should be conducted," Frank said, raising his crystal cut tumbler of Malt Whiskey.

The others joined him.

"Now Daniel, Sean, I have some other business with Ricky," Frank said.

"Of course," Daniel said as he stood up from the table, "See you on Sunday."

Sean nodded and swallowed the remains of his glass.

"I've spoken to my friend in Africa today and he will start needing cars from January. Can you be ready by then?" Frank said.

"I can, no problem. The sooner I know what cars he'll be wanting, the better it is for me to find the right damage repairable car so they can be properly rung," Ricky said.

"Don't worry about all that ringing stuff. All you need to do is have the right cars lined up and delivered to the docks in Southampton. There will be shipping containers waiting. You park them up, shut the door and that's it for you. I will give you a fixed fee for each car you deliver. That payment will take place here in the club every Sunday. It will be me that personally finances this venture and is taking the risk, so it's only right and fair that I take the lion's share of the profits. Once we have a regular flow of vehicles, I will give you the opportunity to take a larger share of the profits by halving my costs and risk," Frank said.

"That sounds very fair," Ricky said. "Have you any idea how many cars we could be talking about?"

"Maybe just eight to ten per week to start with, but it'll need to be closer to twenty-five within a few months. Can you cope with that?" Frank asked, motioning the barman to bring them two more drinks.

"I'll make sure that I can Frank. I think the key thing for us is to keep talking so we can try to manage the business effectively."

"Effectively... I like the sound of that, Ricky Turrell, and you shall manage your side of our business effectively," Frank chuckled "One last thing Ricky. I believe I've made the right decision bringing you in as I have, but you need to understand that there are very serious consequences for letting me down. I'm not going to labour the point... just don't let me down, okay?"

"I appreciate the opportunity you've given me Frank. I will not let you down."

"Right, well I've got people to see and deals to get done," Frank said, waving two lads over from the table behind."

Frank shook Ricky firmly by the hand.

Ricky took his drink and wandered over to where Doreen sat with Daniel and Sean.

"You guys all know each other?" Ricky asked.

"We do," Daniel said. "We get the bigger stuff and Doreen takes care of everything else."

"I just wanted you to know, Doreen, that it looks like we'll be going ahead with those bits and pieces we talked about earlier. We can have a chat in the Arms closer to the day," Ricky said.

"Whenever you're ready," Doreen said.

"I've not seen Jackie about for a while," Ricky said. "Is she okay?"

"Jackie is my little star," Doreen said, her eyes lighting up. "She's doing great and has just got herself a new place down by the park. I don't think she comes into the Arms now."

"I'm pleased she's doing well. If you see her, please tell her that I asked after her," Ricky said.

"I'm with her in the morning. Consider it done," Doreen said.

Ricky waved and walked over to the bar. He ordered a round of drinks for Doreen, Daniel and Sean and asked for a large Malt Whiskey to be taken over to Frank. As he walked down the stairs towards the dance hall, he decided to take one last look around just in case Michelle was there. Once again he checked every bar but she was nowhere to be seen. Ricky left by the front entrance and hailed down a taxi.

"Hello mate," Ricky said. "Can you take me to The Milton Arms on the Milton Road Estate?"

"Yeah, no problem," the taxi driver said.

"Well, that couldn't have gone any better," Ricky thought.

As the car drove through the Milton Road Estate, Ricky caught a glimpse of Kenny outside the Fish and Chip shop. He was talking to Denise. It struck Ricky as a little odd that Kenny would be holding her arm. The conversation looked quite intense.

"Here will do," Ricky said to the driver.

"There you go mate, keep the change," Ricky said, handing him a five-pound note.

"Cheers, thank you," the taxi driver said.

Ricky walked over to the bus shelter and peered around the corner. He could see Kenny and Denise having an energetic conversation. Kenny was shrugging his shoulders while Denise waved her finger.

Then, Denise stepped forward and Kenny began to kiss her on the lips. Ricky wasn't sure where to look."

"*What the bloody hell are you up Kenny? That's Specs' wife and this will cause all sorts of trouble,*" Ricky thought. "*They have a little kiddie together and everything. You are well out of order there, mate. There's plenty of birds about. You don't need to be messing about with Denise!*"

Denise pulled away, turned sharply and took off towards the flats.

Ricky waited several seconds and then called out.

"Kenny."

"Oh, hello mate," Kenny said.

"What are you doing out here?" Ricky said.

"I just had some stuff to sort out. Anyway, how are you? I don't think I've seen you since all that madness the other night," Kenny said.

Ricky shook his head slowly. "I thought for a minute Deano had killed that geezer."

"You ain't the only one. I thought we'd all be up on a murder charge. I mean it's bad enough with Mick being done for assaulting a police officer and possession of a lethal weapon," Kenny said.

"Have they let him out yet?"

"No mate, no bail for Mick. I think he's going to go down. You know, get banged up. Things don't always look like the way they seem," Kenny said.

"How do you mean?"

"I mean look at all this old bollocks with the Bedford Boot Boys. Okay so there's a little tit for tat but it had all gone bloody nuclear with people getting proper hurt and banged up for what... all over some bird?"

"What do you mean some bird?"

Ricky was confused.

"Oh, forget it," Kenny said.

"Nah, nah you've got to finish what you've started now Kenny," Ricky insisted.

"It's almost always over some bird somewhere." Kenny said, rolling his eyes.

"What is?"

"Bloody everything is! Have a think about it. Almost every tear up has some little sort jigging about with legs up to her armpits behind it."

"What does this have to do with the Bedford Boot Boys?" Ricky persisted.

"It's Melanie, ain't it?"

"You're beginning to get on my wick now, Kenny. What are you on about?" Ricky said firmly.

"I told you once that Deano and Melanie can be intense, remember?"

"I do, vaguely."

"Well, many moons ago Deano and Melanie had a bit of a bust up and Melanie has gone off to some party on the Bedford Estate and yes, you've probably guessed it, she's made a play and got off with Clifford Tate. Melanie is one dangerous bird, and she has a thing for the bad boys. Deano has never quite forgiven and forgotten it. It's always there, simmering, just below the surface, so some days they're on and others it can get lethal. Not that I've seen it, but I've heard, if you know what I mean. So, because Melanie has done the business with Clifford Tate, the rivalry between the Milton Road Estate and the Bedford Boot Boys has gone into overdrive with Deano pulling all the strings. I don't really think all this bollocks is about Teds, Skinheads and Boot Boys. Between you and me I think this is all about Deano, Melanie and Clifford Tate and the rest of us are just pawns in the bigger game," Kenny said.

"Bloody hell," Ricky said with a stunned expression. "I didn't see that coming!"

"You've got to keep this to yourself Ricky. I don't want Deano the Dog smashing down my front door and putting me in hospital. It's like I said, this is only my opinion and that doesn't make it a fact."

Chapter 28

"**M**erry Christmas Mum," Ricky said with a broad smile as Caroline opened the front door.

"Ricky!" Caroline shrieked as she threw her arms around him. "Come in, come in."

Ricky closed the front door and followed his mum through to the kitchen. Caroline picked up the kettle and placed it on the cooker.

"Cup of tea?" Caroline asked before reaching into the cupboard for the PG Tips.

"Yeah, that would be great. Thanks Mum." Ricky replied as he sat down at the kitchen table.

Caroline placed the two cups on the table and sat down.

"Where are you living Ricky?"

The mortgage on Ricky's new apartment went through just as Frank Allen had said. All his new furniture arrived as promised by Daniel and Sean along with Doreen's goods. Ricky had the top floor, two-bedroom apartment in Carshalton Beeches. There was an underground car park where he could store rung motors if required.

"I've got a place in Carshalton, Mum, you'd like it," Ricky said proudly.

"Are you eating properly?"

"In between the fish and chips, Chinese take away and kebabs I'm doing fine," Ricky said with a broad smile. "No, I'm just joking Mum. I have a fridge full of proper food and to be honest, having my own space suits me."

"Okay, as long as you're taking care of yourself," Caroline said, reaching over and squeezing Ricky's hand.

"I've got you a little something," Ricky said, reaching into his pocket and producing a small, wrapped, Christmas present.

"Oh, you shouldn't have."

"I wanted to Mum. Why don't you open it now?" Ricky said with a grin.

"That grin will get you in trouble one of these days," Caroline said. "Are you sure? I could wait until tomorrow."

"No, come on Mum, open up your present."

Caroline was wide eyed and grinning from ear to ear.

"I will then," Caroline chuckled.

Caroline carefully unpicked the corners and then removed the wrapping.

"Oh Ricky, what is this?"

"Open it and find out, Mum."

Caroline slowly lifted the lid of the small rectangular box. Inside, nestled in the crushed red velvet was a gold ladies' watch.

"Oh, Ricky this too much," Caroline said.

"Not for you it's not, Mum. Take a look on the back," Ricky said.

Caroline then turned the delicate gold watch over and read:

I Love You Mum Ricky xx

Instantly Caroline's eyes filled with tears of happiness.

"Oh Ricky, this is probably the best present I've ever had, thank you."

"You're welcome, Mum."

"Did you get anything for your dad?" Caroline said as she fastened the gold strap.

Ricky pulled out an envelope with 'Dad' written on the front.

"It's a card with a few quid in it. I didn't know what to get him. You know what a funny bugger he can be at times," Ricky said.

"I'm sure he'll be very happy with whatever you give him, son," Caroline said, still admiring her new gold wristwatch.

"Mum I've got to go. I'm due to meet some friends later for a Christmas drink," Ricky said, getting up from the table.

"Oh, okay Ricky. Merry Christmas and I love you," Caroline said as she kissed him on the cheek.

"Merry Christmas, Mum, I love you too," Ricky said.

As he passed by the front room, he looked in to see a Christmas tree in the corner covered with gold and silver tinsel and shiny red balls. He opened the door, gave Caroline one last kiss on the cheek and left.

"That was the same tree that was up last year and the year before and not one present under it," Ricky thought.

Ricky had left his car at home and taken a taxi over to the Milton Road Estate. Ronnie said that he would be putting some sandwiches and nibbles out and promised to get a DJ for the night. Deano wanted everyone to be there, and it promised to be a good night out. Ricky waited for the bus to pass before crossing the road. He stopped for a few seconds, inhaled the cold night air, and looked up at The Milton Arms pub.

"This time last year I was nothing more than another snotty nosed kid off the estate looking up at Deano the Dog and the Teds, and now I've got my own place, money in my pocket, good clobber on my back, solid friends and respect that's not only from those around the estate. This year, other than losing Michelle, has been good and next year will be even better!" Ricky thought.

The pub door swung open narrowly missing him.

"Sorry Ricky, I didn't see you there."

It made Ricky smile that people seemed to know him and yet he had no idea who they were. He would always nod and acknowledge them. He wondered if perhaps that was how Deano had felt when he first made his mark on the estate.

"No problem, mate," Ricky said.

The Arms had been decorated with coloured hanging tinsel around the bar and over the windows. He could see the cloud of cigarette smoke hanging just above the bar. The pub was packed, and it was still early. He spotted Trudy chatting to two guys, Ronnie pacing up and down the bar, and the two barmaids furiously pouring drinks for customers. There was a Christmas special drinks menu that included a Baileys and Whiskey. At the end of the bar, at his usual table and holding court, sat Deano the Dog. He was surrounded by Teds. In the corner, the DJ was flicking through his vinyls while

'Angel Face' by The Glitter Band boomed through the speakers. Melanie wore a Santa hat and was dressed in a short red Santa skirt with a white fur lined hem and knee-high black leather platform boots. She danced provocatively alongside Kaz and Donna. The twins were dressed as sexy elves in their short green skirts with a red fur lined hem. Their Santa hats were green with red fur, and they wore red high heels. As the record came to a close, Ricky watched as all three girls knocked back their glasses of Baileys and Whiskey.

"What are you drinking Ricky?" Ronnie asked, reaching for a clean glass.

"Merry Christmas Ronnie. You've done a cracking job sorting the place out."

"Now is that a polite way of saying that I've polished a turd?" Ronnie said with a broad grin.

"Would I say that?" Ricky chuckled. "I'll have a pint of Watneys please, mate, and whatever Deano and the boys are having. Can you stick three of those Baileys and Whiskeys on for the girls too?"

"Feeling flush then?" Ronnie asked as he poured the drinks and put them on a tray.

"Nah, just feeling festive. Have one yourself."

"I will," Ronnie replied. "Merry Christmas!"

Ricky handed over a ten-pound note and took the tray of drinks over to Deano, Kenny, Specs, Lee, and Terry and Steve Parker.

"Alright," Ricky said.

"Ricky!" Deano said, shaking him warmly by the hand. "Lee, budge up mate and let Ricky in."

Ricky took a chair from the empty table behind them and joined them.

"Here Ricky, did you hear about Mick?" Kenny asked.

"Hear what?" Ricky asked.

"Mick got weighed off for eighteen months. They did him for assaulting a police officer, possession of a lethal weapon and shed loads more. Some say that he was lucky to have got away with just that," Kenny said

"Christmas dinner in the jug," Lee said. "Rather him than me."

"Mick went down swinging," Deano said. "The man is a legend in my book. I mean who in their right mind shouts out 'fight the filth' and charges into a mass of old bill while they're waving their truncheons. He took out two six-foot plods before being taken out himself. The man is the stuff of legends!"

"It was one old bill, and he wasn't any six-footer," Ricky thought.

"I think we were all lucky not to have been pulled in," Kenny said.

"I would put our Ted Army up against anyone, anywhere, and that includes the old bill. Let's face it, most of them were bullied at school and only join for the uniform and a chance to get revenge on those who messed with them as kids," Deano said.

All the lads around the table nodded.

Ricky caught Kaz's attention while she danced to *'Rock the Boat'* by the Hues Corporation and pointed to the three drinks on the tray. She smiled and waved.

"I think she's looking a bit worse for wear," Ricky thought. *"How many has she had?"*

Melanie, Kaz and Donna came back to the table when the DJ played *'Doctor's Orders'* by Sunny.

"Cheers Ricky," Melanie said, raising her glass.

"Yeah, cheers," Donna said.

"Hmm, Ricky, you look scrumptious," Kaz said, looking deeply into Ricky's eyes.

"Oh, okay," Ricky said awkwardly.

"Get in there my son," Kenny said.

All the lads cheered and held up their glasses with a raucous roar. Kaz raised her eyebrows and smiled.

Ricky smiled back awkwardly.

"Kaz you're embarrassing, Ricky. You're a shameless flirt," Melanie said, shaking her head and winking at Ricky.

"Do you know what I'd like to do with you Ricky?" Kaz slurred.

"Err, buy me a drink?" Ricky said, making everyone around the table laugh.

"I'd like to take you out to the ladies', hitch my skirt up and then straddle that cute face of yours," Kaz said.

"Alright, that's enough!" Melanie said. "You're embarrassing yourself now."

"Ricky doesn't mind, do you Ricky?" Kaz slurred.

"I'm flattered Kaz, you're a nice girl and good friend," Ricky said.

"Friend? Friend? Are you brushing me off?"

"No, I was just…" Ricky said, shrugging his shoulders awkwardly.

"What are you, some kind of poof?" Kaz yelled with both hands on her hips.

"Come on let's go and have a dance," Donna said. "We like this record."

The intro to *'Billy Don't Be A Hero'* by Paper Lace had just started.

"Yeah, come on Kaz," Melanie said. "We can grab these fellas when the slow songs start later."

Ricky watched as the girls led Kaz back to the improvised dance area in front of the DJ's decks.

"You missed out there," Kenny said. "I've always fancied a pop at one of the twins. Either one would be good or…" Kenny paused for a moment, "both together. Now that would truly be something."

"I like them, but not that way," Ricky said.

"How could you not fancy some of that?" Kenny said pointing at the girls swaying their hips in time to the music.

"You're the male version of a tart," Ricky said.

"Nah you're probably right. It's probably got a muff like a hippo's yawn down there," Kenny said, pointing to his crotch. "It'd be like hanging your old fella out the kitchen window. Anyway, what's with all this male tart stuff, can't you see I'm half a dozen pints in? Here," Kenny said to all the lads around the table. "Here, look at the old duffer in the Father Christmas outfit."

All the boys turned to see an older guy staggering over towards the girls. He tripped, recovered and tripped again, narrowly missing a table full of drinks. He rearranged his false Santa beard and began to dance alongside the girls. The lads stood up and began to cheer and clap the old guy on. Others around the pub joined in. It was then that he placed his hands on the tops of his trousers and began to dance with more vigour. As the clapping got louder, the old guy bent forward slightly and rolled his trousers down to his ankles exposing his old tattered grey Y-front underwear. As the pub roared with laughter, the old guy began to thrust his hips back and forth frantically while waving his arms in the air. Melanie and Donna watched as he pranced around to *'You Ain't Seen Nothing Yet'* by Bachman-Turner Overdrive. Kaz, still in a drunken stupor, continued to dance with her head down.

The old guy dressed as Father Christmas lost his balance and accidently staggered into Kaz. She fell backwards, her legs gave way and she ended up on the floor. Her skirt had risen up, exposing her green panties. The lads in the pub cheered as Donna and Melanie raced over to help her back onto her feet. Father Christmas wobbled and then teetered forward and reached out in a bid to help Kaz. His left leg gave away and he fell forward. Melanie and Donna quickly stepped back, leaving Father Christmas to fall face first on top of Kaz. Father Christmas, with his trousers around his ankles and Kaz, were now in a drunken heap on the floor. Kaz was punching and screaming obscenities at the old guy while he tried desperately to push himself off.

"Now that is bloody hysterical," Kenny shouted. "It's times like these you need a camera!"

"Come on buddy. I think you've had enough," Ricky said, grabbing him firmly under the arm and lifting him to his feet. Ricky reached down for Kaz. She pushed his hand away and rolled over onto all fours. Melanie quickly pulled the back of her skirt down while Donna helped her back onto her feet.

"I don't need your help," Kaz spluttered as she staggered towards the ladies. "I don't need anyone's help, thank you very much!"

"I think she might be drunk," Lee said.

"Nah, you don't say," Specs said. "Thank you so much for pointing out the bloody obvious."

"What has got your goat?" Lee said abruptly. "You've had a miserable face on you all night."

"Get lost," Specs muttered.

"Nah, sod that. I'll take it from Deano, Mick and maybe Ricky, but I ain't taking none of that from you," Lee said.

"Alright girls, calm down," Kenny said. "It's Christmas, have a drink."

"What the...?" Deano said as the old guy in the Father Christmas outfit came bolting out of the men's toilet, stark bollock naked.

"He's a streaker!" Kenny yelled.

Everyone in the pub cheered as he ran around the pub with his flaccid old fella swinging about. Ronnie slammed down his drink and marched to the end of the bar. The Streaker saw him and made a bolt for the exit with lads patting him on the back as he ran past and out the door into the night air.

"There's another one for the history books," Deano said. "We've got Lee legging it off down the road with a copper's helmet under his arm in the middle of a punch up with the Bedford Boot Boys.

Terry and Steve not only lay out Fat Pat but are lobbing bottles of drink at all and sundry while I've given that jug-eared bellend Clifford Tate a right good hiding and to finish the year off we have some old fella streaking around the Arms in his birthday suit. Bloody brilliant!"

The lads all cheered and drank from their glasses.

"That's your Denise, ain't it, Specs?" Deano said.

Specs looked up and adjusted his glasses.

"Yeah, she said she might pop in," Specs said.

"She certainly scrubs up well," Deano said. "Here you are, go get her a drink and get a round in at the same time, alright?"

"Yeah, sure. Cheers Deano," Specs said. "Same again?"

Everyone nodded and thanked him.

Kenny leant over towards Ricky and said, "I wonder who is looking after the kiddie?"

"A babysitter I would imagine, mate. That's a strange thing to say?" Ricky said.

"Oh, I was just thinking, you know," Kenny said. "Here, that's Neil ain't it?"

Ricky looked up and saw that Neil was standing by the bar dressed in a black drape suit with red velvet collars, cuffs and pockets.

"Nice drape suit," Kenny said. "I didn't know he'd gone all Teddy Boy on us."

"You ain't the only one," Ricky said.

"You've got to hand it to him though. He's a natural in a drape," Kenny said. "Hold up, have you seen that bird he's with?"

Ricky moved his eyes to the right of Neil. He could make out the shape of a girl with long wavy brunette hair. She wore a knee length brown pinstriped skirt with a matching jacket and heels. As the girl turned to pick up her drink Ricky saw that it was Jackie.

"What the hell is going on? Is Neil with Jackie? Why didn't I know? She looks bloody amazing," Ricky thought.

"Do you want to get that jaw back off the table," Kenny said.

"What do you mean?"

"I heard a clunk and there was you with your gob wide open gawking at Neil's bird," Kenny said.

"Nah, nah, mate you got it wrong," Ricky said.

"Yeah, right," Kenny said.

"No, seriously that's Jackie," Ricky said.

"Jackie? Jackie who?" Kenny said as he squinted to get a better look.

"Jackie, she worked here behind the bar. I've known her for years," Ricky said.

"Well, she didn't look like that when she worked here, or I would have been all over her like a Rottweiler trying to clean the inside of a jam jar lid. Mate, she looks the business!" Kenny said.

Neil and Jackie approached the table.

"Is that you Neil?" Deano asked.

"Hello Deano, are you alright?" Neil said as he nodded to the others sitting around the table.

"Neil, you look the dogs nuts in that mate. Grab yourself a chair and one for Jackie too," Deano said.

"Hello mate, I didn't know you were coming down here tonight," Ricky said to Neil.

"Well, I bought my new clobber and Jackie suggested that tonight was a good night," Neil said.

"Hello Jackie, you look really well," Ricky said.

He could smell the strong scent of her 'Charlie' perfume by Revlon.

"Thank you. I like to look my best for Neil," Jackie said.

Ricky couldn't help his look of amazement. Inside he felt an unexpected pang of sadness quickly followed by anger with a streak of resentment.

"I'm sorry I didn't know. Congratulations, how long have you guys been together?" Ricky said.

"We've got our own place," Neil said.

"Really? Wow, mate. You never said," Ricky said.

"Well other than our bit of business we don't see too much of each other these days," Neil said.

"Yeah, I know and I'm sorry about that," Ricky said.

"It's not a problem mate. Now that Jackie and I are living together we've always got places to go and stuff to do. Jackie is taking driving lessons and I've already earmarked a nice little motor for her when she passes her test," Neil said with a wink.

"What do you fancy Jackie?" Ricky said.

"You mean other than Neil?" Jackie chuckled. "I fancied a Triumph Stag and Neil wants me to have a Sunbeam Tiger. Have I got that right?"

"Yeah, that's right," Neil said with a crafty wink "I found a lovely little motor in need of light restoration. I think that she'll look great behind the wheel."

"I'm sure she will," Ricky said.

"Merry Christmas Jackie," Doreen said as she approached the table. "Here you are darling, a bottle of champagne for my number one."

"Thank you, Doreen. That's very kind of you," Jackie said.

"Are we still okay for an early start on Boxing Day?"

"Yes of course, can't miss work," Jackie said.

"Oh, hello Neil. I didn't see you standing there," Doreen said, looking him up and down.

Neil just nodded.

"You can feel the tension between those two," Ricky thought. *"Either they didn't end too well, or she has the right hump with him seeing Jackie. Oh my God Jackie, you look absolutely stunning!"*

"Neil, that bit of work I was telling you about is on for the New Year. Are we still okay?" Ricky whispered.

"Of course we are mate, as long as you are with me and Jackie," Neil said.

"If you're both happy then I'm happy for you," Ricky said.

"It's funny because Jackie said you'd be alright with it and there was me thinking we'd have some kind of problem," Neil said.

"We're good mates and business partners," Ricky said. "If we play our cards right, we'll have made some serious money by this time next year."

"Jackie, I just can't take my eyes off you...wow!" Ricky thought.

There was a scuffle over at the bar. Instinctively everybody looked up with fists clenched. Specs, Denise and Kenny were standing together. Specs had pushed Kenny several times before throwing a punch. Ronnie was around the bar and between them in seconds.

"You're a bastard and I hate you!" Specs yelled before storming out of the bar.

Deano waved Kenny and Denise over to his table.

"What was that all about?" Deano asked.

"Personal stuff," Kenny said.

"Don't give me personal stuff, Kenny. If I see two of my men having a barny then I want to know about it," Deano said.

"It's okay," Denise said. "It's about time everyone knew the truth. You will know about it soon enough anyway, so I'd rather it came from me."

"What truth?" Deano said.

Denise took a deep breath.

"You don't have to do this," Kenny said.

"She does," Deano said firmly.

"The truth is I should never have married Specs. I was seeing Kenny way before Specs came along and I thought that what we had would never go anywhere. As all you lot know he's a womaniser, so when I accidently fell pregnant, I had to make some tough decisions. Kenny and I broke up and I gave him no reason. He didn't know that I was pregnant. Shortly after that Specs showed interest in going out with me and, well I used him. After sleeping together, I told him that I was pregnant, and he proposed to me there and then. As wrong as I now know that was, I accepted, and the rest you already know. We got married and Specs has been a good husband and father, but I never truly loved him, and I always wondered what could have been had I have been brave enough to tell Kenny that I was expecting his baby. Well, it ate away at me and impacted my marriage to Specs. It got to the point that I had to share my feelings and the truth with Kenny. We talked and talked and decided that we all, as a family, belonged together. I think Specs was beginning to suspect something wasn't right, but every time I tried to tell him either I bottled out or Specs would change the subject. We were all living a lie and it had to come to a stop. So, now you all know, and it's come direct from me and without the usual gossip thrown in to spice things up for good measure," Denise said.

After a few moments silence Deano spoke. "Denise, that was a pretty shitty thing to do a bloke, let alone to Specs."

"I know Deano and I'm sorrier than anyone could ever know, but the truth had to come out," said Denise.

"So, Kenny, what have you got to say for yourself?" Deano said.

"Look, I didn't know alright? But Denise is spot on because had she told me then things would have been different, and Specs wouldn't have needed to be hurt like this. I feel bad for him but then I also feel that we have to be a family unit because it's right for us and the right thing for us as a family," Kenny said.

"Bloody hell, this is going to make things difficult, but with all that said I do understand why you've done what you've had to do, and we only live once and all that old palaver. I'm telling you now though, Kenny, Specs is still a part of us just as you are, so you better start thinking of ways to build bridges. It ain't gonna be easy but build them you will, because we are all: Forever Teds – Teds Forever!"

TEDS...TEDS...TEDS! The boys yelled out as one

The DJ played *'Merry Xmas Everybody'* by Slade and everybody in the pub began to sing along.

"Here, Ricky, tell Melanie I've just popped next door to get my winnings from the bookies will yer?" Deano said.

"Yes mate, of course. Do you want another drink?"

"Same again, cheers," Deano said.

Ricky watched as Deano walked through the crowded pub of merry drinkers. He caught Double Bubble glaring at Deano from the table where he sat alone until he turned his way.

"Double Bubble and Deano must have some kind of history," Ricky thought. *"I can see that coming to blows. One of these days Deano will catch one of his smart arse looks and smash him from one end of the estate to the other."*

288

Deano saw Specs sitting on the seat in the bus shelter with his head in his hands.

"Specs, it's a stupid question I know, but are you alright?" Deano said resting his hand on his friend's shoulder.

"I'm broken Deano," Specs muttered.

"Look mate get yourself over to my place in the morning. Me and Melanie have more than enough grub for three. You don't have to say anything. No need for where, why or how explanations, nothing, okay? Just be among friends at Christmas," Deano said.

"Cheers mate," Specs said.

"Look I've got to get in the bookies and get what's owed before they shut shop. I'll see you in the morning," Deano said.

Specs nodded and stood up. Deano watched as his friend slowly crossed the road and disappeared into the night. Deano marched into the bookies with his betting slip. The counter was clear.

"Hello Stan, I've got me a winner here," Deano announced.

From the doorway a wide-eyed Skinhead ran forward yelling "DEANNNOOOO!" As Deano turned, Eddy Boyce, of the Bedford Boot Boys, thrust his switchblade deep into Deano's chest. The thick crimson blood quickly soaked through to the front of his cream-coloured shirt. Deano looked down at the blade still stuck in his chest and instinctively fired off three punches which all missed their target before collapsing and falling down onto the bookies' black and white chequered tiled floor in a pool of his own blood. Eddy Boyce pushed one stunned punter back against the wall and then raced out of the door and over to a waiting car.

Books by Dave Bartram

with Dean Rinaldi

King of the Teds Inception

King of the Teds II: Unification

King of the Teds III: Infiltration

Coming Soon.

King of the Teds IV: Subversion

King of the Teds V: Misdirectiion

King of the Teds VI: Retribution

Facebook: Dean Rinaldi Ghostwriter Publisher & Mentor

www.deanrinaldi-ghostwriter.com

Printed in Great Britain
by Amazon

23997699R00161